CW01501926

THRILLER WHERE FORBIDDEN TRUTH COULD LIBERATE MILLIONS — OR DESTROY EVERYTHING.

WITHIN

WITHIN

ALAN RHODE

Z

First published in the UK in 2025 by
Zinfandel Publishing, in partnership with Whitefox Publishing
www.wearewhitefox.com

This edition published in 2025

ISBN 978-1-917523-46-2
Also available as an eBook and an audiobook
eBook ISBN 978-1-917523-47-9
audiobook ISBN 978-1-917523-48-6

Designed and typeset by seagulls.net
Cover design by Nathan Burton
Project management by Whitefox

I

WANDERING

How to find our unit is what they first taught me. The entire perimeter knew of Thatem, the boy who had disappeared in the corridors, and neither Mother nor Father wanted their child to end up like Thatem. 'Should the Crier lash you until nothing's left to lash?' Father repeated endlessly, this being the punishment reserved for those who wandered clueless through the perimeter, even though I seldom left our corridor. One could easily lose his way inside the perimeter. Even more so when the lights went off and mute darkness invaded the maze of low-ceilinged passages that wormed into each other in a tentacular mesh. Nobody knew how vast the surround encasing us was, nor whether it was circular, cubical or cylindrical, or in fact shapeless, because no man in the last twenty generations or so had been outside, in the Land of Without, where Sun had annihilated all life.

I had invented a game with the kid of the eleventh unit to the right: who could roll a stone ball the furthest in our corridor. We could only do very short games, though, and just before the lights-out, when the pods of idlers in the corridor scurried to their units for fear of the coming dark. My neighbour always beat me, and I wanted to give up; but then told myself that it was just a matter of trying harder. I didn't know where else to practise my throw in secret, though, if not alone in the corridor at dark, when nobody would see me. But apart from the fact that leaving your unit at lights-out was forbidden – the punishment set at fifteen lashes – I was also damned afraid of the blindness, and so the idea of practising all by myself was abandoned.

My game worsened, though, and I felt the losses even more when the other kids leaned out of their units to watch. Once, exhausted, I threw the ball so feebly that it just dropped right in front of me. My neighbour smirked. The other kids jeered. I ran off home in hidden tears. When I walked in, Father was saying the Tenets, as he always did when, if not engaged with his important duties of keeper, he stayed with us. Often, however, Father went out to mend a light or unblock a vent somewhere in the perimeter, proud to display the red star of the keepers on his robe. He even stayed out in the dark for emergencies. Mother didn't like it. I once saw her crying in her pallet when he wasn't with us. Completely at a loss, I pretended to be asleep.

They often told me that, before I was born, Father had even gone as far as perimeter ᚖᚖᚐᚅᚈ, no fewer than eighty hundred steps from home. This story had made me proud at first, because nobody else I knew back then had reached another perimeter. But later, as I grew ever more disenchanted with Father, I started to believe he just liked to boast.

When I entered our unit, Mother was seated on the floor. Next to her, the usual three boxes. Showing impatience at my lateness, she thrust a ladle inside the first box and poured a red mush onto the ground.

Father stopped the Tenets, and joined us.

'What is it?' I asked, crossing my legs on the floor, a slight wobble still in my voice.

Mother answered: 'Polypeptides. They're good.'

She then opened the second box to take out a handful of stodgy brown textured cubes.

I looked at her, numbly.

'Carbon, hydrogen, oxygen. They're good,' Mother said, the cubes thrown lazily on the floor.

Inside the third box were three flasks containing a thick white solution. *Calciferol.* Necessary to survive without sunlight – Piko had told me – calciferol came in unmistakeable blue flasks that, ever since I could remember, everyone called *bluebottles*. We drank the calciferol from the bluebottle.

The same occurred at every meal: Mother served us the nutrients that were delivered to our unit through a hatch in the wall. While varied in shape, texture and colour, the nutrients were devoid of taste, flavour, smell, and couldn't even stain our robes. As always, Mother and Father greedily devoured the nutrients, uttering wails of pleasure throughout a process that I, on the contrary, found boring. The nutrients occasionally consisted of lozenges, which, being quicker to swallow, I preferred.

'Why aren't we always given the lozenges?' I asked Mother.

'No!' Father, scowling, intervened. 'When I was a child, my genitors told me about a neighbour who only ate lozenges: his teeth fell out. Our body needs variety, as Tenet ᵇ♄⚔ reminds us.'

Mother nodded in admiration of his formidable recollection of the Tenets.

'And remember,' Father added, though not before scooping up with his tongue the patch of floor around him, his eyes narrowed in enjoyment. 'Some men don't respect what they're given, and they are punished with fasting, so that they run out of Juice.'

I shivered at the prospect of the Juice ending, and at the consequences.

After eating the nutrients, we measured our Juice – as always. Father was the first.

'Stable,' he observed with complacency.

Then came Mother's turn.

She smiled after seeing the results.

'Proud of you.' Father patted her shoulder.

I was the last tested. The Juice had remained stable since the previous screening. Mother stroked my neck. I attempted a smile, even though, whenever we tested my Juice, I sensed a mounting fear in them, as though they felt I didn't deserve to retain any inside me.

When the light went out, I laid preoccupied on the pallet – my yearning to practise with the stone ball in the corridor still lingering. The temptation to sneak out in the dark was not new: it had already crept into me on one occasion, when I had refused to participate in the painting of our perimeter.

A Tenet postulates that, with no conceivable exception, all the walls of the perimeters have to be covered in black. Not even a minuscule spot in a different shade is tolerated. I think it is Tenet ꝯꝏ꞉꞉ꞇ. Or, perhaps, Tenet ꞇ꞊ꞇ. I'm no longer sure. Black is meant to remind all of us what Sun did, the Crier said, and we all have therefore to contribute to the perpetual painting of the perimeter. So, whenever they called us, we took our brushes to paint the walls with a sooty varnish of viscous consistency. Some chanted, some recited the Tenets, others were too invested in their brush to do anything else. But, maybe due to the damp, the varnish never lasted, and after quickly flaking and crumbling, it peeled off. A new call would then come for us to start passing our brushes over the cold surfaces of our corridor again and again.

Despite all the chanting and reciting, I suspected our job was meaningless. I never dared to express my doubts though, because Father would've never forgiven me. As a keeper, he took a special pride in supervising the coating of our perimeter. He meticulously inspected the work, and if the paint was somewhere a bit thinner, he would yell at us, threatening to call the Crier for proper punishment.

The black varnish released a strong odour, an acrid stench that crawled up through the nostrils, causing me to fall sick. The disgusting smell of pigment survived in my nose so long that, often, the periods where I lay exhausted on my pallet lasted more than the clammy varnish on the walls. I was the only one having this problem, it seemed, and this made Father suspicious, I guess. So, he thought mine was just a trick to avoid the coatings. Once, after a call was made, I asked him to let me stay in our unit, for I had just started to recover after a long bout of nausea. He went wild. 'You, selfish kid! Putting yourself first. What's your little sickness against the highest duty to work together?'

I feared he might slap me, as often happened, but Mother intervened.

'Father is right, Boz,' she said. 'You must help us. Remember: a little pain cleanses the mind.'

I nodded, unconvinced. Shortly after, the light went out. When it came back, I reluctantly began painting the bit of wall assigned to me. I was paired with a much older neighbour, a harmless good-natured man. 'Cheeky paint ... no matter how much of it you apply ...' the good-natured man said, as he moved his brush left and right against the wall, apparently enjoying the futility of our work. It was true: I had done that bit of wall on innumerable occasions. I didn't comment, though, nor even dare to nod, because Father was patrolling the corridor, and I didn't want him to see me questioning our task.

I was already dull and dizzy: the varnish. The sickness quickly grew unbearable. My legs strained to hold me up, and my arms felt so numb that I couldn't get the brush to draw a straight line. I must have looked very weak when I staggered into our unit, right before the dark, and Mother's eyes showed signs of compassion at my slightly chattering teeth. Father, in the middle of his Tenets, didn't notice my struggle, or simply didn't care.

The coating was to resume at lightbreak, but I couldn't carry on with it. So, writhing on the pallet, I devised a plan to evade the blackwashing, and put it to immediate execution: when Mother and Father fell into their usual comatose sleep, I rummaged inside Father's satchel, where I found his torch and the key to the shelter. I took them and stole out of our unit. The shelter wasn't far: a large, sealed room meant to protect us if another plague hit the perimeters. No plague had spread through our perimeter since my birth, but those who had suffered through it in the past, like my genitors, remembered the gruelling agony of the disease pursuing them. So, if a new plague spread within the perimeter, the only escape for the uninfected residents would be to lock themselves in the nearest shelter, hoping that nobody inside had yet contracted the virus.

Outside of an emergency, no one was granted access to the shelter, but all keepers held a key. Most crucially, shelters were exempted from blackwashing. My plan was to hide there while the rest of the perimeter was being varnished. The shelter contained masks, nutrients, medicines, and everything else needed for survival, even for long. Mine was an act of rebellion in breach of multiple Tenets for which Father would surely make me repent, but I was a wounded child who could see no alternative.

As I poked my head out of the unit, glancing left and right at the expected dark, my feet stood firmly anchored to the imaginary line that separated me from the corridor, aware that nothing would be the same once that line was crossed. As I hovered by the door, cold sweat dampened my stiff chest, but, for all the inner turmoil, the amusing contrast between my heart's choking beats and Father's quiet snorts wasn't entirely lost on me.

I crossed over the threshold. Out in the corridor, I switched the torch on. Endless rows of doors stretched ahead on either side. All units were silent, the idlers inside fast asleep. It seemed incredible to me that, in shameless defiance of more Tenets, I was wandering through the corridor at lights-off. I thought of Thatem, the boy that went missing, and wondered if he, too, had left home to avoid carrying out a duty.

The nauseating stench of fresh varnish reinforced my will to continue my flight. I was confident I wouldn't get lost. Father had forced me to memorise the path to the shelter. After no more than twenty steps, though, a hand clutched at my right shoulder. I jolted forward, then turned round.

'You want to ruin us?' Mother, enraged, muttered.

'I can't take it anymore,' I said.

We stood there, in the middle of the corridor: Mother overwhelmed by incredulity at my actions; me expecting the worst.

'Come back, or no way will I be able to save you,' she urged, waving her torch.

We returned to our unit. Unaware of his son's unruly behaviour, Father was still asleep. When the light came back, I heard them whispering. So, I thought Mother was giving me away, but I was wrong, I guess, because the only consequence of my attempted escape was that, from then on, they allowed me to avoid the coatings. I had achieved my aim but, due to Mother's early intervention, I would never know whether my brave plan would have worked or not. I'm sure that this sense of unfulfillment bore a role in later events.

Shortly after my incident with the stone ball, on my way to the choir room I met the neighbour of the eleventh unit on the right. After spotting me, he and two other kids exchanged knowing glances. I nodded, uncomfortable. They said nothing, but stared. As soon as I had walked past them, the kids burst into mocking laughter. I was alone, conscious that when a pack of kids teased you, they wouldn't easily let you go. It had already happened. For a reason that escapes me, I thought again of Thatem, and wondered whether he had left home to run away from a pack of kids.

The second call to the choir had been yelled, so I picked up the pace. Failing to attend a call to practise the hymns meant a serious violation of Tenet 3♂, and I didn't want to be lashed by some bailiff, or by the Crier himself.

When I walked in, many ranks of dark-robed kids already occupied the large room. The minister of the choir, disturbed by the echo of my shy steps, glanced at me with contempt. As before every practice, the minister sat on a cathedra elaborately carved with an intricate multitude of animal shapes. The chair was so heavily covered with engravings that, for all my attempts during the many practices, I still hadn't identified all the animals. One of the images, etched near the right armrest not far from a conch's spiral shell, was clearly a large caterpillar. Squinting, I also thought I could make out the contour of a tiny jerboa, abruptly interrupted by the armrest's edge. Yet I failed to recognise the other engravings, including a flattened shape with two rows of legs that had caught my attention earlier on.

I found a place at the far end of the last row. I instantly noticed that all our robes were pristine. It was no accident, as ahead of a choir practice new robes were delivered through the hatches of our units. When no practice occurred for a long period, however, the robes slowly grew rumpled and musty, until a foul stench invaded the corridors, and our units.

Upon standing from the cathedra, in the silence of the room, the minister began to move his hands in the air with extreme solemnity, as if to pull towards him the hundreds of young voices that began singing at his sole command.

Sun betrayed us. *We worshipped him – put his radiant light at the centre of the Universe – sacrificed our children to his power – yet our endless prostration was in vain.* ***Sun betrayed us***. *He scorched our lands – emptied the lakes – burned our skin – forced men to seek refuge inside the land. We allowed him to dictate our* *lives – believing that no mortal lip was worthy to pronounce his name; yet Sun showed no mercy in leaving a multitude of dried corpses rotting under his vicious rays.* **Sun betrayed us.** *But our Fathers did not surrender: they created a sacred place for the few survivors. We still thrive in harmony here, protected from the fatal heat of Sun, sharing our lives, abiding with the Tenets.* **Sun betrayed us.** *Long gone are the blue skies, plush forests and fanciful animals that the capricious Sun judged best to annihilate for no reason. We sometimes feel lost, secluded, but we are not alone: because Earth is still our friend, and we shall merrily descend into Earth, through our Descent, at the end of everything.*

We knew the hymns by heart. I enjoyed singing, though I struggled to find a sense in reprising the same chants at every practice. I would've liked to learn new hymns, even compose them, but the Tenets forbade it. I had to concede, however, that when we all sang together was one of the rare moments where I felt less isolated from the other kids. Chants marked our existence inside the perimeter. We sang the hymns to salute the end of every darkness, while coating the walls, or to show repentance in front of the Crier. Refusing to chant was a gesture of disobedience, an act of insolence, or interpreted as a sign of insanity.

As we practised, I looked around the choir room. Hairless heads shrouded in identical dark robes, we all looked alike. Under Tenet ꞓꞙ꞉, growing hair was forbidden. So, at every lightbreak we endured the agonising process of pulling out the hair from the entirety of our body. For an unknown reason that nobody ever dared to question, the Crier, with his long purple hair and huge purple beard, was the only one allowed to grow hair.

The dull rolling of the kids' eyes, singing together as one, was a measure of their subjection to an imposed uniformity: unable to build something of their own, forced to follow a prescribed existence. Although you can't miss something you can't imagine, I now understand in hindsight how that cauldron of rotten energies and unborn dreams engendered in the kids a restless urge to find prey to persecute.

One kid looked different, though. Standing in a nearby row, he was alone in not singing – and, to my amazement, he didn't even pretend. A sturdy build, flat nose and jutting jawline; the kid glowered. His robe was stained. I was sure he had been among those jeering at me in the corridor. Feeling observed, he gazed back in sullen response. I looked away.

After the closing hymn, the minister of the choir, barely looking around, slowly walked out of the room. Silence was no longer mandatory, and the kids felt free to move with disorderly haste towards the exit, the solemn harmony of the preceding chants supplanted by a brassy rhythm of squeaky voices.

In the crowded corridor I spotted a nice boy I got along with.

'Boz: the Juice may nourish you,' he said. 'I haven't seen you in a while.'

'The Juice may nourish you, too,' I reciprocated. 'I've been unwell.'

'Have you ... heard, Boz?' the nice boy asked, lowering his voice.

'About what?'

'There's a new kid. He comes from ᑯᙓᘖ ...'

'Perimeter ᑯᙓᘖ ... *Breathitt*,' I whispered to myself.

'Yes ...' he replied, looking around furtively. 'Breathitt. Men are so evil there that even the bailiffs avoid it ...'

My chest began heaving. Unnerving stories about Breathitt abounded. Dreadful accounts of men engaging in violence, murders, and other heinous deeds, in most cases with no other reason than the banality of evil. I had heard tell of lone women whose only purpose was to give men pleasure – a despicable practice that made Mother's face glower whenever she heard about it. And while, since when the bailiffs ensured steady supplies of food, human flesh was no longer eaten in our perimeter, cannibalism was said to be still common in Breathitt.

I somehow knew that the kid I had been exchanging glances with during choir was the newcomer from Breathitt. 'His name is Bruttho,' the nice boy added in such a feeble voice that I had to read his lips. 'They all fear him. He's already formed his own pack.'

'How many?'

'Twenty kids, maybe more …' The nice boy paused, looked around, then added warily: 'One kid refused to join the pack. Bruttho cut off all his fingers. He's mad.'

A sudden outburst behind us made me turn. Hawkish grins on their faces, five or six kids were pointing in my direction.

'Let's go get him!' Bruttho yelled, emerging from the crowd. The other kids around him shouted at me.

Everything happened so fast. I looked at the nice kid, who had already drifted a couple of steps away. 'Go to your unit …' he whispered, trembling, more a plea than a recommendation.

I bolted off. One of the fastest kids in the perimeter, I could still make it to the only safe place: my unit. Entering someone's home without their permission violated Tenet ꝑꝏ, and I was sure nobody would dare to do it. I reached the end of the crowded corridor (I still don't know how I avoided crashing into anyone) before running into a second corridor. I took a quick look round. Roughly fifty steps behind, Bruttho and three kids were pursuing me. I gritted my teeth, pushing myself to go even faster. I took the fourth corridor on the left, the eleventh on the right, the second corridor again on the right, then the eighth to the left, careful not to lose either my speed or the way to my unit. I glanced behind again. Bruttho was still chasing me, but at least I had lost the other three kids.

Despite all the sweat dripping off my body, and the rattling fear that Bruttho might catch me, I came up with a plan and, putting it into action, swerved into a large storeroom with three different exits (I had accompanied Father there at least twice). Inside the storeroom, I took the exit that would lead me into a narrow by-corridor close to home, hoping that Bruttho would pick another one. He did so.

I was already in our corridor, but still hadn't slowed down when, ten steps from home, I tripped over my robe, and entered our unit in a flying leap.

My unforeseen landing in the middle of the room startled Mother, who was staring at me, bewildered.

'Boz ... ?'

I lay on the floor, gasping for air.

Suddenly, Mother looked past me. I turned around. With one hand holding up the canvas curtain, Bruttho stood on the threshold. Panting, his features working furiously, his eyes left me to take in the small room. Evidently prone to ignoring boundaries, Bruttho was tempted to trespass but, coming somehow to his senses, desisted.

The canvas curtain dropped down.

'Boz ... ?' Mother whispered again in disbelief. Nothing like that had ever happened. I lowered my eyes, and she asked no more.

When, not long after, the light switched off, I writhed on my pallet, searching for impossible solace, conscious that when a pack of kids chose you as their prey, you needed to act before it was too late. I had one of my plans ready, at least: I would beat my neighbour at the game with the stone ball to regain dignity in front of Bruttho and his kids.

I decided my training would begin immediately. I snatched up the goggles that Father used for urgent maintenance works in the dark – not the torch, this time – so that I could see in the dark up to a distance of one hundred steps without being noticed. The only issue was that Father's goggles were a bit loose on me. A minor problem, I deemed, and, after grabbing the stone ball, I pulled the curtain up and went out. A diffuse light inside the goggles replaced the surrounding obscurity, helping to assuage my fear of the dark. I rolled up my robe's sleeves, knelt, and threw the ball low ahead with all my strength. The stone ball hissed while rolling dynamically on the floor. I stood up and walked forty steps to gather it.

Not a bad start, I thought.

Walking through the corridor to get the ball, I observed the stillness around me. Idlers were sleeping in their units, the only noise being that of the air whistling out of the ceiling vents. I completed another hundred throws, 'til my arm ached. I was improving. Back to our still-dark unit, I placed the goggles in Father's satchel and returned to my pallet. I was so excited – no less for my disobedience of a Tenet than for my progress with the ball – that I couldn't close my eyes. If Father caught me, I knew he would hit me very hard. When the light went on again, I felt drowsy, but also couldn't wait to be back in the corridor with my stone ball during the following lights-out.

I trained at every lights-out until, with the stone ball reaching up to eighty steps, I knew I could beat my neighbour under the amazed eyes of Bruttho. Still, I wanted to perfect my throw. So, the next time it was dark, I placed myself at the centre of the corridor, breathed deeply, imagined a straight line in front of me, took a four-step run-up, and threw the stone ball. As it left my hand at full speed, I had a feeling this might be my greatest throw yet. Very soon, in fact, the round shape went out of sight. Marvelling at my own achievement, I trotted down the corridor in search of the ball. I had covered almost one hundred steps, but, oddly, the horizon remained empty. Either the ball had travelled more than two hundred steps, or someone had taken it; but no one other than me, I believed, would venture into the corridor at lights-off without permission. The Crier meandered occasionally through the dark, but I preferred not to consider the prospect of encountering him. I gazed left and right, seeing no movement. All units were quiet, hidden behind the static curtains. I kept walking, my concern mounting: where was the stone ball?

I had reached at least three hundred steps when I finally saw a blur in the distance. I drew closer, squinting. It was indeed the stone ball, immovable,. at the centre of the corridor. How could the ball have gone that far? I didn't know. Fearing some kind of trap, I slowed my pace – and, had the ball not been necessary to execute my plan, I would've left it there. As I bent down to pick it up, a blinking red light at one corner of my goggles signalled motion: a slow movement coming from a vacant unit on my right. No sooner had I jerked my head up in the direction of the red light than I saw a long-lived man standing inside the curtainless room. Standing in profile, shrouded by a saggy robe, his bulging eyes were aimed at a corner of the room hidden from my view. The man didn't acknowledge me at first, but, as I continued staring, his gaze slowly moved in my direction, revealing how the half of his face previously covered from my sight had been completely obliterated, as if by means of a knife engraving his skin, or from fire scorching the tissues, or through acid melting the bones – or on account of all such evil deeds at once.

Whether the disfigured man's stare was hostile or not, I couldn't judge, for I broke into a run, and my sudden dash caused the goggles to fall to the floor, next to the stone ball. I ran blindly in the direction of our unit – the sight of the monstrous man having given me such a fright that there was no longer room for fear of the dark. After running hundreds of steps, my arms outstretched against any invisible obstacles, I stopped, reassured by the lack of footsteps behind me. Our unit wasn't far, I knew, but finding it without the goggles would be difficult. I had to reach home before the silent return of the light, otherwise my genitors would notice my absence.

I was in trouble. But memory, the great memory of those who cannot read or write, came to my rescue. I suddenly remembered when, as a child, I had secretly etched the shape of a scarab on the stone jamb round the door with Father's chisel. They had never noticed it, so the tiny etching should still be there. With my hands, I inspected each jamb in the long row of units to my left. I had checked at least thirty jambs in vain, and thus begun fearing that one of the damned coatings might have covered the engraved scarab, when, at last, my fingers met the rugged cut-out. I was home.

II

SCARABS

'Boz?'

Piko, the faint hint of a smile on his face, held up a weathered slate in his right hand. The answer wasn't difficult. With its luminous green dorso and clubbed antennae, the painted image portrayed a figeater, my favourite among scarabs. Piko put the slate down, and gave me another one, the last from the deck prepared for our class. I wasn't so confident about this scarab: the red line stretching under the dark shield could belong to a toadflax, or maybe an alder. I went with the first.

'Boz: your memory never fails you,' Piko observed, laying the slate down on the table. 'But, given your passion for scarabs, I shouldn't be surprised.'

We had dedicated many classes to scarabs.

'Are you sure no scarab has survived outside?' I often asked him.

'No. Sun burned all forms of life outside these walls. The Land of Without is empty, barren' was always his unequivocable answer.

'Maybe there are scarabs inside the perimeter, then?'

'Nobody has ever seen any form of living creature within these walls,' Piko sternly replied. 'Other than humans, of course.'

Entrusted with the duty of teaching me in depth how nature had thrived in the Land of Without before Sun's betrayal, Piko was my Master of the Known. Even though nobody in twenty generations or so had seen a living being other than men, a circle of privileged kids were yet selected to learn the features of the very creatures that Sun had obliterated, and I was among them. Our efforts wouldn't be in vain, we were told, because Sun would eventually restore life on Without and let men finally leave these corridors to admire a harmless blue sky once again.

We often paced together through the corridors, Piko sharing with me his incommensurable knowledge of a past that no longer existed. He had taught me about changing seasons, the pollination of flowers, of how larvae turned into butterflies or glaciers created rivers, and so many other marvels of nature. Entomology, ornithology, ichthyology, bromatology, scatology, eccrinology, palynology, acanthochronology, and a multitude of other sciences were all at the end of Piko's calloused fingers, despite the fact that he had never seen the wondrous phenomena he taught about. He had in fact acquired his lore of nature through the massive collection of slates or from the accounts of some other Master.

Piko was a man of conversation. I often saw him around the perimeter talking with those who sought his advice or simply enjoyed his eloquence. Curious by nature, he didn't merely deploy his intellect to study a long-gone world, he also observed everyone and everything around him. So, if anyone could tell me more about the disfigured man, that person was Piko. But I couldn't confess to him about my wanderings in the dark. Piko was extremely respectful of the Tenets – no less than Father – and he would never tolerate my actions.

'When I was walking to the choir room, I met a strange man …' I told him a half-truth while he was putting the slates back.

'Yes?' he said, gently raising his voice from one of the furthest shelves. I couldn't see him, but I could hear the muffled clank of the slates being laid down in careful order.

'Yes. A man with half of his face missing,' I said, contemplating the horror of my story. 'It was monstrous. Who is he?'

The clanking sound ceased, but Piko gave me no reply, and, back at our table, just said that the next class would teach me how carnivorous plants devoured insects.

As I was heading out, Piko prepared to measure his Juice. The men of the perimeter were all utterly anxious about their Juice, but Piko more so. He tested his Juice between every class, and even interrupted his teaching for that purpose. His was an obsession, but I wasn't sure what had caused it: maybe he feared the Descent or, perhaps, curious as he was, he longed to see what would happen afterwards.

At the end of the short way back from his unit, I found something unexpected on the floor. The stone ball. Because of the Egyptian scarab painted on the smooth surface, I knew it was mine. How had the ball returned? None of the kids would ever bring it back to me. The disfigured man? Or was it, even more unsettlingly, a magic sphere with self-moving powers? I nonetheless took it home.

The nutrients were already on the floor.

As we ingested a white powder, the content of which I didn't bother to enquire about, I said: 'When I was walking to the choir room, I met a strange—'

'Have you seen my goggles?' Father, not listening, asked Mother. 'I can't find them.'

I shuddered.

Mother gave me a quick glance.

'No,' she replied.

'Perhaps I left them in the storeroom. I will check,' he said, without taking his eyes off the nutrients scattered on the floor.

'What were you saying, Boz?' asked Mother, who always listened.

'Nothing, nothing,' I whispered, lowering my eyes. I no longer deemed wise to confide in them about my encounter with the disfigured man.

'Someone told me of noises in the blindness around the third corridor on the right,' Father said, his eyes still on the nutrients.

Mother glanced at me again.

Before going to our pallets for the sleep, we tested the Juice.

Upon seeing his results, Father's eyes sparkled.

He was stable.

Then it was Mother's turn.

She smiled sweetly after seeing the results.

'Proud of you,' Father said.

Then we tested my Juice.

'Something must be wrong,' Father said after the results. 'We need to try again.'

Mother didn't speak, but I could sense a sudden worry in her.

We tested my Juice again.

The results didn't change.

I was beginning to frighten.

A third attempt, with likewise no improvement, followed: my Juice had dropped.

In the preoccupied silence of the room, I stared at the results. It was common for the Juice to dwindle imperceptibly between screenings, but not to plunge. Only some grave reason could lie behind such a huge leak of Juice.

Father was pacing back and forth, agitated, muttering what, I couldn't make out. Then, as if he had just experienced a sudden realisation, he switched to outright rage, and, having grabbed the vase with the fern that stood next to his pallet – the sole ornament in our unit – he threw it against the wall. Vase and fern parted ways, but bounced back intact.

'It's your fault!' Father yelled.

I looked at him, puzzled.

Mother was crying, her sobbing covered with ease by his screams.

'They punished you for missing the coating …' he scolded. 'You and your damned excuses!'

I had already heard about men suddenly leaking large amounts of Juice. They said that a huge loss of Juice could only follow the violation of a Tenet, but I wasn't certain this was true. What I knew, for sure, was that all these men had ended up badly.

'You'll make amends!' Father screamed. 'You're nothing but trouble!'

I made a largely useless effort to explain that it wasn't my fault (although I wasn't too sure). Mother had meanwhile moved to another corner of the room, her back turned, and she was busying herself with some futile chore, pretending not to listen.

I had been caught unprepared. What I had always taken for granted – life – was now in peril. Maybe my leak of Juice was a singular event and, if this was the case, I wouldn't have to worry. But if the Juice diminished again at that pace, my Descent would begin earlier than expected; and, even though I wasn't as curious about life as Piko, I did still want to continue existing. I feared that the loss of Juice might be a consequence of my wanderings in the dark. I felt so at fault for my breach of the Tenets, and for the pain that Mother was suffering because of me. My hurt was compounded when, in the ensuing darkness, Father, from his pallet, whispered: 'Is he really our son?'

I couldn't make out Mother's feeble reply.

When the lights came back, Father had already reached a decision on how to address the serious matter afflicting our family: he would ask the zookeeper, who owed him a favour, to assign me some chore at the zoo after my classes with Piko. Finally useful to the men of the perimeter, his son would be spared further losses of Juice – Father believed.

I still remembered my first visit to the zoo as a child with Piko – especially the moment when we had entered the largest room. There, a creature with smooth dark brown skin was pacing on two feet inside a wide cage made of glass. I could easily see from a bulging band covering her upper bosom and a thin cloth around the hips that the creature was a female.

She didn't react to our presence.

'Piko,' I asked him. 'Didn't you tell me there are no surviving creatures ... that Sun killed them all? That only mankind has survived?'

'Indeed, Boz,' he replied, appreciating both my memory and curiosity. 'She is a Congoid, and belongs to mankind.'

I had never seen nor heard of a Congoid before.

'But she's not like us ...' I observed.

'Her skin is darker, her nose flatter, her lips protuberant,' Piko replied. 'But her anatomy is not much different from that of our women.'

'But why is her skin so dark?'

Piko answered with a question. 'Do you remember, Boz, when I showed you a map of Earth before Sun dried up all the Oceans?'

'Yes, I remember.'

'The Congoids come from Africa, a place where sunlight was so fierce, even before the apocalypse, that their skin had already turned dark. It was from the land of the Congoids, indeed, that Sun began the destruction of Earth.'

'And what are we?'

'Caucasoids.'

I had listened to his explanation in silence, watching the Congoid run on a wheel fixed to the floor to train her body, while in the centre of the glass cage a large table hosted various piles of slates, presumably serving to strengthen what Piko said was a rather weak mind. In a corner stood the pallet where the Congoid slept, not far from a squatting hole that led to an uninspiring transparent box laid under the cage.

I had never returned to the zoo since.

'Your father says you're lazy, that we need to straighten your back,' the stout zookeeper warned in a sullen tone that betrayed his overall disinterest in the task. He clearly didn't want me around.

'Listen to what you've got to do,' he instructed, pointing at the cage.

The Congoid was still there.

'When the zoo closes, you must clean the cage and

empty the shit-box. Always remember to lock the cage and the entrance to the zoo when you leave. If I find out that you've forgotten to do what I say, I will whip the crap out of you. Understood?'

I already hated him, but at least he didn't want me to black-wash the zoo.

'Ah … I was forgetting …' the zookeeper added. 'When you finish with the cage … you also need to do my room …'

The glass cage was relatively well kept, but his unit, I suspected, had never once been cleaned. As the zookeeper snored loudly, slouched on a chair with his filthy feet propped on a stool, I got through ten rags, and even had to use a putty knife to remove all the dirt accumulated on the floor. I was tempted to use the putty knife on his feet also.

The Congoid hadn't aged much since my visit with Piko. On that occasion, I had noticed a couple of long scars on her back, which had now grown in size and density to create a tracery that extended almost to her shoulders.

I went to the zoo before every dark. While I always studied her actions as I cleaned the cage, the Congoid didn't take any notice of me. She was used to seeing staring Caucasoids, I presumed. While I was there, she ran on the wheel, or sat at the table, engrossed in examining her numerous slates.

She was much taller than me, but I didn't feel in the least intimidated, for her eyes displayed calm and patience, qualities much needed to survive an entire life within a glass cage. After a while, I got into the habit of thinking aloud when I was there with her. The zookeeper always retired to his room soon after my arrival, and we were left alone inside the cage. 'Don't try to talk to her,' he had once warned me, after hearing my voice in the cage. 'She's sly and devious. And there's no point: Congoids don't understand us.'

I didn't follow his order. Even though she couldn't grasp what I said, I opened myself up to the mute guest of the cage. She didn't seem sly and devious to me. I spoke of my loss of Juice, my issues with Father, whom I could no longer stand, and of the other problems in my life. As I spoke, she kept doing what she was doing, or sometimes glanced at me. Despite the silence, I enjoyed her presence. I could feel lonely at home, especially if Father was in, and outside with the other kids, too, but never with her.

Meanwhile, visions of the disfigured man haunted me in the sleep. I wondered if he, like the Congoid, belonged to another human race. Perhaps he had escaped from a zoo. But I couldn't ask this sort of question of the zookeeper, unless I wanted to receive a good whipping for my insolence.

Apparently proving the wisdom of Father's decision, after I started visiting the zoo, my level of Juice remained stable. The arguments with him stopped, Mother seemed relieved by the renewed stability of my Juice, and life in our unit was returning to its dull normalcy.

Once, among the usual muddle of the Congoid's table, I noticed a rectangular board, chequered in turquoise and brown, with an equal number of bee- and scarab-shaped pieces on the surface. It was a board of senet, a game at which I was quite good. By instinct I drew closer to the table. The zookeeper had warned me not to touch it, as this in particular would upset the Congoid. But, as usual, I didn't follow his instruction, and picked up one of the well-crafted cones to observe it in more detail. From her wheel, the Congoid saw me. She jumped down and moved threateningly in my direction. Up close, she looked even bigger. For the first – and last – time, I felt intimidated by her. I dropped the piece back on the board and took a couple of steps back. The Congoid paused. She looked down at the board, then straight at me, a clear thought materialising in her mind – confirmed when, having cleared some space around the board, she pointed. The Congoid wanted to play.

It was the first of many silent rounds of senet. She was very good. I wondered with whom she had learned to play. From her behaviour I concluded that, before meeting me, the Congoid had considered herself unbeatable at the game and was now disappointed in seeing that I was at her level. We both took the game very seriously, and both hated defeats. When I won a round, she would close her eyes and clench her fists so as to prevent her inner rage from flowing out in a violent outburst. On one occasion, I almost laughed at her insane reaction to a loss, but wisely stopped myself.

The incident with the Juice had distracted me from Bruttho, but not him from me. I heard his pack had now grown to a hundred kids, blindly obeying his orders in unquestioning reverence, and that he was keen to punish me. Bruttho couldn't afford for his pack to see me escape unharmed; he had to set an example.

The moment of retribution came in the shape of three kids ambushing me around a bend. They had been waiting. Two held my arms, the third slapped me. Yelling at the top of my lungs, I tried to break free with all my strength, but it was useless, as nobody around helped me. I noticed an armband stitched to the kids' sleeves, a sign that – as I would soon learn – identified those belonging to Bruttho's pack.

'Shut up!' one of the kids shouted as he gripped my right arm even harder. Another elbowed my stomach, prompting me to realise how vain any further resistance would be. My arms firmly in their grip, we all walked together through dozens of corridors to reach a far zone of the perimeter unknown to me. It was nothing like our corridor. The walls, whose black coating had entirely worn off, were smeared with patches in oxblood colour, while many of the units had been torn apart. The light was dim, and the air reeked of stale piss. We strode through a corridor where a host of kids, armbanded like my abductors, idled around. On seeing me hauled ahead, the kids burst out laughing. Just one, the nice kid with whom I had spoken after choir, watched us with a look of apprehension, empathising with my dreadful fate. We reached a unit which differed from the others, for the colour of the curtain hanging on the door was oxblood, not grey. It was Bruttho's den. One kid raised the painted curtain, another pushed me in. On the far side of the large room, a throng of kids stood in a circle around Bruttho, sat up straight on a cathedra, his big hands placed on the armrests. They had stolen the engraved cathedra from the choir room, and covered it in oxblood.

The kids dragged me in front of him, released my arms and, as they joined the others in a wide circle, left me there alone. My legs shook under my robe. Bruttho looked at me, caressing the carved handle of a curved knife placed on the right armrest of his new throne. I avoided staring back, so that he wouldn't think I was defying him, and my eyes naturally landed on the curved knife. I suddenly felt like an idiot for having believed that my improved game with the stone ball might ever save me.

'Boz, you run fast …' he said in a calm tone.

I nodded, though I wasn't sure I should've done so.

His accent confirmed, as I had been told, that Bruttho came from perimeter 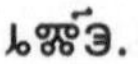. Breathitt: the ugliest of places. I was very good with accents. I could even tell in which corridor someone lived. Not that I had ever met someone with a Breathitt accent before, but I had heard others imitate it.

'You know why you're here?' he asked.

I didn't nod this time. Just stood there, mute, still feeling like an idiot.

'I want you to join my pack,' he said.

I was surprised. I had thought that Bruttho wanted to punish me, yet he apparently meant me no harm. But why would he want me in his pack?

I looked at the other kids, trying to read their reactions. They stared at us in silence, seemingly more ill at ease than me.

'So?' Bruttho insisted.

The thought of the kid who had lost all his fingers after refusing to join the pack influenced my answer: 'Yes.'

'Good,' he commented, without the hint of a smile.

One of his kids approached me. Brandishing a long nail he used to stitch the oxblood armband to my robe, he pricked me. I twitched in silence. When the sewing was complete, the kid raised my arm up. Encouraged by Bruttho, the entire room howled. I smiled, although still unsure that the pack really meant me no harm.

'Let's have the food!' Bruttho shouted. His kids yelled. Many other boys poured in from the corridor. Soon, nutrients of all sorts covered the floor, more for each kid than their genitors might ever give them. Before every lights-out, indeed, each unit was delivered only an amount of nutrients sufficient to feed that unit, and storing nutrients was not allowed. Observing the kids trampling over a thick layer of edibles – an abundance hard to justify – I wondered where Bruttho had stolen all the nutrients from.

I found myself eating next to the nice kid. After devouring everything he could without lifting his eyes from his full hands, he spoke: 'You were wise, Boz. Nobody says *no* to Bruttho.'

I ate reluctantly. Piko, to whom I was heading when the kids had taken me away, was already worried, I was sure. And the thought that I wouldn't see the Congoid for who knew how long saddened me. Moreover, even though I had accepted Bruttho's invitation to join his pack without undue persuasion, I felt uncomfortably less at liberty now that I belonged to it.

'But what does he want me to do?' I asked the nice kid.

Before he could answer, Bruttho silenced the room, announcing with solemnity that he wanted us to sing a new hymn with him. Silence followed. Knowing that the Tenets prohibited new chants, the kids peered at each other with ill-concealed unease.

Yet, Bruttho sang with conviction:

We, the kids, are tired. We want to eat and sleep more. All these rules are killing us. Kids shall do everything they want. We are nothing, let us be everything. The domination of the grown-ups is about to end. The kids will conquer all units, perimeters, clusters. We will finally have our own rules, play in the dark, stop pulling our hair out, beat the kids who aren't with us!

The pack refrained from accompanying him in the chant, but when Bruttho ended his short hymn, they yelled, banging the walls with their hands in a frenetic rhythm, throwing hand-fuls of nutrients in the air. As they continued eating, I couldn't say whether their enthusiasm for Bruttho's words was real, nor whether they enjoyed the tasteless nutrients, or whether all of it was done to flatter him.

No single Tenet prevented a kid from building his own pack, at least not that I knew of; yet it was clear to me that Bruttho was acting way beyond what the Tenets might ever allow. He was planning a rebellion. Without question, he would soon face the Crier's harsh punishment.

As the kids gobbled the food, the boy who had stitched my armband on, whose name was Tiruyte, walked around the room to light the many candles lining the walls. I remembered seeing those candles shelved in the storeroom.

Darkness was approaching. We all could somehow feel it; even though blindness was never announced, and measuring time was forbidden by Tenet ৪৬, the frequency of the dark was sufficiently regular for us to develop an instinct for when the light was about to go off.

'He'll order us to leave,' the nice kid warned me. 'Only Bruttho and his chosen ones stay in this room once the lights are out. The others sleep in the corridor.'

As predicted, the lights went off.

'Out!' Bruttho yelled.

The kids uttered a soft groan of disappointment, for they would have preferred to stay in the den with the light and the nutrients, but still hastened to the dark corridor. I was walking out, too, when Bruttho, beckoning me, said: 'Boz, stay here.'

The kids hummed. I saw disbelief in most eyes, and envy in those who had to leave. I regretted parting ways with the nice kid, even if only for the lights-out, and felt bad for being favoured over him. We touched hands, then he went away with the others in forlorn silence. Only six of us remained with Bruttho, the others being much older and bigger than me.

The flickering candlelight cast shadows across the walls. In the dim light of the room, Bruttho lorded over us from his oxblood throne. We sat silently around him. For a moment, I cherished being among the chosen ones – but it didn't last long.

'We aren't ready for the sleep yet, agreed?' Bruttho asked in a high pitch.

Cupping their hands around their mouths, the kids howled furiously. I was probably expected to join the bawling, but I didn't.

'Good …' Bruttho said, pleased with the noise.

He looked at me.

'Boz … your initiation must now begin …'

The other kids howled again, even louder.

I held my breath; it had indeed seemed too easy, I thought.

A kid stood up from the circle. He drew close. 'Go over there,' he said in a low tone, pointing towards one remote corner of the room – at a low arched doorway I hadn't noticed before.

I hesitated.

'Go!' yelled Bruttho, impatiently, waving the curved knife in the air.

I had no other choice than to do as I was told. So, as the kids thrummed in evil anticipation of what was to come, I walked hesitantly towards the arched doorway, dreading the unknown fate that awaited me behind the flaky wall. I feared someone might be lying in ambush with a bucket of hot tar, or that I would have to face the disfigured man again. As I reached the rounded doorway, quivering at the darkness of a small room now visible ahead of me, I turned around but, lacking the courage to even look in Bruttho's direction, I resolved to walk in. Once inside, I paused, waiting to adapt to the near-dark, only slightly penetrated by four or five candles. I soon discerned a tiny shape, standing head-bent by the opposing wall.

I moved closer. Curiosity, outgrowing fear, powered my movements. The room felt cold, a sensation that I knew had to come from within me, because the temperature inside the perimeter never changed. I got to within eight steps of the immobile figure, whose face was entirely covered by a cowl. I, by contrast, was in full view, and the disparity made me feel naked and vulnerable. Suddenly, however, as if to put me more at ease, her hands rose to pull down the cowl.

A girl.

She was beautiful, even more so than the girls I had seen in perimeter ᖯᕈ̃Ꝫ, where Father and Mother had taken me to find a female I could eventually have a child with. I hadn't seen one since. No girls lived in our perimeter; only mothers. Families giving life to a daughter were deported to other perimeters.

With her smooth skin and complete lack of motherly weariness in her eyes, I doubted that the girl before me was a childbearer. She then must have come from another perimeter. Her calm detached look told me that she posed no threat, and the occasional laughter coming from the kids in the large room sort of reassured me, too. I was expected to talk, I knew, but it was my first moment alone with a girl.

She spoke first.

'Boz?'

Unlike the croaky sounds made by the boys of the perimeter, especially the older ones, the girl's voice was soft and even.

'Yes,' I whispered, her knowledge of my name unexpected. 'What's your name?' I asked.

'Flox ...' said the girl, a little surprised at my interest.

'I've never seen you around ... where are you from?' I asked. 'ᴸᵅᵌ.'

Breathitt.

She had come with Bruttho; but I couldn't believe how her gentle features, smooth dark hair, and thin, delicate lips had all survived that ghastly place intact.

'Is it as ... terrible ... as they say?' I asked.

She didn't answer. 'I'm here to bring you joy,' Flox declared, untying the cord of her robe to gently drop it to the floor. The gesture brought back to me those stories about lone women in Breathitt committing their lives to giving men pleasure. I had always envisioned these benefactresses as quite withered and coarse, so thinking that Flox, with all her youth and composure, could be one of them disturbed me.

'Breathitt ... is it that bad?' I repeated, curtly. I could tolerate my Master of the Known ignoring my questions, but not a girl from Breathitt. Also, I wanted to decline her offer of pleasure, about which I had reddened a little.

Flox looked at me in slight amusement: the other new members of the pack had surely shown a more enthusiastic response to the prospect of intimacy.

'It's dangerous,' she answered. 'Men are slaughtered even before ending their Juice ...'

I smothered a groan at the image.

'Our men aren't evil,' she claimed. 'Violence is just a need. There's no hymns, no zoo, no spectacles in perimeter ᴸᵅᵌ. There's nothing of nothing. You don't understand how privileged you are, here. My people need violence if they don't want to become any madder than they already are.'

Was Flox saying that, just as I entertained myself by playing senet with the Congoid, for the same purpose a man in Breathitt would take a stick to bash his neighbour's head in?

'It's not that our people are evil,' she repeated. 'It's the Crier.'

'What?' I asked, incredulous. How dare she say that the Crier was malevolent. He had saved us from Sun! He fed us! The Crier was our future!

'I know why you're looking at me like that,' she said in response to my bewilderment. 'I, too, believed that he was our saviour. But after what I saw … I opened my eyes.'

Flox had acquired a stern, yet no less controlled, expression. 'Right after I was born, Mother ended the Juice,' she said, her eyes staring past me as if trying to go back in time. 'It's painful … not remembering her face. Father was a strong man, the toughest of the perimeter. He did all he could to make me feel safe. At every lightbreak, he hugged me tight, then left our unit to find food. We aren't spoilt like you. Nobody brings us food in perimeter [illegible]; we must find a way to quell our hunger.'

I had never considered eating the nutrients a privilege – quite the opposite. But at least I'd never had to work to get them. And if you ended the food, as Father said, you ended the Juice. So, I was privileged – at least more so than those of Breathitt.

'When he went out for the food, Father left me alone; even for long,' Flox continued. 'But he always came back, and with him came one can of food. It was fine to stay by myself. I recited the Tenets. I felt safe: the others feared him, and no one would ever touch me, not even that neighbour staring at me in the corridor. He freaked me out with his toady eyes …'

I resisted the curiosity to ask her which species of toad her neighbour was from. After all, I doubted any Master of the Known was spreading knowledge through the corridors of her savage perimeter.

'I was terribly curious of where Father took the nutrients from,' Flox continued. 'But when I asked him, he said: "Only men must know about these things." I was upset. We always shared everything; why shouldn't I know this? So, I wanted to find out on my own where he got the food.'

I understood how she felt. I knew only too well how unbearable curiosity could be.

'I followed him,' she continued. 'The toad saw me, and he instantly understood what I was up to. Still, I carried on following Father through the corridors.'

I was getting to like Flox even more: she had done precisely what I would've done in her place.

'Father walked five hundred steps, turned right, walked another three hundred and fifty steps, bore left, then right after two hundred more steps. He reached a group of men going into a room. When they saw him, they made space so that he could pass. One even patted him. I was so scared to stay alone with all those strangers – and I really wanted to see what was inside – so I sneaked in, even though I knew I shouldn't be there.'

'What did you find inside?'

'The room was full, and I could see nothing with all those idlers around me. I looked left and right, in search of Father. Then, the men's noise grew stronger. They were shouting at something I couldn't see. I made my way to the edge of the crowd. Small as I am, and with my cap on, nobody saw me. I almost reached the front … when …'

'When ... ?'

'Father. His back to me, he was standing in the middle of the crowd. Opposite him, at no more than six or seven steps, was another man. He stared at Father as if he wanted to kill him. The idlers were shouting at them to start fighting, but they kept their distance, and just moved in a circle, putting up their fists. I was upset: why was Father fighting with a man instead of searching for food? Then came the sound of a horn. The men roared. I covered my ears against all the noise. Father and the other man took off their robes. I couldn't believe it when I saw an iron shift wrapped around Father's trunk. I had never seen it at home. The other had on a mail full of tiny golden bells that made an eerie sound when he moved.'

A sudden noise startled us. Flox paused. A couple of Bruttho's kids had come close to hear what was going on inside. We stood silent. Soon after, the kids, hearing no moan of ecstasy coming from our room, went back to Bruttho, disappointed. Flox resumed: 'The big man lunged forward, but Father ducked and avoided him, three or four times. I hadn't known he could move so fast. I peeped out from behind two men. I didn't want him to see me; he would've been angry or, worse, become distracted. The man tried to hit Father again, but lost his balance, and was throttled. He tried to break free, kicking his legs out left and right, trying to elbow Father, but he was done for. His head dropped. He was unconscious, or dead, already. Father let him fall. Then he stood still, looking down at the man on the floor with no pity. The idlers cheered, raised his arms, swarmed around him. They hid my view. I was afraid. When the horn blasted again, they all moved away, and I saw Father standing there, his robe back on, holding a large can. The man on the floor was covered with a wrap. That is how I found out how Father got the food for me.'

Altogether, Flox had discovered her father, the only man she could rely on, wasn't the man she had always thought he was, and that blood lay behind the food she shared with him after every lightbreak, and from then on her life could never be the same.

'He didn't see me. I followed him, back to our unit, through a shortcut to arrive first, so that he wouldn't suspect. The toad was waiting, of course, staring into the corridor. I looked at him threateningly, then whispered: "If you tell Father, I will tell him that you tried to play with me." He went back to his cubicle. From then on, when Father left home, I followed him, and watched him kill a man in exchange for a large can of food. The pull was stronger than me: now that I knew what Father did outside home, I had to go with him. If they harmed him in one of those duels, I wanted to be there at least, stroking his head, telling him how much I cared ...'

'What happened to him – was he murdered in a duel?'

'No, he was always the one to kill. He was the strongest. That's why everyone respected him,' replied Flox, slightly annoyed by my insinuation. 'Even in his last duel, he gouged the other's eyes out. We all clapped and yelled. Yes, me too; I was getting used to violence, almost enjoyed it,' she said calmly, reliving that gruesome memory. 'But, as Father held the large can of nutrients in his hands, the yelling in the room suddenly changed. There was no longer exaltation in their screams, but fear. Men scuttled away, stumbling into each other, trampling those who had fallen to the floor, caring only about themselves. I didn't move. A lump rose in my throat. The room was almost empty when I saw a man with a long purple beard, a huge man, clomping among the idlers. He wore a purple cloak and had a whip in his hand …'

'The Crier!' I shouted. The description fitted with the stories Father told whenever he threatened to call him.

'Yes …' Flox nodded, lowering her eyes, that memory still a cause of pain. 'The men were rushing off because of him. I wouldn't have thought it possible, but … Father, too, was scared. The Crier unfolded his whip. Father waited there, shaking, but didn't run away. The Crier waved his whip in the air, cracked it against the floor, warming up the lash …' said Flox, finally losing her composure, a tear sliding down her cheek. 'The first whipping reached Father's legs. He screamed, then tried to snatch the whip, but he didn't make it, and a second lash cut his shoulder. The third lash was to his face. He bent forward in pain, and the Crier lashed him in the back one, two, three times, before I had to look away; I just stood there, crying inside at each crack of the whip. Men were coming back into the room. They were enjoying all of it. One, craving more, whooped at every lash. I stood in silence, even though I wanted to shout, and soon Father, too, fell silent. Nobody dared to get close to the Crier, but all the men in the room screamed in awe at his ruthless execution of Father.'

Flox paused. Her lips were trembling. It was too much to bear. I felt pity for her, but also wanted to learn what happened next, and so I asked.

'The Crier raised the whip in the air and yelled: "The Tenets prohibit duels!" … and that was it. He walked out of the room without another word. I rushed to Father. Lying on his stomach, blood all over his back, he was still breathing.

When he saw me, his eyes reduced to slits, he knew that I had seen everything, and groaned. I called for help, but the room was empty. The can had also gone. I stroked his head, told him how much I wanted him to live, but soon his eyes … closed.'

Flox had found herself alone in Breathitt, with a Tenet to justify her Father's death. For all our quarrelling, I couldn't imagine living in the perimeter without Father and Mother, because, at the time, I still thought I could count on them, and they ultimately gave me a sense of protection.

'I wanted to stay close to Father a bit more and … cry … cry. But now I was on my own, with nobody to help me. I was in danger. I still feel guilty for having left him on the floor to run home, even if I had no choice. When I arrived home, I searched his things. I found a curved knife. At first I couldn't bear even to touch the handle, but then I found the courage to grab it. There were still some nutrients: two cans – they would last for a while. I had some time to work out what to do. I felt a bit safer now, and finally cried all the tears I wished I had shed on Father's body. Then, holding the knife tight in my hand, I fell asleep. When I woke up and looked around, the first thing I saw was the toad. He was standing right by the door. My heart was pounding. "They told me what happened," he said, a grin on his face. I had never heard his croaky voice before. "Why are you here?" I asked. I wanted him gone. "I can protect you – you know?" he said. "I can give you all the nutrients you want." "I've enough food," I said. "It will end," he said. "Soon you will beg me for the nutrients." He went away. I was happy that the toad had left, but he was right: my nutrients wouldn't last forever. I didn't know where to get more of them. So, I tried to eat as little as possible: one tablet of polypeptide, a spoon of calciferol and one strip of phylloquinone before every dark. That was my ration. I stuck to it. I began losing weight. I was having vertigo. Still, one can of nutrients ended. I hoped someone would save me. I didn't know who – I was alone – but I had hope. I kept dreaming of Father. Every time I woke up, I was afraid to open my eyes and see the toad. I filled my life by reciting the Tenets. I wanted to believe in a reward. When the second can ended too, I gave up the Tenets. It was useless, anyway. I had stopped measuring the Juice long before. Hunger was already gnawing at me when I begged the other units for food, but nobody helped me. They all said that Tenet ꗏꔫꕔ prohibited us to give nutrients away, that I should find a way to get the nutrients by myself. One neighbour was kind enough to allow me to lick his floor, but the others didn't care. I was lying on my pallet, weak, desperate, hopeless, when the toad appeared by the door with a little can in his hand. He started to shake the can gently, snapping his tongue. "Do you want it?" he asked. Exhausted, I nodded. "You know what I want from you?" I didn't say anything. "I just want to play," he said. I had already played with a boy, but didn't want to play with this old toad. I had no choice, though. So, I played with him. It was awful. The smell of it was awful. But after playing, he gave me the little can. I ate the nutrients in a fury. My teeth scratched the can. But the nutrients didn't last long. The toad came back with a new can. We played again. He gave me the can. He visited me over and over. I was alive, but in agony. I wanted to end the Juice, so that I would never have the toad touching me again; but I also wanted to survive, so I accepted the food, and what followed. But I was no longer the same person I had been before the toad touched me.'

I groaned, clenching my fists. Had I been in the position to, I would've killed the toad for what he had done to Flox. But, apparently, someone had beaten me to it: 'It had been going on for a while when a kid sneaked inside the cubicle. The toad was lying naked on my pallet. Absorbed by his cravings, he didn't notice him. The kid took my knife from where I had placed it after Father's death, next to the pallet, and when the toad bent down to kiss my body, he stabbed him in the back. I will never forget the sudden look of pain and surprise in his eyes. The kid stabbed him twenty times. Father's knife had finally served its purpose. I celebrated all those twenty gashes. The bastard spat blood everywhere. After completing his job, the kid took the little can of nutrients and gave it to me, reaching down for my hand. "I'm Bruttho. Come with me. We must leave," he ordered. I followed him; he was my only way out of hunger and pain. We travelled through many perimeters. Wherever he went, Bruttho built a pack. The kids adored him. Every time, he stole nutrients to share with all the kids and with me. He can be very generous, Bruttho. When we ran out of food, we moved on to another perimeter. When grown-ups tried to kill him, Bruttho stabbed them with Father's knife. He's very strong. He reminds me of Father.'

Why was Bruttho taking Flox with him, perimeter after perimeter? So that she could provide joy to his kids? Was giving pleasure away a condition for Flox to survive, just as the toad had once imposed on her?

'Now you know why I believe the Crier is evil.' Flox interrupted my brooding. 'He took everything from me. If Father hadn't been forced to fight other men for food, he would still be alive. The Crier forced him to fight for food, then killed him because of this.'

I liked Flox, very much, but I still believed that nobody should judge whether the Crier was right or wrong. It was a serious violation of the Tenets. We had simply to accept what the Crier did.

'Boz!' Bruttho shouted from the other room. 'Come here! Enough with the joy!'

The kids of the pack laughed.

'You must go,' Flox whispered.

Her eyes smiled, but not her lips.

I didn't know why Flox had shared her sad story with me. It was normal in Breathitt, perhaps, but in our perimeter we seldom opened ourselves up to others.

'Why have you told me all this?' I asked.

'You're the first kid who's ever asked for my name,' she answered.

I was cherishing the moment between us, but I really had to go back to Bruttho.

'I've one question,' I said. 'In your wanderings, have you ever met a kid named Thatem?'

She seemed amused. 'I've never heard this name.'

Once back in the large room – even though the greatest part of me was still with Flox, and was already determined to help her escape the condition she was in – the kids urged me to eat more nutrients. Bruttho himself took a bowl, filled it with three handfuls of yellow powder, a couple of large spoons of red paste, some brown mess, then had it brought to me.

'How was the girl?' one boy whispered, timidly, among the overall noise. 'I haven't tried her yet.'

'Unforgettable,' I said. 'She shared everything with me.'

'Oh …' The kid blushed.

I was absorbed in my thoughts when Bruttho, raising his head from his mound of nutrients, addressed me.

'You're the son of a keeper, right?' he asked, a reddish liquid trickling down from his busy mouth.

I didn't know where he was heading with his question, but I didn't want Bruttho approaching my family again, so I found the courage to give him a square, angry look.

'I know you are,' he continued, oblivious to my reaction.

'Your father holds the key to the shelter.' Bruttho was revealing his true intentions towards me, and why he had asked me to join his pack. 'You must bring it here. We need it.'

He wanted to ransack the shelter. Bruttho had taken a huge stock of nutrients from some other place but, judging from the greed of his pack, it was coming to an end. The candles, too: they would need more of them in case the bailiffs cut the lights out in the part of the perimeter that had fallen under Bruttho's control, and the shelter was stocked with them.

I didn't want to steal Father's key. Even though we didn't get along well, I was reluctant to betray his trust, especially without it being necessary. Also, the nutrients in the shelter were meant to feed the perimeter in case of a plague, not Bruttho's greedy pack. He just wanted more things to swallow before leaving for another perimeter with Flox, abandoning these kids to the beatings of their genitors.

I didn't want to take part in a purposeless rebellion.

'No. I will not help you.'

The kids stopped eating, and dropped the nutrients on the floor.

Bruttho stood up, removing the curved knife that had once belonged to Flox's father from a pocket in his robe.

The shocked kids screamed.

I thought their screaming was in reaction to my imminent slaughter, but I was wrong.

A large shadow on the wall, he had arrived unnoticed. Next to the door, cape down over his shoulders, mouth bared in a repellent grin, was the disfigured man. The ruin of his face was even more appalling in candlelight. Opposite the empty half of his mouth stood two short arches of intact pearly teeth, ready to sink their sharp edges into our flesh, while scarce patches of white hair speckled his wrinkled head.

Bruttho paused. The curved knife fell into the soft pile of nutrients on the floor. His eyes, invaded by dread, never left the disfigured man, while from beneath his robe a yellowish dribble reached his shaky calves.

Bruttho's den was now quiet. The other kids had run away through a door in the back, leaving Bruttho and me alone with the disfigured man, who, turning his battered face towards me, said: 'You must go home, Boz.'

III

DESCENT

The good-natured man with whom I had once painted a bit of wall suddenly ended his Juice. After repeating the measurement in the futile hope of a mistake, because no result was ever reverted, the man came to accept an unavoidable destiny. He was muttering something mournful about his Juice in the corridor when the undertakers arrived. He nodded, downcast, then followed them towards his Descent. I was there. I saw everything.

The man had no woman, no child, and siblings are forbidden within the walls, so Father believed it appropriate to show him our deepest sympathy by attending his Descent. And, most of all, despite his stern warnings against curiosity, Father was in fact a prying man.

I had never attended a Descent. When we arrived next to the bronze manhole, the good-natured neighbour was there, surrounded by the undertakers and five or six idlers. With some effort, for it was very heavy, the undertakers raised the rusted lid from the manhole to drag it aside. Deep scratches around the hole revealed the frequency at which it was uncovered. Around thirty candles on a hanging candelabrum were the only source of light in the room. The last light this man would ever see.

He leaned forward to stare into the darkness, then looked up at those around. Hope and a sense of liberation should pervade whoever commences the Descent, Tenet ϬӠ϶ postulates, but the good-natured man appeared rather more forlorn than joyous at entering the manhole. For fear of plunging inside, I kept myself a couple of steps behind the others. Even though the idlers were by now crowding the room, I could still see the descending man – albeit intermittently – through the thickening wall of dark robes. Standing before the open manhole, the man sung his ode.

He who is of Earth belongs to Earth. Soon my flesh will merge with the soil, my blood with the mud, and I will become as one with mighty Earth. My Descent is about to start. Safe inside the bowels of Earth, Sun will cease threatening me. I will no longer suffer fear, pain, strain, torment. Life comes from Earth and returns to Earth.

As the man sang, I looked at Mother, and knew right away what she was too afraid even to contemplate: that the next Descent might be mine. I couldn't tell anything from Father's eyes; he stared, impassive, at the manhole.

Midway through the hymn, the man, whose robe was now stained with the copious wax falling from above, suddenly stepped into the hole. To my amazement, he didn't disappear. I leaned forward in a hurry to see, and discovered that his feet had met the first step of a narrow stairwell previously hidden from my view. I had never seen a stair, at the time. Chanting alone, the man slowly walked down another step. Then another. Four or five steps followed, until he was out of sight. His quavering voice grew distant, feebler, swallowed by the hole. The throng of idlers were silent. Soon the undertakers drew closer in short steps, took the bronze lid and covered the hole. No more sound came from below. The wax now fell on the lid, punctuating the stillness of the room. The good-natured neighbour's journey into Earth had begun – the only certainty being we would never see him again.

Upon watching that man disappear inside a dark hole, I dared to ponder whether Thatem hadn't lost himself inside the perimeter at all; perhaps he had undertaken the Descent, and we simply didn't know it. What an absurd theory!

After the function, I met with Piko for our class. When I walked in, he was ferreting around in the shelves to prepare the slates. We sat down by his stone table, on which he laid the slates.

'What's troubling you, Boz?' he asked slowly, yet abruptly.

Piko has seen into me, again. It was embarrassing, whenever it happened, because I felt nude. And it was dangerous: not all my thoughts conformed to the Tenets, and opening myself up to Piko, to Father and Mother, to anyone inside the perimeter, was a source of peril.

'I've just attended a man's Descent …' I told him.

Piko nodded, as he always did when he approved of my reactions, when he believed I was responding in the manner a boy should.

'My first Descent … I still remember …' he commented with soft eyes. 'A man was leaving his family. I found it difficult to accept. He had a child, who cried so loud when his father walked down. No matter what she did, the mother couldn't stop him from crying. I, too, began to cry quietly. Then, a woman standing next to me whispered that I should be merry – not sad – because that man was about to become a single

thing with Earth. It was not his end, she said, but his comple-
tion. And he would finally smell the soil, something precluded
for us living within these walls. 'In sorrow, yet joyful,' she said.
The kind woman was right. I found solace in her words.'

Hungry to learn, I always tried to extract as much knowledge as I could from Piko.

'What happens during the Descent?' I asked.

'You go back to where everything began.'

'And there is no returning?'

'No, there isn't.'

'And we can't hear them … ?'

'No. Unless they want us to know they are still there; in
that case, they make the floor quake.'

I nodded. It had happened on three or four occasions:
the ground trembled, walls shook, things fell on the floor. I
was just a child when it first happened. I had rushed under
Mother's robe. She told me not to worry, that everything
would be fine, but she didn't say it was the men from underneath who had shaken the land so violently. Without the
privilege of a Master of the Known, she probably didn't know
what had happened underneath.

'We borrow life from Earth, we must give life back to
Earth,' Piko warned. 'When we still lived outside, humankind
believed that ending the Juice meant ascending to the realm of
the skies. How foolish. As if someone could exist in an imaginary place so high above. And, of all places, the sky, from
where Sun later perpetrated his annihilation of all life!'

'Really?' My eyes widened.

'Yes, Boz. What they already had was not enough for them.
They needed to believe in other worlds, in creatures without

flesh, in spirits departing from bodies. The Land of Without was not sufficient. And the more implausible the stories, the more they liked to believe. Sometimes, I ask myself whether Sun punished men for their greed ...'

He quieted himself. The bailiffs could lash him for this heresy – he knew it. Under no circumstance, in fact, did the Tenets allow a man to justify, even in part, what Sun had done to the creatures of Without. Never. A thick silence ensued.

'It's getting late. We must start our class,' Piko urged.

He took a slate with the image of a scarab I had never seen before. Shiny black thorax with ochre markings, elongated and robust legs, red tips to its antennae.

'A Nicrophorus,' Piko, observing my silence, revealed.

Magnificently displaying its chromatic splendour on a broad leaf, the Nicrophorus had a squarish, yet well-proportioned body. Along with its delightful appearance, nature had also bestowed this marvellous scarab with a noticeable resourcefulness. The Nicrophorus, indeed, fed on carcasses, which its antennae smelled from a distance. It then transported the carrion to a safe place on its back, where it burrowed into the carcass. As soon as the fur was removed, the Nicrophorus excavated the soil from underneath to slowly bury it. After, the scarabs mated on top of it and the female deposited the resulting eggs in the carrion, so that the larvae could be fed with the remains.

I was taken by Piko's detailed account of such gruesome diligence. Yet my amazement soon blended with melancholy, brought on by the awareness that no scarab had survived Sun's heinous burning of Without. Maybe some scarabs had found refuge under the soil and their descendants were still crawling around, I liked to imagine, but my theory couldn't be shared with Piko; he always reiterated that no creature, besides humans, had avoided extinction – and he was, by now, annoyed with my frequent mulling over the possible survival of scarabs, and said that my continuous questioning might be interpreted by the Crier as a sign of arrogance.

Piko painted the slates for his archive with great dexterity. He occasionally visited other perimeters, when allowed by the bailiffs, to meet the most distinguished Masters of the Known, examine their collections of slates and copy all the illustrations of eukaryotes that he found worth of remark. Jealously attached to their slates, Masters of the Known never lent them to anyone, so Piko had to pull a cart through the corridors laden with thin brushes, every colour of pigment and loads of blank slates.

He needed to be very accurate in his craft, Piko always reminded me, because the differences between species were often so fine that even a little imprecision in copying could result in daunting confusion. He often lamented how the long periods spent painting in miniature with a magnifying glass had damaged his eyes. His was a taxing duty, Piko enjoyed repeating. Although I wasn't predestined to become a Master, he did allow me, on occasion, to try my hand with a slate, thinking that my talent for drawing deserved to be nurtured, in any case.

I was privileged in being under his guidance, and my good fortune had come from being the son of a keeper who had negotiated with a bailiff so that his child would be assigned to a Master. Most kids were left without an education on the past treasures of Without, and I should always be mindful about my privilege, Piko reminded me constantly. Once, when I questioned why I was learning about a lost world, he frowned, then replied: 'We are helping you build yourself.'

He was right: if I wasn't like all other idlers, I owed that to him.

Not all the other Masters were as skilled or precise as Piko was. In fact, he sometimes found two slates portraying the same species that featured discrepancies due to error. In these painful moments of uncertainty, which disrupted his otherwise harmonious studies, Piko hastened to our byzantius in search of older slates that could resolve the conflict.

The byzantius was the archive where all the slates painted by Masters of the Known were stored after their Descent. Over many generations, the galleries of the byzantius had grown into an immense labyrinth of images and information, so vast and chaotic that visitors in search of the truth about past life in the Land of Without often ended up losing their way – and their minds – among the millions of slates. On those occasions where I had seen him leaving for the byzantius, Piko indeed returned a different man: tenser, obsessed with things that seemed meaningless to me, and even more frightened about losing his Juice.

After the class, I stumbled into the nice kid.

He no longer wore the oxblood armband.

'Boz: the Juice may nourish you,' he said.

'The Juice may nourish you,' I replied.

'You were right to oppose Bruttho,' he said, informing me that the entire pack had deserted Bruttho after the appearance of the disfigured man. I had wondered for a while if the whole experience was just a dream: Bruttho, Flox, the disfigured man. But the nice kid was confirming the opposite.

'Where's Bruttho now?'

'Dead …' he replied. 'When the monster arrived, we all pelted down the corridor. Bruttho was left there alone, and the monster ate him.'

I shivered, my breath coming less and less easily. Had the disfigured man really fed on Bruttho? It was atrocious. Perhaps Thatem, too, had shared the same terrible fate.

I had to leave the nice kid for a very important reason: Flox. I had been thinking about her ever since, but because of my dread of the disfigured man, had lacked the courage to return to Bruttho's den to see if she was still there. Now, if Bruttho had really been killed, and she was alive, Flox needed more protection than ever. I ought to look for her.

The way to the den clearly stored in my memory, I hurried to reach the large room where Bruttho and his pack had been feasting. The floor no longer bore any trace of the heaps of nutrients that had covered it while I was there. Who had cleaned it? Had I dreamed everything? My doubts were coming back. The oxblood cathedra was still there, though: it hadn't been a dream. I rushed to the other room, hoping to see Flox again so that I could save her – without asking anything in return. But, to my dismay, nobody was inside.

IV

MOZART

After our class on mermaids, Piko asked: 'Do you remember, Boz, when you told me of a man without a face?'

Heat surged through my body. I hadn't expected he would bring the matter back up.

'Come with me. I want to show you something,' Piko said.

We left his unit, taking the third corridor on the right, the second on the left, the eleventh on the left again, then the fourth on the right. We finally strode through a dim corridor with metal doors dotting greyish walls. I had never been there. In that moment, I asked myself why they imposed on us the onerous duty of coating and recoating the walls of our corridor when entire swathes of the perimeter had never been black-washed at all. I couldn't ask Piko, though.

We reached the twelfth door of the corridor. Piko pulled out a large key from his robe's pocket, which he inserted in the lock and rotated twelve times to the right, then three to the left. The door opened. We stepped inside. Barely illuminated, the room was filled with shelves, each of which was completely stocked with slates. Owing to large rusty fans running on the walls, there was less damp here than in the corridor, but the room bore the smell of time immemorial.

'You are the first to enter my vault,' he said.

I hadn't known before that Piko had a vault. Since he never wanted to part with his slates, I had always believed he kept all of them with him, in his unit.

'This is the place where I preserve what I cannot afford to ruin or lose,' he said.

I looked at him, but said nothing.

He moved towards the far end of the room, beckoning me to follow.

We reached the last shelf. He made a bit of room there by moving a group of slates to the left, another group to the right.

A tiny hole in the wall came into view.

Piko pulled out a second key, opening what seemed to be a secret vault. With extreme care, he withdrew a box from the narrow aperture to place it on the shelf. The container was made of a white material, the identity of which I couldn't determine, and the surface was covered with intricate engravings. A marvellous work of carving, I judged – even better than Bruttho's throne.

'Numidian ivory,' said Piko, aware of my cluelessness. 'A material made from elephant tusks,' he added, foreseeing with pride the effect his unsettling revelation would have upon me.

I sighed inside. I had never seen anything made from animals. I wanted to touch the box, to see whether it would feel like stroking an animal. I couldn't believe I was looking – in some way – at an … e-l-e-p-h-a-n-t.

'Men killed elephants to get ivory,' Piko later revealed.

'To eat it?' I asked.

'No. They just enjoyed looking at ivory, and touching it.'

Killing an elephant to touch it? Absurd. It seemed a silly, evil behaviour to me.

'Ivory is very resilient, much more than wood used to be,' Piko added.

I knew what wood was – the matter of which trees were made – although no remains of wood had survived the burning of Earth.

A third key allowed Piko to open the ivory box. Inside, there was nothing but a single slate, which he took out with a gentle but firm hand and laid on the cleared part of the shelf. I examined the weathered slate questioningly, because it was unlike the many slates Piko had showed me during our classes. The slate wasn't painted with three or four colours applied in narrow strokes, as usual, but was instead dotted with tens of colours, all merged together in a meaningless design. The lowest part of the slate was covered with a mess of yellow-greenish points. The centre featured a group of crooked squares, rectangles, and thick black vertical lines, arranged in no particular order. The uppermost area, painted in azure and grey, was slightly better, in the sense that I could discern – or, at least, I believed so – a sky with clouds. I had seen a clouded sky with Piko at the museum, where a copy of the last existing ferrotype of the Land of Without was preserved. Thrifty as he was, I doubted Piko himself had wasted all those pigments on that chaotic slate.

'The man who painted this image is of a deranged mind,' he said, reading my confusion. Then, he began his story: 'At the seminary, I shared my cell with another young novice. He, like me, aspired to be a Master of the Known. He was bright, perspicacious, had a profound understanding of the Tenets. He didn't have any friends, as far as I knew, and was without genitors. We grew close, talked a lot, wondered together about the past mysteries of Without. I remember we asked ourselves how one place could have been arid and hot at one time, and wet and frosty at another.'

Whenever he recalled his period at the seminary, Piko's expression lost itself in a strange haze of warmth and melancholy that made me feel even closer to him. 'We even had a fiery discussion about who would win in a fight between a leopard and a chimpanzee,' he continued. 'The leopard would take the chimpanzee by surprise and kill him right away, I said. A chimpanzee wasn't so easy to be caught off guard and, with all the strength of his arms, would strangle the toughest of leopards, my fellow novice argued. He was gifted, perhaps too gifted, for my fellow novice held all kinds of weird ideas. He even believed that, just as we talked in our cell, trees could communicate between themselves too; not with words but by propagating seeds and issuing scents through the air. I laughed at him. He didn't take it well. There was no end to his fervent imaginings.'

I listened, enraptured, and envied the fortune the young Piko had to be able to share his wonderings on animals with someone else. There was, in fact, no kid with whom I could fantasise on the past life of Without, and the old Piko was open to teach me, not to listen to my conjectures about nature.

'As part of our discipleship, we spent long periods acquiring knowledge at the byzantius,' Piko continued. 'He – like you – having a particular interest in scarabs, was deeply invested in the classification of various species whose existence was recorded only at the byzantius. I was helping him. On one occasion, I fell ill, and couldn't travel with him. He went alone. But when he came back, my fellow novice was a changed person. His mind was consumed by some kind of fury. He was detached, absorbed in incessant thoughts, and writhed fearfully in his pallet during the sleep.

'All of a sudden, it was like being alone in the cell, for he had lost all desire to talk to me, and we were growing estranged. At first, I hoped he would go back to being the same man he was before the byzantius, but it was futile. When I asked him what was happening, I saw a spark in his eyes. For a moment, he seemed his old self, and plucking at my sleeve, asked me to sit down. Then, placing himself very close to me, he whispered from the corner of his mouth a most insane idea. He said that, contrary to what all of us believed, the Land of Without hadn't been destroyed by Sun. It was a deep-rooted lie, he claimed. The truth was that men had destroyed Without with their own hands to feed their insatiable greed, choking the air with dark fumes spread in the atmosphere, tainting the waters with poison, filling the soil with filth, and slaughtering all animals. I listened – aghast. He seemed so captivated by his mad conjectures that I didn't dare to contradict him, and I asked where he had learned what he was telling me. Plentiful evidence was available at the byzantius, he replied, but only for those willing to unearth it. He had brought something to our cell, he said, and I was shown this very slate you are now looking at.'

I examined the splattered colours in front of me more closely, but failed to see how they might prove anything about the end of life in the Land of Without. I expressed my doubts to Piko, who nodded. 'According to my deranged friend, these long dark strokes that you can see here – yes, right here – were steel tubes designed to spread noxious fumes into the atmosphere,' Piko said, pointing repeatedly at the upper part of the slate with his long-nailed little finger.

'Why would men ever do something like that – biting the hand that fed them?' I asked.

'That's what I thought,' Piko answered, nodding again. 'This wasn't one of his usual eccentric theories that made me smile. It was pure heresy, a folly for which the Crier might execute him, and I risked being suspected as an accomplice. But there was more ...'

'More?' I asked, incredulous. What I had just heard was already beyond belief.

'He claimed that the Land of Without is still habitable,' Piko added, his neck twitching nervously, agitated by the mere recollection of such a blasphemy. 'Yes, he said that. He kept repeating how the Crier made us believe that the Land of Without was unfit for life, but it wasn't true. People could still survive there. People lived there ... he believed ...'

I didn't know why Piko had decided to share his fellow novice's follies with me, but this wasn't the kind of secret I wished to be part of. As occurred too often, though, I wanted to learn more.

'What happened to him?' I asked.

'He left the seminary. We never met again. But I learned that he was determined to prove his theory. He wanted to find a way to the Land of Without, so that he could see what lay outside with his own eyes,' Piko revealed. 'I don't know how, perhaps by digging a hole, but he eventually found an opening to the Land of Without. And the moment he tried to satisfy his insatiable curiosity, the man poked half of his face out, and the burning rays of Sun mangled it. He was punished for nurturing his own delusions!'

I suddenly understood, now, where his story was leading me to.

'Yes … Boz, the terrifying man you met is … my lost friend!'

The sudden, unexpected mention of the disfigured man allowed his image to take frightening shape in front of me. I saw him, right there, as if he were with us. I screamed through the dead calm of the vault. Piko pressed his hand against my mouth. 'You must be wary of him, Boz … he still wanders aimlessly, trying to draw others into his heresy …' he warned, staring into my eyes, preoccupied as I had never seen him before. 'You must avoid him, for he can be very persuasive, or you will meet his same end. His ideas are powerful and dangerous. You must avoid him … his name is Mozart … Mozart the Heretic!'

No longer able to bear his intense stare, my eyes darted everywhere. Only then did Piko remove his hand from my mouth. He warned me not to tell anyone what he had just revealed because nobody would believe me – or, even worse, they would think me mad. A tense silence fell between us and, after leaving his vault shortly after, we went our separate ways.

Piko's revelations about his fellow novice, irredeemably lost to a path of heretic folly, had shaken me, and even put a damper on my joy of seeing the unexpected remnant of an elephant. It had never occurred to me that a man might think to reach Without, nor that a way to get there even existed. I was grateful to Piko for his determination to protect me from Mozart, but still couldn't understand why Mozart had chosen me, and for what evil design.

Suddenly, I remembered that I needed to go to the zoo to complete my chores. I hastened my pace but, when I walked in, a dreadful sight diverted my thoughts from Mozart, at least temporarily. Inside the glass cage, her back bleeding, the

Congoid was crouched on the floor. I could guess what had gone on, but didn't know what to do. I put some detergent on a cloth, and offered it to her, but she gestured a refusal. If her wounds weren't promptly cleaned they might get infected, and an infection would most likely mean an agonising death. As she wouldn't be able to clean her back without my help, I applied the cloth myself to one of her fresh cuts.

'No ...' she moaned, withdrawing. 'It hurts.'

'What? You can speak ... ?'

'Yes,' she whispered, and from her scared reaction I gauged she was terrified the zookeeper might have heard us; but he carried on snoring in the other room.

'Why have you always been silent, then, while I talked to you ... ?'

'I'm not allowed,' she said, pointing her quivering arm at the zookeeper's room.

'But why has he lashed you?' I asked.

'I refused to play with him,' she replied in a soft voice, without even turning to me. 'I always refuse to play with him. And I will never allow him to play with me.'

I thought of Flox and the toad – a burning anger rising in my chest.

'You should let me clean your back, or it will get worse,' I said.

She nodded, sobbing a little.

I gently passed the cloth over the tangle of wounds on her back.

'I'm grateful to you,' she whispered. 'What's your name?'

'Boz. And yours?'

'I don't have one.'

I glanced at the entrance to the zookeeper's room with apprehension. I wasn't sure I was allowed to help her in any way.

'This was the punishment for when he said I was making too much noise,' she told me when I pressed the cloth against an old scar.

'Making noise how?'

'I don't know. I was just running on the wheel …'

So far I had simply hated the zookeeper, but now I was beginning to think he deserved a fate like the one meted out to Flox's toady neighbour.

'That's for when I smiled at a visitor …' she said while I cleaned another old scar.

She shared the miserable story behind each of her wounds. There is only so much that a human being can tolerate, and she had gone past it. But we needed to be careful: if he saw us talking, the zookeeper might well add another scar to the collection.

'It must be tough, living inside a glass cage,' I commented, nothing cleverer coming to me.

'I don't know of any other life,' she responded. 'I was born inside a cage, in another perimeter. Then, they moved me here.'

'Don't you ever get bored?'

'No – I like to observe the visitors to the zoo. They're convinced I can't understand them, or that I don't notice what they do in front of this glass; but it's the opposite … I remember everybody and everything.'

She had said that because it was true, I felt, not just to boast about herself.

'Do you remember me coming here the first time?' I couldn't resist asking.

'Yes. I remember when you came here with an older man …'

'Piko, my Master of the Known …'

'Yes. And he said that my brain is weaker than my body. That I don't have much memory. If only I could talk … he would see …'

I smiled. It didn't happen often.

'Why don't you have a name?' I asked.

'I don't know,' she answered. 'Nobody ever gave me one.'

'I will give you one,' I said, sensing the growing confidence between us.

'Yes?'

'Yes. I will call you *Daffodil.*'

'I like it.'

I began cleaning the cage, for the zookeeper could wake up at any time, but continued talking to her. And, from then on, whenever I went to the zoo, even though Daffodil listened in silence to everything I said, without showing emotion, and pretended I wasn't there, I knew it was no longer the same as before.

I had acquired a friend.

V

THESPIANS

When the light went on, Mother was always the first to rise. She intoned the same unchanging hymn, did the prescribed squatting in her rayon shift, donned a robe and, only then, awoke us.

I was thus surprised when, after a lightbreak, I saw Mother still lying in her pallet.

'Mother?'

Mother didn't respond.

I called to her again, drawing closer.

She remained still.

I jiggled her body, and she opened the eyes, but for a blink only.

I went to Father.

He was kneeling, saying the Tenets.

'Father?'

Eyes fixed on the wall ahead, he continued with the Tenets without acknowledging me.

'Father?' I tried once more.

He paused, annoyed by the interruption, raising his eyes sternly.

'You shouldn't interrupt the Tenets – I've told you,' he warned. It had occurred twice when I was a child, and on both occasions he had made me kneel on gravel for the length of an entire lights-out to mark my disobedience.

'I think Mother has a problem,' I said.

He looked at her, immobile on the pallet, then resumed the Tenets.

I went back to Mother, and kept trying to shake her from the torpor, but it was useless. She must be suffering from some illness, I thought in alarm.

I went to look for Piko, whom everybody in the perimeter called when someone fell sick, hoping that his deep knowledge of animals might extend to humans.

I stopped in front of his canvas curtain.

'Piko: are you there?' I whispered.

No answer came back. I called his name again, raising my voice, but in vain.

I decided to go in.

Piko was there, engrossed in testing his Juice. He looked at me with an air of contempt.

'Piko, Mother is sick,' I explained in a hurry, so that he would understand why I had entered his home uninvited. I don't know whether it was my hastened justification or because his Juice had tested fine, but the look of disapproval quickly left him. He followed me with a satchel of tools.

Piko examined Mother. As if aiming to communicate with her body, he slowly raised her eyelids, touched her ashen neck, felt her pulse, even took a handful of hair strands from her head to examine them with a magnifying glass, and observed the symptoms of her illness with attention. Seeing Piko's formidable brain invested in trying to heal Mother reassured me. With him in the room, Father, too, decided to take the matter seriously. He ceased the Tenets and came over. We observed his actions intently, but Piko never spoke, nor did his bowed head give us any indication of Mother's condition. He only paused a couple of times, gathering his thoughts over some conjecture on her illness, but then shook his head almost imperceptibly so as to dismiss it, resuming his inspection. Finally, with a tone between solemnity and sadness, Piko stated his diagnosis: 'Gipokaltsiyemiya.'

Father winced.

I knew the reason. Gipokaltsiyemiya was an illness whose remedy was easy to state, but difficult to obtain: twice the normal allowance of calciferol. With nutrients strictly rationed, and exceptions not admitted – even for the sick – Piko couldn't have declared a worse diagnosis.

Despite his compassion for our family, which he showed by patting me gently on the shoulder, Piko could do nothing other than leave the unit in gloomy silence. Father and I were left alone, brooding over the cold and undeniable fact that without the missing ration of calciferol, Mother would never recover.

Father paced back and forth, observing her drowsiness, probably trying to find someone to blame, as he did by habit whenever trouble and difficulty came to him. But on this occasion he couldn't single out anyone responsible for the fact that our lives were to change irrevocably for the worse.

I stood over Mother. From then on, apart from my classes with Piko or the chores at the zoo, throughout her illness I never moved away from the pallet. I fed and cleansed her because, even though occasionally awake, she was too weak to do anything for herself. I, who had never been able to stand still for long, was always there by Mother's side.

Cherished memories with her resurfaced.

When Mother had shortened my first robe, for instance.

'It's too long,' she had said. 'If you run, it will trip you up.'

'Why would he have to run?' Father had argued, not at all enthusiastic about her idea.

'You know how children are,' she had murmured.

So, from then on, when a new robe was dropped into our hatch, Mother always took up her shears to shorten it. And it was indeed without the hindrance of a long robe that, free to run through the corridor, I became one of the fastest kids in the perimeter. Father remained staunchly against all this cutting and sewing but, despite painstaking effort, failed to find a Tenet on which his finicky opposition might rest.

It was Mother who once saved me from a small pack – three of them, in fact – trying to cover my body with tar: a most favourite game among kids. On hearing my desperate screams, Mother ran to the corridor. A mother's intervention wasn't usually enough to scare off a pack of kids or dissuade them from perpetrating a wrongdoing, but in that circumstance she had the brilliant idea of bringing with her no less than … my stone ball. As soon as she saw the marauding kids, and the bucket of smoking tar threateningly close to me, my yelling mother threw the ball into the pack, hitting one of them in the head. The other two kids ran away, dropping the smouldering bucket on the floor. After caressing my pale face to ascertain that I was fine, Mother asked for my help to drag the collapsed kid to our unit. There, she took care of him as if he were her second, prohibited child. The kid soon recovered, and he left our home, though not before expressing profuse gratitude to Mother – his attacker – for the care shown after the attack. He had even hugged me. I believe that my passion for the stone ball sprang from this heart-warming episode.

Mother was now the one in need of care. Lights-out after lights-out, the lack of change in her condition wore me down. Although he was very tried, Father didn't take any action to change the course of events. He didn't beg the neighbours for more calciferol, and nor did he plead with the bailiffs to deliver more, because he considered asking to be privileged over the others to be a behaviour disrespectful of the Tenets – one that might cause his disfellowship.

To alleviate my wait, Piko asked me to copy one slate that he had recently borrowed from the byzantius. Though I was very far from matching his drawing skills, yet I could at least find some relief from my ordeal. The slate depicted what I thought was the most elegant of scarabs: a seven-spot ladybird. Although I would never tire of admiring her shiny red wing cases, marked with seven black dots, I knew well that the *Coccinella septempunctata* had been a widespread scarab before the apocalypse. So, I struggled, at least at first, to understand why Piko had borrowed such a common slate. But a further examination of the image removed my doubts: the painted scarab featured nine dots instead of the customary seven. Was this a mere drawing error in the long chain of transcripts, or was it, instead, evidence of some unknown species of scarab?

While I still enjoyed the exchanges with Piko, conversation with Father had shrunk to the least possible. We ate on the floor in silence, then he went back to the Tenets or left the unit for some maintenance work. When he did speak to me, he sounded angry. Perhaps he had begun to suspect that my refusal to participate in the coatings might lie behind Mother's illness. In fact, I felt no guilt at all, and my only regret – if any – was that Bruttho was no longer with us: he would happily have given us some calciferol for Mother.

When foam suddenly appeared at Mother's mouth, Father, no longer willing to see her worsen, finally acted.

He went out of the unit and came back a short while later with a bluebottle. 'A man owes me a favour,' he said.

We gave Mother the calciferol, careful not to spill a single drop on the floor. She trembled a bit, but then, as if nothing had happened, fell back to her wretched sleep.

We waited for what felt a very long while, during which she didn't show any sign of awakening. Father and I glanced at each other, confused, lost, upset at seeing no progress. For the first time since my early childhood, I cried. A lot. Father, too, was on the edge of shedding tears, but resisted.

Had Piko's cure failed?

The lights went out.

I was distraught, yet too exhausted not to doze off. I dreamed of walking alone in the corridors at lights-out. Despite having no torch or goggles, everything was illuminated by a soft blue glow. I walked, aimlessly. My legs were leading my body to an unknown somewhere. Yet, I wasn't worried, just relieved by the numbing powers of the dream, a place where I could not feel the pain of Mother's illness.

'In the sleep, a low moaning rose from nearby.'

'I'm scared …'

The voice of a kid.

I walked towards the young voice calling for help, originating from behind a canvas curtain.

Past the curtain was a small round room, deserted, with a narrow circular manhole at the centre.

The feeble voice came from a cavity in the manhole.

I found myself three or four steps away from the hole.

'Who's there?' I asked.

The echo of my voice resonated all around.

With no apparent reaction to my presence, the moaning persisted.

'Who's there?' I repeated.

The sound from below ceased.

Had I scared the kid trapped inside the cavity away?

I stepped forward, reaching the edge of the manhole, but didn't have the courage to look down inside.

I was asking who was there, again, when ... a bare arm sprang out!

I stepped back with a scream.

While the feeble begging for help continued, the protruding arm of the kid spasmed before me. It was so skinny, so lithe, that I feared it might detach itself from his body and fall on the floor. I wanted to rescue the kid, but didn't know how: the cavity was too narrow to drag someone out of it. Not that I had a real opportunity to save him, for the sudden return of the lights in the perimeter brought me out of the sleep.

Still unable to sever dream from reality, I was about to cry for the fate of the imprisoned kid when, opening my eyes, I saw Mother standing on her feet. Incredulity, swiftly joined by bliss, invaded me with such vigour that no other sentiment could find room within me. Father woke up, too. The unexpected sight of Mother squatting on the floor as if nothing had happened instantly erased the miserable veil that had covered his face during her illness, bringing a spark of light to his tried eyes. We approached Mother, both screaming and jumping in circles with joy.

She was weak, but smiled, and hugged us.

Father told her about the cause of her ailments.

'You'll never have to worry about the calciferol – never again,' he reassured her.

'Who should I be grateful to?' she asked, holding on to a sleeve of his robe, afraid to lose her balance.

'Someone owes me a favour,' he briskly answered.

Mother didn't enquire more, and asked instead about my classes with Piko.

'I'm helping him draw animals,' I replied with true enthusiasm.

I took out the slate with the nine-dotted ladybird for her to see.

'How beautiful ...' Mother commented.

I didn't consider my portrait particularly well-executed but, unlike me, Mother had set her eyes on only a handful of slates throughout her entire life, and was thus unable to form a proper judgement on my drawing.

'I can do better,' I said.

'Is the Master also teaching you the azbuki?' she asked with enquiring eyes.

'No. He says I'm not ready. But he will teach me, eventually.'

Mother nodded in approval.

Father took her under his arm, and smiled at both of us.

Our family had never been, and would never be, that close again.

'The spectacle! The spectacle has arrived! Bebro's with you!' came shouts from the corridor, accompanied by a rattling sound that broke our fleeting intimacy. We raised the curtain to look in the corridor. There, a thespian, so short he barely reached my chest, trotted merrily, dragging behind him scores of rolling cans of all colours attached with a thread to his pied coat. I had never seen many of those hues, and didn't even know their names back then. I didn't know how he made it, but the man was able to produce a vibrant rhythm with the cans by simply moving, stirring and raising the thread at his whim, making a very difficult performance appear easy, as only those who master their own craft can do.

'The spectacle! The spectacle is waiting for you!' he shouted.

'I want to watch the spectacle …' Mother whispered with a sparkle in her eyes.

Though he deemed most thespians to be despicably prone to heresy, in that circumstance Father couldn't avoid nodding back. So, we set off in pursuit of the thespian and his musical cans. Father held Mother's hand, while I followed close behind. Many idlers left their units to join us behind the trotting man. He never turned, but led his increasing group of followers to a large room, already crammed with idlers, at the end of which stood a wide platform covered by a colourful striped curtain. When we strode into the room, the man had already vanished into the growing crowd that looked up at the platform with excited anticipation.

'I want to get closer,' Mother said.

Again, Father couldn't say no to her eager, almost pleading tone, and so we moved towards the stage through a multitude of swishing robes.

We didn't have to wait long before the cables lifting the curtain began raising the canvas. As the stage was revealed, the crowd sighed in great, yet slightly perturbed, expectation: because nobody could be sure that the spectacle about to begin would be righteous. An improper word, a forbidden image, even an unusual body movement were indeed sufficient to violate one of the innumerable Tenets that regulated our lives; and showing enthusiasm towards a blasphemous spectacle was likewise deemed against the Tenets. I saw more than one bailiff among the crowd.

A replica of a small room occupied the entire stage. There was one pallet, a desk, a latrine, a fern, the hatch on the wall. It reminded me of Daffodil's cage. A large painting of a moonlit sky loomed over the platform, meaning that the spectacle was set in the Land of Without, at night-time, before the apocalypse.

'What's that?' asked Mother, pointing at a framed hole in a wall built on the stage.

'A window. People in the Land of Without used windows to look outside,' I said.

'Oh!' she commented. 'So many things you know.'

'I learned it from Piko,' I told her.

Right then, coming out from a narrow corner of the plat-form still covered by the curtain, a young woman entered the stage. She wore a blue tunic and a voluminous green wig. The lady looked left and right with apprehension, sobbing heavily, then neared the window. She laid her hands on the ledge and stuck her head out, pretending to gaze into the far distance, amid the sudden silence of the idlers.

'Cardenio ... Cardenio ... where are you?' the lady asked plaintively. '... I'm here for you,' she then whispered, looking down at the attentive crowd with a sad expression. 'I've been waiting for you … and I'll always wait for you … but when are you coming back?'

Covering her face with both hands, she continued sobbing.

From the opposite side, a man walked stealthily on to the stage. He was the short man who had called us to the spectacle with his musical cans. The cans had gone, and he now wore a yellow curly wig that looked very amusing on his plump head. The crowd chuckled at him.

Unaware of the man's arrival on the stage, the lady resumed speaking to the missing beloved with a broken voice: 'Cardenio … the food is ending! We used to grow carrots, potatoes, leeks and cauliflower in our garden … but the soil is so parched that no green is taking root anymore. What has become of the water that we fetched in abundance from the backyard well? Vanished: even the bottom of the well has dried up. The animals have shrunk to their bone, and died. Only one lamb survives. Will we follow the same fate?'

Mother stared at the stage, possessed by the scene, and hardly ever had I seen her so entranced.

After a pause, the man with the yellow wig spoke.

'Bologna … Bologna … why are you crying?'

The lady gasped in surprise. '… You scared me,' she said after recognising the man. 'I didn't hear you coming. How did you get in?'

'The gate was open,' he said, looking around inquisitively. 'You should be careful with all these rascals and looters … they will steal any food remaining in the abandoned farms …'

'Someone must've forgotten to latch the gate. There's nothing to worry about, in any case; thieves wouldn't find much food here …' she lamented. 'What we hadn't eaten already was robbed by the servants who fled the farm.'

'What are you doing all alone by the window?' the man enquired.

'I'm waiting for my Cardenio … he still hasn't returned from a long journey.'

'What journey?' the man asked, drawing closer to her.

'He went to see his uncle in Siberia.'

'Siberia?'

'Yes. His uncle owns a large farm in Siberia. It's rich with fields, vines and cattle. Hopefully, he will let us live with him. Cardenio could help with the harvesting. I could cook and do the housework.'

'What is an uncle?' Mother asked, drawing her mouth close to my right ear.

'An uncle was the brother of a mother or a father in the Land of Without,' I replied – having learned this, too, from Piko. The illness had definitely changed her; she was really enjoying asking me questions, and that hadn't been the case before, when Mother had always restrained her curiosity.

'Siberia is far away,' the man on the stage commented with a dry, almost derisive tone.

Not welcoming his dismissive remark, Bologna added: 'Cardenio heard from a traveller that sunrays are not as vicious and ruthless in Siberia, that people can still grow food there. So, he left to join his uncle. He will come back with two strong horses, and will take me there with him.'

The man drew a bit closer.

'A rather audacious undertaking … may I say …' he commented.

'We don't have alternatives,' she replied. 'Soon this land will be uninhabitable. Sun is destroying everything. Every night, when Sun gives us some respite, our remaining servant has to walk a long way just to fetch half a glass of murky water from the pond.'

'It's terrible … I know …' the man admitted, taking a few steps further in her direction. 'But Cardenio was irresponsible in leaving a lady of your beauty alone. And the journey to Siberia? He can only move at night-time, for the heat during the day is so prohibitive. It'll take him a lifetime. And the horses? They wouldn't survive the double journey. What a madness!'

On hearing this, Bologna burst out crying again.

Trying with all his might to show a guilt that he didn't feel, the man caressed the sleeve of her dress.

'I don't wish to hurt you, Bologna …' he said. 'I just want to be sincere and honest with you. Neighbours are meant to help each other.'

He passed Bologna a handkerchief, and waited for her to wipe her tears before revealing his ulterior motive. 'You're no longer safe here. You should move to my farm,' he suggested. 'We still have plenty of food … and money …'

Fortunately, Mother didn't ask me what money was, for I wouldn't have known how to respond.

Bologna blushed and, as if holding his handkerchief might represent some sort of commitment to her unrequited pursuer, gave the item back, staring at the farmer with steely coldness.

'No … no! Once back, Cardenio will certainly look for me,' she said, trying to convince herself, too. 'And if he doesn't find me here … he will think I've abandoned him. If he learns that I'm staying at your farm … he will think that … that …'

'That ... what?' asked the man with a lascivious look.

'That I am playing with you ...' she said, cringing at the image.

Upon hearing her suggestion, the man stuck his tongue out rather pathetically, and let out a groan of pleasure.

The crowd laughed boisterously at his lecherous smirk.

'Go away ... !' Bologna yelled.

The man didn't appear discouraged by her open refusal. 'Come live with me, Bologna,' he insisted. 'I have six farms, food, servants. Everything you no longer have. And you should forget Cardenio; he must be dead already.'

The man grabbed her arm. Bologna screamed, trying to break free.

'Your food will end ... Sun doesn't forgive,' he said, threatening her with an unsurmountable truth. 'I can protect you, and save your life. Come with me!'

I was suddenly reliving the misfortunes of Flox. I could see her on the stage, pestered by a toady neighbour who made use of her hunger and loneliness to satisfy the cravings of his flesh. Since our encounter, Flox, the only girl I had ever talked to, had indeed been a constant presence inside me. And I still asked myself if I could have done more for her, and shivered when imagining her being killed by Mozart, although I wanted to believe she had escaped death.

'No ... no ... no!' Bologna yelled at the man, interrupting the wanderings of my imagination.

At that moment, someone stole on to the platform from the rear. He didn't look stocky like Bruttho, quite the opposite. And, instead of a knife, he held a large bucket in his hands. The kid, unnoticed, drew close to the farmer and threw the full contents of the bucket over him. A red liquid suddenly covered the man's face. Almost blinded, the farmer ran round in circles, wiping his sticky head in a frenzy, unable even to shout, and rushed off stage to the crowd's jeers.

'My lady … are you harmed?' the newcomer asked once the noise had abated.

'No … my faithful servant …you saved me. I don't think that naughty farmer will ever come back. But what did you throw at him?'

'The blood of our last lamb, my lady …' he replied. 'His bony flesh will serve to feed us for a little while … but we need to find other food.'

'If only my Cardenio was here with us …' Bologna looked at the crowd with serious, yet wistful, eyes.

'I will now cook the lamb's meat for you,' the young servant said before leaving the stage.

Bologna was, once again, alone.

Then, a prolonged rustling, alternated with a short tapping, could be heard. The crowd watched the stage in thrilled anticipation. I looked around. Everybody, including Father and Mother, was enraptured. Bologna looked to her right. Hesitantly, she moved towards the source of that sound: the window. From there a young man surprised the crowd by leaping into the room. His breathing was laboured, and his clothes torn and soiled.

'Cardenio!' Bologna cried, worried by her lover's appearance.

The two embraced each other.

'Bologna … I missed you so much. I've risked my life to come back here.'

'What happened?' she asked, caressing his azure wig.

'After a long and tiring journey, I reached my uncle's farm,' he said. 'But I didn't find what we had hoped for. The land was parched, sterile, barren. Scarcely any trace remained of the abundant crops or of the lush vines that used to grow on the hills around, where I used to see my cousins as a child. The farm looked desolate, and the heat was even worse than here. Only one person still lived at the place: a boy. The boy told me that my uncle, to whom he had been a loyal servant, was long gone. Then he led me to the farm's pantry, where some food remained. Starving, I devoured an entire loaf of rotting bread, and fell very ill afterwards. But the boy took care of me, sharing what little water he had, so that I could get back on my feet.'

'The Juice may nourish this boy!' Bologna yelled. 'He saved your life!'

'True!' Cardenio nodded. 'And the generous boy told me of a large pond not far away from my uncle's farm that, he believed, still had water. So, we left for the pond. And it was there that we found two scrawny horses drinking the dregs from the bottom. We took the horses, and I asked the boy to join me.'

'So … he's here?' Bologna asked, eyes wide.

'Yes, he's waiting outside.'

'Tell the boy to come in! Sun is about to come back, and it will soon be dreadfully hot outside,' Bologna urged. 'I want to show him how grateful I am to him for saving you from certain death!'

Cardenio nodded, and shouted out loud: 'Come inside, boy!'

After some further rustling, the lean shape of a boy entered the stage.

Despite the male disguise, and a giant yellow wig, I immediately recognised her, and my relief in discovering that Flox
was still alive was no less than the surprise at seeing her part of
the spectacle.

Bologna took the pretend boy's hands in hers. 'Cardenio
and I will never leave you. You must stay with us, if you would
like to,' she offered.

The boy nodded in shy acceptance.

'Bologna: while on our way back, we heard that most of
the survivors have found shelter somewhere,' Cardenio said.
'They are gathering the last available food and medicines, and
people there don't rob each other. We should try and find
them. Staying here is too dangerous ... Sun will soon turn so
fiery that I fear he will even burn the wood of our walls. We
must all leave, Bologna!'

'Yes, but you and the boy must first rest, my Cardenio,'
Bologna said, gently extending the palms of her hands forward,
inviting him to slow down. 'It's almost day. We should leave
at night-time, when Sun is gone. And the lamb our servant is
preparing will soon be ready. You both need to eat after the
long journey. Let's go to the kitchen.'

Cardenio agreed, and the three moved towards the rear
of the stage.

As the curtain went down for the end of the first act, the
crowd roared. They were enjoying the spectacle. Wishing to see
how the story went on, a woman yelled: 'More, more!'

Mother was happy, even though she didn't join the others
in yelling – she never raised her voice, at least not outside
home – while a hint of enthusiasm made Father's eyes appear
less impenetrable than they normally were. Suddenly, though,

the screams of excitement in the room were accompanied by another sort of yelling.

'A' oot!' a bailiff shouted in rage.

Bailiffs, by the dozen, began hitting the idlers with their sticks. The crowd stampeded to the exit, the screams now of pure fear. I heard children crying, and mothers cursing the bailiffs. Some idlers already lay on the floor, grunting with pain.

Father took Mother's hand. 'We must go,' he urged.

Mother reached for my hand, but she didn't find it. I wasn't prepared to leave: having already abandoned Flox once, I wouldn't do it again.

'Mother: we'll meet at home,' I tried to reassure her.

As she glanced at me, bewildered, I started off towards the platform, while Father pulled her to the exit. We both turned repeatedly, as if this might be the last opportunity to see each other.

Parrying a couple of blows from the bailiffs, I reached the platform and, not without some strain, climbed it. The striped curtain had been removed. The platform was deserted. I ran to the rear, where I saw a long rope that, fastened to a pillar at one end, had been unrolled to reach a deep pit behind the stage. I climbed down the rope. At the bottom of the pit was a narrow opening in the wall. I followed the rope through the opening, crossed an empty room, and ended up in a wide corridor.

'Boz!' I heard a call from halfway down the corridor.

I looked ahead.

Flox.

She sat perched on the edge of a tumbrel. Knowing that tumbrels were ritually used to ferry idlers on their way to the

Descent, a shiver ran through me. But when Flox beckoned to me with an unexpected spark in her eyes, I knew she was fine.

The man who could make music with cans was holding the tumbrel's long shafts. He turned to me. His face was still covered with red paint. 'Hop on, my dear Boz! We're leaving,' he invited me. Pleased to learn that Flox had mentioned my name to him, I jumped on. She had taken off her wig and bundled it with the other stage clothes in one corner, next to the folded striped curtain, and put her dark robe on again. Ahead of us stood a second tumbrel, where Bologna and Cardenio, still wearing their stage costumes, were seated. They both waved at me. Squatting between the tumbrel's shafts, and looking at me with the kind of curiosity kids have for one another, the boy playing Bologna's servant waited to pull the other tumbrel.

'I always play the part of the villain ... but I'm not!' the red-faced man was keen to inform me. 'My name's Bebro.' Then he turned forward again, and began dragging the tumbrel, his short but thick legs lumbering over the ground.

I sat on the edge, opposite Flox. After our first conversation in the dim room, I had thought of her constantly, tormented by many fears, including the concern that seeing her again might disappoint me if she wasn't up to my memory's expectations. That had been a foolish concern, however, because her commanding beauty had nothing to fear even in full light.

'I came back to look for you, but you were gone,' I said. 'I didn't want to abandon you. I've thought a lot about you.'

Bebro was listening, but I didn't mind.

'I thought about you too, Boz,' Flox replied, with the hint of a smile.

I blushed.

'Right after you left, I heard the kids yelling in the other room,' she said. 'I had never heard Bruttho screaming in fear before. The noise didn't last long, though. After, there was only silence. I couldn't find the courage to leave the room. I stayed there, waiting. I only left when I was so hungry that I really needed nutrients. But none was left. The kids had all gone. The floor was clean.'

'What have you done since?'

'I started wandering through the corridors, looking for nutrients. I was alone and starving, like when I lost Father.'

I lowered my eyes.

'Don't be sad, Boz. That's when I met them. They rescued me.' She smiled with her eyes.

'The spectacle! The spectacle! Join us!' Bebro suddenly shouted into a new corridor. 'Bebro has arrived!'

The families of idlers peeped their heads out of the units, staring in amazement at the stocky thespian with a painted face. He smiled back with no hint of shyness. His enthusiasm couldn't hide the strain of pulling the tumbrel, though, nor the wrinkled face.

'Shall I help you?' I offered, pointing at the shafts.

With profuse gratitude, Bebro accepted.

'You don't mind staying with us for a bit?' he asked after we had switched positions.

'Sure. I will be glad to,' I replied, my hands clutching the tumbrel's shafts.

'How did you meet Flox?' he asked. 'Are you from Breathitt, too?'

'We share a friend from Breathitt,' I replied, mindful not to allow the memory of Bruttho and his curved knife to unsettle me. 'But I'm not from there.'

'Can you perform on a stage?' he asked.

'Never tried ...'

'You should,' he replied. 'Later, I will tell you my story.'

The tumbrel was heavier than expected but, with the talkative thespian soon asleep, at least there was no conversation to bear. I walked thousands of steps, softly whistling all the way, hiding my efforts so that Flox, observing me in silence from behind, wouldn't think me weak. I glanced at the other tumbrel, where Bologna and Cardenio, who had now removed their wigs and put on their robes, gently whispered to one another, holding hands. Their closeness apparently outlived the spectacle. After noticing the sudden change of puller, they smiled at me in encouragement.

'I will tell you where to stop, Boz,' Bebro, refreshed from his sleep, suggested after a while. 'We must camp somewhere near: the dark is close, and we don't want to be caught unprepared, do we.'

We stopped in a large hallway between corridors, delineated by four symmetrical pillars. Cardenio alighted from his tumbrel to unfold a bundle of tarp that, with the participation of the entire troupe, quickly developed into a voluminous tent. I didn't know where we were: someplace far, perhaps even in another perimeter, because the corridors were much narrower and more winding than those of our perimeter. But I wasn't the least worried about staying away from home. I enjoyed being with Flox, and with the thespians.

As we sat in a circle in the tent, whose tarp blocked out the light coming down from the ceiling, Bebro put five of his cans in the middle. He removed the lids, and I was thus allowed to discover that the cans not only served to make music, but also acted as handy food containers. With the versatile cans moving from hand to hand, and the nutrients shared in equal parts among us, the light-hearted circle of thespians buzzed animatedly.

'Did you like our spectacle, Boz?' asked Cardenio, sitting on the floor, right in front of me.

'It's called *Dead of Night, Life of Men*,' Bebro interjected.

'I enjoyed it very much,' I said, praising all of them. 'But why did the bailiffs interrupt it? There was nothing inappropriate, in my opinion.'

'I don't know. They never let us end a spectacle,' Bebro replied. 'They let us begin, yes, but then shut it down after a single act.'

'They know that, in the end, idlers need entertainers,' said Cardenio. 'They just don't want us to tell stories about life in the Land of Without.'

'I've spent my life doing spectacles, and the bailiffs have always closed them down,' Bebro lamented, yet in a tone more fiery than glum. 'I've pulled the tumbrel to each and every corner of all perimeters ... and it's always the same trick with the bailiffs.'

'Who makes up the stories?' I asked, trying to feed a nascent curiosity about the thespians and their forbidden spectacles.

'Yours truly,' Bebro answered.

I was impressed. I looked at the others, who nodded, pleased to vouch for Bebro's precious talent.

'How does this story end? I'm curious,' I asked him. 'Do Bologna, Cardenio and the boy escape Sun?'

'Sorry to disappoint you, Boz, but I've no clue,' the experienced thespian exclaimed, still chewing some nutrient.

'I just write the first act of my spectacles. Sadly, I've never needed more than one act. But you can still imagine by yourself how the following acts would have gone on, right? Can't you?'

I was not in the least disappointed by his answer. I actually liked the idea of creating an end for his story, one that was all mine. Perhaps I should become a thespian, I thought, and make my own spectacles.

'Boz: you must join our troupe!' Bebro proposed, raising a bluebottle.

I was left in silence. He, like Piko, was reading my mind, it seemed.

'You'll travel through the perimeters, have fun, and eat more than at home,' he added. 'A nice existence.'

Everybody in the tent looked at me in anticipation of my response.

'Let him eat the nutrients in peace,' Cardenio intervened, seeing me blush. 'First he fled the bailiffs, then carried the tumbrel's weight; he must be dead tired!'

The circle laughed. I blushed again.

Flox, sitting next to me, stroked my left sleeve. I blushed even more.

'Flox told me that you had just met once ... you must really like each other ... your feelings seem so pure ...' Bologna whispered, a tear running down her left cheek.

'Who ever loved that loved not at first sight?' Cardenio whispered back.

'How do you get the nutrients if you're constantly moving ... ?' I asked, aiming to divert the attention away from my reddened cheeks.

'Families,' Bebro answered. 'When we pass through the corridors, they come out to bring us food. Maybe half a fistful of nutrients each. Not a big sacrifice for them, and it keeps us going.'

That's in breach of Tenet ৪৵ৣৡ, I thought, but didn't say.

'So, Boz: I promised I would share my story with you,' the verbose, yet intriguing, Bebro said. 'Well, I haven't always been a thespian. After many ordeals – which, if you allow me, I'd rather not describe at the present moment – I ended up being one of those idlers in a corridor. Not that I enjoyed that life so much; the others kept pestering me due to my … smallness … I was prey to so many packs of kids in the corridors … you wouldn't believe …'

I naturally assumed a sad expression because, after my experience with Bruttho and his pack, I could definitely relate to his pain.

'All changed, however, when the kids of the corridor played another of their heinous tricks on me,' he continued, the others listening in respectful silence (though I suspected they had heard his story more than once). 'After tying an iron chain around my chest, the kids pushed me back and forth between them like a stone ball. I smiled, at least at the beginning, for I was used to their jokes, and still hoped the silly prank wouldn't last long. But they went on. I grew dizzy, and the chain was beginning to hurt me. I asked them to stop, but nothing. I yelled, but nothing. When a kid threw me against a wall, and a searing pain hit my shoulder … I really saw red! I gave them a murderous look, but they didn't care, laughing even louder. I couldn't take it anymore: I took a large breath, and pressed my arms against the chain with all my strength. But the chain was too tight, too hard. I tried again, shaking and drooling like a madman, but ... nothing. I had lost all my confidence, and was almost crying like a baby, when I realised that the chain was slackening: only a tiny bit, but it had loosened. So, I widened my tied elbows until the bulging veins on my forehead were almost exploding. The strain seemed to last forever, and I was about to faint when ... clank! The iron chain fell to the floor, broken. Nobody was laughing now. They all looked at me, incredulous. And, from that moment on, they left me alone.'

Bebro had gained the respect of a pack of kids by breaking an iron chain. What a resourceful man ...

'What had happened made me think,' he continued. 'I wondered if I would be able to break a chain again. So, I decided to conduct an experiment. I asked a neighbour to tie me with an iron chain, exactly like the nasty boys had done. He was a bit surprised, I must say, but helped me. I tried to break free from the chain again, but I failed. Something was missing: the rage. I needed it. "Upset me," I demanded. He goofed around. His plain stupidity was upsetting me already, but I needed more rage. "Upset me, idiot!" I yelled. He looked around, baffled, not knowing what to do. Then his eyes sparked – I believe for the first and last time in his life – and he kicked me with his foot, yelling "Midget!"

'He had done it. If I had seen red with the kids, I was now seeing black. He had said that one damned word he shouldn't have. Devoured by rage, I pulled the chain with all my strength and ... clank! I had freed myself, again. I thought I had found how to break the chain at will, but I needed to see whether it really worked. So, I asked the neighbour to tie me again. Once wrapped in the iron chain, I concentrated, and thought: Bebro – midget – Bebro – midget! And the chain broke for the third time without effort! Even the neighbour was ecstatic!'

The troupe, who had respectfully followed Bebro's story, suddenly burst out in clapping and yelling. I did the same, until I had no more breath, and my palms ached. Bebro bowed his head in gratitude. He didn't stay silent for long, though. 'So, I had found out that by breaking a chain I could finally get men to appreciate me,' he said. 'I immediately gathered as many chains as I could, and began wandering through the corridors with my neighbour. The idlers liked my gimmick as much as I liked their celebration. Occasionally, one would approach me to ask: "Can I join you?" One man I met was able to walk on his hands. I said: "Come with me." That's when I started to build my troupe. But, after a while, the idlers got tired of the iron chains. I had to find something new, and came up with the trick of the cans. I still use them to draw attention to our spectacles. In time, the spectacles became more sophisticated, with a plot and many thespians, as you can see them now.'

Then, Bebro paused, and I somehow anticipated that his story was about to change mood. 'I was performing a spectacle that the idlers were enjoying when I received an unexpected visit,' he continued in a quieter tone, darting fearful glances around. 'A man dressed in purple with a folded whip ...'

'The Crier!'

Bebro nodded at me, and I instantly looked at Flox – who, her eyes already moistening, was destined to soon relive her past pains through Bebro's story.

'He walked towards me; all the idlers were running away,' Bebro said. 'I had only heard about the Crier, but never seen him before. He's very tall – and I mean really tall, not just in comparison with me – and intimdating. When he was near enough, he unfolded the whip and … slash … hit me on my right wrist …'

Bebro, who told his own story with solemnity, as if part of a spectacle, showed me his wrist, which hosted a single, though deep, scar.

'Then he went away,' Bebro said. 'The Crier could have killed me, had he wished. But he just whipped me once. And it was from then on that the bailiffs began disrupting my spectacles. They hadn't done it before. It's the Crier: I've never seen him since, but the bailiffs are doing what they know he wants them to do.'

Flox laid her head in the crook of my arm, prompting a fluttering in my chest. I was suspended between the pleasure of protecting her and my fear towards the Crier. For some reason, I was sure my path would eventually cross his.

After the meal, we cleared the floor, then the boy distributed the bedrolls. He even had a spare one for me, which I unfolded next to Flox's, slightly away from the others. Not much later, the lights went out. Flox and I writhed in our sacks, each waiting for the other to speak first. I didn't want to tell her what had happened in Bruttho's den after I had left, because I didn't want to sadden or scare her by describing Bruttho's death at the hands of Mozart. Bebro's mentioning of the Crier had already unsettled her enough.

All the others in the tent were sleeping.

Bebro snored, even louder than the zookeeper.

'I like Bebro,' I whispered.

'He's a genius,' Flox replied.

I hummed in approval.

When Bebro was a child, Flox told me, he was already so gifted that the Masters of the Known encouraged him to enter the novitiate. And that's what happened, even though the Masters eventually ousted him, long before his induction. When I asked the reason for his expulsion, Flox replied that Cardenio, who had told her the whole story, was unsure. Apparently, the Masters hadn't enjoyed Bebro's habit of asking questions. But someone had told Cardenio a different story, in which the Masters had expelled Bebro for his failure to grow in stature. Or, Cardenio had also heard, the cause lay in one slate where Bebro had painted a rose in the shape of a woman's breast. In any case, the rejected Bebro had found nothing more desirable than dedicating his vast talent to the creation of spectacles set in the Land of Without before the apocalypse. Spectacles that the idlers liked very much, the bailiffs less so.

Flox told me that the whole troupe had been very caring, and had made her feel secure, almost as much as her father once had. They all owed to Bebro, in some way: Cardenio, sentenced to three hundred lashes in perimeter ⱵꙄⱵ after they found out that he measured time, had saved his own skin by joining the troupe (no more spectacles in perimeter ⱵꙄⱵ, though). Bologna had just lost her genitors under a collapsed ceiling when Bebro saved this poor girl left stranded in tears. And the boy: Cardenio suspected he was Bebro's son, but without specifying on which grounds his suspicions lay.

'Will you follow them?' I asked, not entirely comfortable at the prospect, because even though I appreciated how they had taken care of her, I would rather she didn't travel away from me. I wished I could join Bebro to become a thespian, if only it didn't mean abandoning Mother now that she was better, and renouncing what Piko would soon teach me, at last: the azbuki!

'I'll leave them as soon as the light is back. And you must come with me, Boz,' Flox whispered urgently.

I asked why, confused.

She didn't say anything else other than that I should trust her; and I did so.

VI

HERESIES

After promising the persistent Bebro that I would take some small part in a later spectacle, Flox and I parted ways with the troupe, heading towards a destination that, despite my insistence, Flox didn't want to reveal.

I had skipped my class with Piko, missed the chores at the zoo, and my genitors were surely worried about me, but I was determined not to let the prospect of punishment ruin the joy of being with Flox. As we journeyed together through the corridors, I felt a growing force expand inside, a strength so powerful that not only I, but also everything around me, seemed unable to resist it, while a pleasant new warmth, enveloping my whole body, rendered me immune to fear or hesitation.

When, after twelve corridors, I recognised one face among the many idlers, I was sure we were back in my perimeter – if we had ever left it. Flox wisely kept her cape down: girls didn't habitually walk through the perimeter, at least not without a child, and we didn't want to raise the suspicion of the bailiffs. If they found her, she would be deported to Breathitt.

We finally reached the corridor that had accommodated Bruttho and his pack, our journey ending in the large room where the kids had been feasting before Mozart's intrusion.

Just as I was wondering why Flox had brought me back there, she gestured towards the smaller adjoining room in which we had first met.

'He's waiting for you,' Flox said, implying that I was to go in there alone.

I had already been through the same situation with Bruttho but, trusting Flox infinitely more, I walked with confidence towards the archway, without even turning once.

I stepped inside the narrow room, just past the entrance.

A tall, shrouded shape was waiting by the opposite wall.

Despite the near-darkness, I recognised him without effort.

'Boz ... come here.' He beckoned me with the jangly voice that only added to his intimidating appearance. I was still afraid of him, although less now that, by revealing his former friend's life of passionate delusions, Piko had made Mozart the Heretic less of a stranger to me. I walked forward, standing far enough away from him to avoid seeing the grisly details of his face.

'I asked Flox to lead you here. And she did it,' Mozart said, annoyingly pleased.

I frowned. I didn't like to consider any relationship between her and this insane man. A tense silence ensued.

'Do you feel something for ... Flox?' Mozart asked, sounding pleased in pronouncing her name.

'What have you done to her?' I asked, instead of answering. I feared he might have forced her to play with him.

'I saved Flox,' he responded, in control. 'She was alone, with no food. So, I asked a most trustworthy man to take care of her: a thespian, surrounded by a very loyal troupe, who performs his brilliant spectacles throughout the perimeters.'

Bebro: they had met in the novitiate, I guessed, both eventually failing to become Masters of the Known.

'Why am I here?' I asked impatiently. I wanted to hear what he had to say and then run off, so that he wouldn't infect me with his contagious insanity; but I would also have to persuade Flox to leave him, and that might call for a whole lot more work.

'You're here because I have a mission for you – outside,' he said.

'What is a *mission*?'

'I would say it's a difficult task that a brave man completes when he has a purpose to believe in.'

'And what should I do for you that I believe in so much?' I asked, a little irked by his presumption.

'I cannot tell you, yet,' he replied calmly.

I glanced at him and, despite the distance between us, noticed the geometrical precision with which Sun had destroyed no less, and no more, than a perfect half of his face. I didn't know what was worse: the atrocious punishment inflicted on him or, perhaps, his rejection by the men of the perimeter. My only certainty was that I didn't want to meet the same fate.

'It's impossible to reach Without,' I blurted. 'And thinking about it is already in breach of the Tenets.'

'So, we are both in breach,' he said.

Annoyed by his comment – somewhat perceptive, I had to admit – I looked at him askance.

'A path to the Land of Without exists,' he argued, unsurprised by my tangible hostility. 'And I know how to reach it.'

If Mozart's intention had been to unsettle me, he had achieved his aim. But I didn't want to let him use my innate curiosity towards Without to plant the seed of doubt in me.

'Even if a path to Without existed, why should we ever follow it?' I countered. 'No life is waiting there: only burning heat. And even if Sun didn't turn our bodies into ash as soon as we stepped outside, famine or drought would quickly kill us.'

'Have you seen such holocaust with your own eyes?' Mozart asked provocatively.

'No – my eyes have only ever seen these walls,' I replied.

'Quite,' he confirmed. 'And aren't you tired of these damp corridors? Of dreaming about a past that you haven't even touched with your own hands? And wouldn't you be eager to learn more about the Land of Without, if you could? Aren't you curious to see what is inside the outside?'

I was very annoyed by his arrogant, though persuasive questions. 'And you: have you ever been to the Land of Without?' I asked, unsure whether my question was designed to provoke him, or to conceal the fact that I knew what Sun had done to him.

'More than one man has been there, and returned,' he answered without answering. 'That's what caused all those plagues.'

'What do you mean?'

'Every man who comes back from the Land of Without,' Mozart said, 'brings with him all sorts of bacteria, germs and viruses, which spread through the perimeters, killing so many of us. It wasn't body hair that caused the plagues – as Piko wrongly told you, I suspect.'

Mozart knew my preceptor. He had been watching us. I trembled in the dark.

'Who do you think feeds us?' Mozart asked, with no apparent connection to the preceding conversation.

'What?'

'Where do the nutrients come from?'

'The bailiffs give us all the nutrients we need,' I replied.

'Yes. And the nutrients are cleverly formulated: they nourish, but don't fatten us, and let men survive without sunlight,' he continued. 'But if Piko has prepared you properly, you should know that before the apocalypse – as they like to call it – all food was ultimately created by plants that converted sunlight into sugars. No sunlight would have meant no food. We needed it. So, if Sun has become so heinous as to burn everything around him – as they like to say – how can we still have food? And the filthy air that we get through these rusty vents …' he added in a raised voice, pointing a hand to the ceiling. 'Piko has no doubt told you how plants and plankton were the sole creators of oxygen in the Land of Without. But if Sun has burned all forests, and emptied all oceans – as they say – without plants and plankton there shouldn't be any air for us to breathe. Don't you see?'

His twisted reasoning, insane but not entirely illogical, tantalised me. However, I wasn't going to allow Mozart the Heretic to refute Piko's precious teachings, or question what Father and Mother had told me since I was born; at least not yet.

'You cannot prove what you say,' I replied. 'It's just theories.'

'You will help me to prove them.'

I shook my head, so dumbstruck by his presumption that I was unable to respond, not even to say that I would never become his accomplice. Never.

'I have devoted my entire life to finding the truth.' Mozart filled my silence. 'I was a friend of your Master. We liked each other, but we fought, and then grew estranged. He never accepted that, unlike him, I long for more than just learning about the past; I want the truth about … the present!'

His voice still echoing in the room, Mozart slowly drew a couple of steps closer, allowing me to see a large necklace hanging over his robe. Almost entirely obscured, I couldn't tell what stone it was made of, but I was yet able to make out three identical shapes converging towards a wide orange sphere embossed on the surface.

'Scarabs …' I whispered in delight, staring at the necklace.

'Yes.' Mozart nodded, pleased. 'I've had dreams about them since I was a child.'

I, too, had often dreamed about scarabs. Hercules, Goliath, *Agra liv*. In sleep, I tried to capture them, but always failed because the scarabs ended up crawling into somewhere inaccessible. And I occasionally dreamed about them without even closing my eyes: more than once I had glimpsed a scarab crawling up a wall only to quickly realise, with sadness, that it was just a figment of my imagination. I really wanted to touch a scarab, to feel its movements on my hand, and to sense the freedom that lightness and speed had bestowed upon it. Piko said that scarabs could move very fast.

I didn't share my feelings with Mozart. I didn't want him to know we had something in common. But our similar passion for scarabs had stirred my curiosity. 'If a scarab creeps into a man's dreams,' Mozart said, almost reading my mind, 'it means that the Land of Without is calling that man. Dreams tell us what is still to come. Hasn't Piko taught you about the purpose of dreams … ?'

Feeling at fault for my ignorance, my head shook in silence. Despite his lunatic heresies, I had to admit that in a way Mozart

seemed to me already a man of some authority. When Piko
had warned me about his powerful ideas, I had glimpsed in my
Master a form of respect for his strayed friend, a sort of guilty
admiration that I was beginning to understand, at least in part.
I can say with hindsight that it was Mozart's courage that first
impressed me; and his willingness to sacrifice of everything he
had, even a portion of his face, to prove his truths.

'What are the scarabs joining with?' I asked him, looking
at the necklace.

'They are embracing Sun,' he replied in a most normal tone.

I recoiled, not only because portraying Sun in image is
forbidden by Tenet ᴣ%̄, but also because any proximity between
the scarabs and Sun was no more desirable to me than the
thought of Flox having to depend on Mozart. 'It's impossible.
Sun killed all scarabs!' I yelled. 'They should flee the sunlight,
not embrace it …'

'You're wrong, Boz,' he replied, calm yet firm. 'Sun would
never harm a scarab. It was Sun that dispatched scarabs to the
Land of Without as heralds of life during night-time, when
Sun rests. For this purpose, Sun gave them all the greatest
powers – crawling, digging, swimming, flying. So, the scarabs
can only be grateful to Sun, and not fearful of him.'

I tried to speak, but he interrupted me. 'There is life
outside, Boz. The apocalypse is a mere invention.'

At hearing another blasphemy, I wasn't sure whether to
oppose it or simply not react, for talking to Mozart about
Without had already made me feel as if I was somehow partak-
ing in his madness – an awkward sensation that I wanted to
suppress, and quickly. I couldn't see any reason why we would
have been told a lie about Sun, I ultimately argued.

'Your mission will be, indeed, to find out why,' he declared.

Mozart's insistence ate at me, and elicited a harsh response, which I still regret. 'I will not let Sun destroy my skin,' I said, looking straight at his misshapen face for the first time since my arrival in the room.

'Who told you it was Sun?' he replied, his voice hardening. Silence.

'It wasn't Sun,' he said. 'The Crier did it.'

I looked at him in suspicious wonder.

'I had just left the novitiate. The Masters hated my theories. They called them arrogant. I was studying in my unit when the Crier and two other men came in. They tied me to my pallet, and the Crier began his torture. *He* did this to me. Coward. I couldn't even defend myself. Then, they made up the story of Sun's punishment to scare the other novitiates away from the truth about the Land of Without.'

I was left thrown. Everything was happening so quickly.

'There's life outside, Boz,' he repeated. 'But, if you want to find it, you must first look beyond these walls. You must learn to look not at the things that are seen, but at the things that are unseen.'

He paused, then said with greater urgency: 'Scratch them with your nails, hit them with your fists, or just yell at them, but don't let these damned walls choke you!'

As Mozart shouted, Flox hastened into the room. But it wasn't Mozart's animation that had drawn her inside.

'The bailiffs,' she whispered in alarm. 'I saw them in the corridor. They're searching all the units.'

'You must go. Both of you,' ordered Mozart. 'If they find you here with me, they will lash you to death.'

'And you?' I asked, without actually knowing why I cared about his fate.

'We will meet again, Boz,' said Mozart, giving me the half-smile available to him.

Flox took my hand, and we left the room. We walked through the corridor at a slow pace in order not to attract the attention of the bailiffs, whose voices I could hear not far behind us; but, apparently, they were on the lookout for someone else, or they simply didn't notice our presence, because nobody tried to stop us.

We travelled through seven corridors, then Flox turned to me.

'It's not safe for you to be seen with a girl, Boz,' she warned.

I liked Flox's concern for me very much, but I didn't want to abandon her again, and I told her so.

'I will not be alone, Boz. The thespians told me where their next spectacle is. I will join Bebro and his troupe there.'

I couldn't possibly bring Flox to our unit, and she was right: walking together was putting both of us at risk. So, for all the pain our separation would bring me, I agreed that she should go with Bebro, with whom she would be better off, at least for the moment.

Just before parting from me, Flox drew close to rest her lips on my forehead, and her brief gesture swept all the uncertainty away.

'Yes, you can take care of yourself, I know,' I whispered with a soft smile, even though she hadn't said anything in that regard.

So, I walked home alone, and, despite my resistance, Mozart's voice slowly invaded my thoughts. I couldn't just ignore his words. Not that I would be so mad as to search for the Land of Without. And if I ever tried to reach it, I would do so only to fulfil the burning desire to see a real scarab with my own eyes. If they still existed. How could Piko be so sure that no scarab had survived? He had never been outside. I was tempted to believe in the existence of more than just these damned corridors, but the mere imagining of a place that I wasn't allowed to visit pained me deeply. Gripped by sudden guilt, I shook my head to dispel the heretic thoughts, yet they would come back to haunt me, I was sure, no later than the next class with Piko.

When I reached our unit, Mother was alone.

As soon as I went in, she started in my direction, yelling my name, reaching out to touch my robe to make sure I was real.

I hugged her.

When Mother asked why I had abandoned her after the spectacle, my elusive answer was that I had hidden somewhere for fear of the bailiffs, and had returned home only when no longer in danger. To my surprise, she nodded, convinced by my lie. She would never have accepted such a lame excuse before the illness.

When Father came home, and saw me there, he behaved as I had expected. He seemed relieved, at least at first, but then a veil of anger came over his face. He, like Mother before, asked where I had been and, once I had repeated my lame excuse, slapped me in the face. Mother, shocked, didn't understand why Father had done that. But I knew why.

'I was talking to a neighbour,' he said in a dry tone while he surreptitiously removed a bluebottle from under his robe to hand it to Mother. 'He saw you pulling a tumbrel of thespians through the corridors.'

He tried to slap me again, but I ducked to avoid his large hand.

'You know what the bailiff, or even the Crier, could do to us if they saw you with those damned thespians? And what if the neighbour tells on us?' he asked, enraged, though in a low voice so as not to be heard outside. 'Haven't you seen what shameful spectacles they put on?'

I thought his scolding was unfair. They were a nice bunch of performers, after all. I was grateful, at least, that nobody had told him about Flox; he would never accept me helping a girl from the corridors of Breathitt, who moreover had pleased so many men, to hide in our perimeter against the Tenets.

I had a question for Father; one that I knew he wouldn't like.

'Why did the bailiffs stop the spectacle?'

He looked at me, inquisitively.

'I didn't see anything against the Tenets in it,' I continued, defiant.

Mother, watching us both, couldn't bear the tension. She burst into tears.

Father stared at me with unbridled hostility. He didn't have the answer. He just called me arrogant, then flounced out of the room.

Mother had moved to a corner. I got close and caressed her smooth head from behind, but she didn't react, continuing her feeble weeping. The whole situation was so depressing that I had to leave the unit. At first, I headed towards Piko's unit, but then realised that I wasn't prepared for a confrontation about my missed class; I'd had enough of being scolded for no reason. So, I went to the only place where I was sure they would all leave me alone: the museum.

Always deserted and left unattended, the museum consisted of a large circular room, at whose centre stood a suspended iron panel. The panel was occupied in its entirety by a ferrotype showing the last existing image of the Land of Without. According to Father, every perimeter had a museum, and every museum displayed just that one item, the last existing image of the Land of Without; lest we forget.

It was an overcast sky, Piko had told me the first time, seeing my eyes squinting at the ferrotype in the vain effort to make out its content. He had then hovered his right hand over the blurred illustration, trying to define, with the tip of his index finger, the contour of each cloud among the inextricable mesh of grey and white shades.

Thinking of the wondrous objects awaiting us, I hadn't closed my eyes in the lights-out before my first visit to the museum. But, when we finally entered, I had been disappointed that of all marvels nourished by the Land of Without before the apocalypse, the only item the museum displayed was no more than an unfathomable greyish mass. But I had returned there many times since. Because, despite their inscrutability, or perhaps exactly because of it, those clouds attracted me. The more I looked at the cloudscape, the more I longed to understand what lay behind it.

'You must learn not to look at the things that are seen, but at the things that are unseen,' Mozart had told me, and I pondered his cryptic words while, still distressed by my quarrel with Father, I stared at the mysterious, overcast sky. But Sun had punished humans for their greedy desire for a better world in the skies, and for believing in creatures without flesh, Piko had once said. Wasn't I similarly breaching the Tenets with my curiosity over a place I had never seen, and which no longer existed? Was my own life not enough?

'Boz.' I heard my name whispered in the empty room.

Mother.

She came up behind me and gently laid her hand on my shoulder.

I turned, and her still-wet eyes smiled at me.

She looked at the ferrotype.

'I remember it. I saw these clouds at the museum of my perimeter when I was a little girl,' she said. 'Mother took me there once. I asked to go back, but Father told me that the museum was reserved for men. I wasn't allowed a second visit.'

Mother spoke of this episode as if what her genitors had said was a reality that had to be accepted, no matter how unpleasant. I doubted she had ever asked herself what was beyond those clouds, or that she would ever wonder about it.

Neither of us spoke for a while, and we watched the blurred cloudless sky, so distant in space, so distant in time, while innerly lost in our family's struggles.

I then broke the silence. 'I don't understand why Father has it in for me …'

'He doesn't have it in for you,' she softly replied. 'He just wants you to follow the Tenets. He doesn't want those awful thespians to lead you astray. Have you seen what outrageous spectacles they put on?'

Mother was repeating what Father had said, despite having seen her with my own eyes enjoy the spectacle before the bailiffs' interruption.

'But I liked the spectacle,' I said to provoke her.

'You must be careful. Curiosity can be dangerous, Boz,' she told me.

I didn't reply. I didn't know how.

'You are privileged, Boz,' she continued. 'Father didn't have a Master of the Known. He is worried that you will lose your privilege. Or, even worse, your Juice.'

Mother made me feel guilty about my decision to avoid Piko, and fearful of another loss of Juice. So, I left the museum to find my Master. I had to confront him, in any case, sooner or later.

He didn't ask what had happened, but solemnly warned me not to miss more classes, as it had happened twice already (once was when Bruttho's pack had kidnapped me), and a third would not be tolerated. That would mean losing the azbuki forever. My heart pounded.

Shortly after, as I listened to Piko explaining why borers burrowed into the bark of trees, it suddenly came to me that it wasn't the fear of being scolded that had lain behind my reluctance to see him. The truth was that I had known I would be tempted to ask him Mozart's dangerous question: *how can we still breathe without plants?*

I didn't ask him anything like that, evidently, because Piko wanted me to answer questions – not to raise them. For the entire class, nonetheless, I sensed Mozart's disturbing presence with us, as if he were there to question everything Piko said.

'When will we start the azbuki?' was my only question, at the end of the class. Piko had taught me about the past life in the Land of Without, but not the azbuki.

'You are almost ready, Boz,' he said. 'Almost ready. But not yet.'

I nodded, though I was disappointed. I had been waiting for long. Very long. The azbuki would allow me to read the slates, to learn more about scarabs, to visit the byzantius with him. Even though I had a better memory than all the other kids, the azbuki was still unknown to me, and this lack of knowledge made me feel incomplete.

I was heading out of his room when Piko called me back. Perhaps he had changed his mind about the azbuki, I hoped. Instead, he said: 'I've seen your mother in the corridors. She seems fine.'

Piko appeared pleased, but also perplexed about her improvement. 'She's feeling better,' I replied. I couldn't say that Father was regularly bringing her bluebottles hidden under his robe. Less than happy to observe that his diagnosis might have been wrong, Piko mumbled something before going back to his slates.

VII

BOREDOM

'To the s … ! To the s … !'

When the confused shouting first reached me from a distance, I briefly hoped that Bebro was back, and Flox with him. But it wasn't the thespians that were coming to us.

'To the shelter! To the shelter!' the panting man yelled.

The idlers rushed out of their units. Father took Mother's hand, Mother clutched mine until it slightly ached, and we left home. The mass of robed bodies rushing to the shelter was already so thick that those pouring into the corridor were instantly swallowed up. Men trampled children under the agonised eyes of their genitors, who had to abandon them on the ground so as not to be crushed themselves. If a plague was already in the perimeter – and I'm sure we were all thinking it – we were bound to get infected.

'The shelter! To the shelter!'

The man's screams were barely audible in the deafening noise, and the smell of the fresh sweat already lingered in the stale air. Among the moving crowd I glimpsed one of Bruttho's kids. Trailing behind his genitors, crippled by an unknown danger, the kid no longer looked that threatening. He saw me but, too captured by fear, didn't react.

We needed to hurry. There wasn't enough room for everybody inside the shelter, and the gate would soon close, leaving many of us outside. It took us some three hundred steps to reach the entrance. The crowd there was so dense that, in the struggle to get in, we pushed hard against those in front. Unable to bear the crush, a woman screamed in pain, then fainted. But the crowd kept her body upright, holding us back, so Father was forced to swiftly push the unconscious woman aside, where she finally dropped on the floor and disappeared. But we got in, we got into the shelter!

When the bailiff by the gate decided the shelter was full, he raised his stick and, with no warning, began hitting those scrambling to get in. Meanwhile, other bailiffs moved to shut the gate. But they struggled, for those still outside resisted with all the force of desperation; a closed gate would indeed mean their end. Only after many attempts did the bailiffs lock it – severing, in the process, three fingers of a man unwilling to remain out in the corridor. I stood ten steps from the gate. I saw everything. Those outside didn't give up, though. Banging on the gate with their fists, they produced a relentless noise that gave us shivers. Nothing could be done from the inside to stop them, and the thumping on the gate unnerved us throughout our entire stay in the shelter.

A mother and a father who had forced their way in, only to realise that their child was still in the corridor, begged a bailiff to open the gate so that they could go back to him, even if leaving the shelter meant never returning. The bailiff shook his head with distracted attention, but the two insisted, until he had to silence them with his stick.

We were given one bedroll each. Soon, I could see no end to the many lines of unfolded bedrolls covering the entire shelter. Mothers and children sat on their lumpy sacks, while men gathered in groups at the centre. The height of the ceiling, at least ten times greater than anywhere else in the perimeter, turned the buzz of the crowd into a deafening whir that made me feel even more small and insecure.

'What's happening outside?' Father hastened to ask a small gathering.

'Nobody knows,' a man replied. 'I asked, but they didn't say. They told me to go away!' he added, pointing at a surly group of bailiffs not far off.

'It must be a plague,' another man whispered, as if his low tone might diminish the issue. 'That's what the shelter is for.'

Others nodded in agreement.

'No!' a man interrupted. 'I heard that packs of kids from Breathitt are raiding the perimeter. That's why we're here!'

'But why are we hiding, instead of fighting back?' another argued. 'It doesn't make sense.'

'It does,' replied the first man. 'The shelters are what they're looking for. If we defend the shelters, the packs will go away. They're here only for the food.'

An invasion from Breathitt; it made frightening sense. What if Bruttho and Flox hadn't been alone in coming to our perimeter? Maybe hundreds of ravenous kids were already looting our units. And Flox: was she part of the plot? I didn't believe so.

'What ... what if ...' I started, '... they keep delivering nutrients through the hatches, even if we aren't inside? The packs will take over our units and stay – as long as there are nutrients – forever.'

The whole group, Father included, turned to me. Unless asked, a kid wasn't permitted to address men. But they were too worried about what was going on to scold me and, ignoring what I had just said, they simply carried on talking. But the men could not deny, at least to themselves, that my fear was well founded. I went back to Mother, though not before over-hearing another group speaking about descended men suddenly coming back from beneath to kill everyone – all because of one undertaker who had failed to close a manhole properly.

When his group broke up, Father came back to us, saying that there was nothing to worry about. Soon, he promised Mother, we would be back in our unit; and, in any case, the shelter had plenty of food; and, if the worst happened, the bailiffs would protect us. Yet, for all these reassurances, not knowing what lurked behind the iron gate slowly began to eat away at us.

While the nutrients were being distributed, Father approached the bailiff who had beaten those genitors culpable only of caring too much for their son. This bailiff, I noticed, was acting very authoritatively with everybody. 'I'm a keeper,' Father told him, pointing to the red star on his robe. 'I believe another pair of hands could be of use to you.' The bailiff looked at him with mild surprise. He might well have gone for beating Father for his audacity but, after rolling his eyes in lazy thought, he approved his request, and told him to help distribute the nutrients.

The one good thing about the shelter was that there were no tools to measure our Juice. As long as we were there, I would be spared my genitors' fear over my results. Given his obsession with the Juice, I wondered how Piko, who I hoped had reached some other shelter, was coping with the uncer-tainty. At the end of our last class, he had told me that I would begin learning the azbuki in the next one, but the call to the shelter was ruining everything.

The rumbling at the iron gate never subsided, not even in the dark. Despite some inner resistance, we alll gave in, sooner or later, to the temptation of glancing at the closed entrance. I don't know why, but some even pressed their ear against the cold iron to hear the suffocated pleas coming from outside. I didn't, because I knew that, had I gone to the gate, a deep pity for the excluded would have haunted me, and I would have kept going back to the gate, again and again. Hoping in vain to get back to their lost child, the two distraught genitors never moved from the entrance.

The worry of the unknown threats waiting in the corridors sufficed to keep my mind occupied, at first. But, as lights-out followed lights-out (four hands would've been needed to count them, had I been allowed), boredom seeped in. I missed all that I had outside: the expectation of meeting Flox in the corridors, Piko's classes, my games of senet with Daffodil. I waited for something new to happen, but it didn't. There wasn't much to occupy me, other than listening to those around me spiralling with their fears.

'A bailiff told me that we're here because Sun has cracked the walls,' one man said. 'His damned rays are already inside. Here ...' he said, pointing at the sturdy walls of the shelter, '... it's the only safe place.'

The idlers murmured.

'No, it's the Crier,' another man revealed. 'He wants to punish us for that damned spectacle. We're in punishment.'

After a while, I ceased bothering even to listen.

A large pack of kids had formed eighty steps from me, and were busy with some game. I approached them.

'The Juice may nourish you,' I addressed the kids.

Most of the kids didn't acknowledge my arrival; only a couple of them glanced at me, coldly.

'Can I join in with your game?' I asked.

The answer came from Tiruyte, the kid in Bruttho's pack who had sewn the red armband to my robe: 'Na, Boz. My genitors don't want me to talk to you. They say you're a friend of the thespians. Go away!'

I was surprised that this kid, who had helped Bruttho ransack the perimeter, now cared about his genitors, and their lack of trust in me. He probably didn't have a choice, now that he was back in captivity. After his harsh dismissal of me, the other kids even ceased to look, pretending I didn't exist. I left in silence, and went back to my sack.

Doing nothing was worse, though. So I began wandering around the shelter. I wasn't alone in having to cope with boredom, it seemed: as well as the many groups that formed then broke up, aimless streams of idlers crossed the shelter constantly. Some didn't find anything better to do than occupy the queue for the latrines, which became swollen with idlers that didn't need to be there. But the queue shrank to nothing when the dark was near. In fact, nobody wanted to remain alone inside the latrines when blindness arrived: because if anything bad happened to them there, nobody would come to the rescue.

The orders were clear: wandering around the shelter in the dark was forbidden. And even if anyone wanted to breach the rules, it was impossible to go anywhere without light.

On one occasion, we were given proof of how dangerous the latrines were in the dark. From our bedrolls, we heard screaming. A woman had failed to come back before the lights-out, and was now begging for mercy. Each of her cries knifed me in the gut. I wanted to help her. I am sure others felt the same. We all listened in silence to her screaming, although I could also hear the soft cries coming from Mother's sack and, of course, the relentless thumping on the iron gate. Having to stay still, unable to share my pain with someone else, only made it feel worse. Eventually, the exhausted woman stopped screaming, and expressed her agony only through a dwindling weep. When the lights came back, she had long ceased making any sound at all.

Leaving their bedrolls as soon as they could, three women rushed to the latrines. I was about to follow them, but Mother begged me to remain with her. She was still coming back from gipokaltsiyemiya and, not wishing to upset her, I thus stood by my bedroll. She didn't deserve more pain. Despite the unbearable stench, the rescuers searched hundreds of cubicles before finding the woman huddled on the floor – I was later told. They carried her back. She could barely walk, her head lolling, her tired eyes no more than two slits.

As I followed the woman's stilted movements, my attention was suddenly diverted by the sight of a bailiff walking out of the latrines almost unnoticed, glancing in all directions other than where the woman was. I could see the guilt in him; even though I couldn't recall which Tenet prohibited men doing bad things to women – maybe there wasn't one – everybody knew it to be wrong. As soon as I learned that the woman was alone in the shelter because her man hadn't made it through the gate, I was certain that the bailiff had preyed on her for this very reason, and he had to be conscious of his own evil.

The poor woman's ordeal distracted me for a while, but then boredom resumed, more threatening, and not only for me. A few on the inside had started banging on the iron gate, for they wanted to leave the shelter, whatever it took.

Even ingesting the nutrients – a process I had always found tedious – was now a welcome occupation. I waited eagerly for Father to distribute the nutrients before each lights-out. I would make the meal last as long as I could. Against the bailiffs' orders, Father brought not one, but two bluebottles each time, handing the second to Mother in secret. I was so desperate to occupy myself that I would have even been willing to blackwash the walls, had they allowed us.

Apart from boredom, I was also consumed by the anxiety that distance might take Flox away from me. Perhaps her flesh had already been offered to someone else – I feared – and she was already with child by then. Or Mozart was harassing her at that very moment. Or she had been killed by the plague. More than once, even though it was impossible, I thought I saw Flox inside the shelter. What hurt me the most was being powerless, unable to protect her. At first, imagining we would reunite to have a child together eased my suffering, but it didn't last. So, after a while, I began an internal battle not to think of Flox – a battle that I never won, as her image kept chasing endlessly round in my mind.

Eventually, an event close to my sack distracted me. A woman with child began her pains. Soon after the labour had commenced, a group of mothers came to her. After clearing some space around the bedroll so as to hide the woman from all curious eyes, the mothers reassured her, brought her clean clothes, massaged her belly. One mother even got some thebaine from the shelter's pharmacy to ease the woman's pain. For once, the bailiffs, ill-equipped to address what was occurring, didn't intervene.

Little by little, the moans of pain grew louder. I couldn't see much through the encircling mothers: just the woman clutching some arm for relief, or a mother whispering occasional calm reassurances to her. Once again, I had to endure the torment of hearing the cries of a woman – although this time caused by the hand of nature. I knew it might end badly. It had happened before: abandoned women dying alone in their units while giving life. But she had the mothers caring for her.

It didn't take long before the shelter got bored of watching the birth of a child. The idlers stopped looking in her direction, and carried on as if nothing was happening, even showing some intolerance for the woman's noises. But the mothers didn't abandon her. They took turns. I kept watching, hoping that I would see a tiny bit, at least, of a child coming to life. It would prepare me for the moment when Flox would make me a father.

I really hoped Flox had reached the thespians. She would be fine with them, this I knew, in a safe perimeter far away. I was sure Flox would return to me once the alarm was called off, so that we could decide what to do. I thought of Cardenio and Bologna on the stage, reunited after a long, perilous journey, and felt the pleasant warmth inside me once more.

I recalled when, so overjoyed at meeting Flox a second time, I had told her that I didn't want us to part ever again. There, lying close together under Bebro's dark tent, I had felt her shy smile. 'It is not up to us – at least, not just us,' she replied, struggling to come to terms with her emotions. Flox was difficult to understand because she was at moments tender, at moments cold, and this contrast made her even more irresistible to me.

'I don't care. I will do everything I can,' I said, somewhat taken aback by her dry response.

'I know …' Her voice had acquired a warmer tone. 'And I like it. I've been feeling so alone after Father's death. I kept looking at the door, at every door, hoping he would come back. Even when the toad was all over me, I still glanced at the door hoping to see Father. I felt so alone. Bruttho protected me, but he wouldn't have given his life for me. Then, when you walked into that dark room, and didn't want what all the others had wanted from me, I knew you were different, that you were there to give, not to take. Suddenly, I no longer felt so alone.'

Then, at hearing my sigh of happiness, she must have imagined the corners of my mouth rising, and my strong will to live for her. I've never forgotten what she said under Bebro's tent. And, inside the shelter, the memory of her helped me to keep going.

There was no end to the monotonous thumps on the iron gate. Even their intensity remained the same. But we eventually grew used to them; and, in fact, had the sound from the gate ceased, we would have missed it because, in the end, the noise reminded us how life still continued outside of the shelter's walls.

I often thought of Mozart, too. Even though his madness still frightened me, sifting through his theories helped my mind to fight boredom. Usually, I resorted to Mozart after a lengthy count of all the species of scarabs known to me, or after squatting and stretching twenty times in a row, or when all other available remedies had been exhausted. I remembered Flox telling me of those in Breathitt using violence to alleviate boredom. I didn't want to follow their path, for sure, but I didn't want to go insane either.

I wondered, once more, how Daffodil had survived an entire life inside that dreadful glass cage. I had asked her this very question when we last met, right before the call to the shelter. 'Curiosity saves me,' she replied. 'I listen to everything they say in front of my cage – I already told you – and meditate on their thoughts. You've helped me, too, by sharing your hopes and fears with me, Boz. I like the way you feel about Flox. You're putting her needs ahead of your own, you would do anything for her. I also see that you hate your father, Boz. This is wrong; this hatred will only harm your mother, if she feels that you bear hostility towards him.'

'But you hate the zookeeper ...' I objected.

'True. But he has done to me what he has done, you know.'

We both stood in silence. I regretted my comment.

'And I have them,' Daffodil resumed, showing the faintest of smiles as she eyed a pile of slates on the table. 'They keep me company. I can learn so much from their images and words.'

'You can read the azbuki? Really?' I asked, surprised, trying in vain to hide my envy.

Daffodil nodded.

'Where did you learn to read?'

'The previous zookeeper ...' she replied.

So, a zookeeper had taught Daffodil what my Master of the Known was still refusing to teach me. It was upsetting. But then I realised that, of all people, it didn't make much sense, and wasn't even right, to be envious of Daffodil.

I had noticed that the slates weren't always the same. They kept changing.

'Who gives you all these slates?'

'A wise and generous man. He comes here once in a while, when I'm sleeping in the dark. He whistles to wake me up, then he passes me the new slates through that opening in the cage and I give him some slates back. The zookeeper doesn't know about all this, and if the pile grew bigger he would realise. I've spoken to the generous man briefly, but never seen him. It's too dark when he visits me. He hasn't been here for a while, actually, and I am now getting tired of looking at the same slates. But mind: the zookeeper mustn't know.'

I nodded. I wouldn't tell anyone.

'The old zookeeper taught Mother and me how to read. None of my ancestors ever learned how to read since we came inside ten generations ago, Mother said.'

'You met your mother?' I asked, widening my eyes.

'Yes. We shared this cage. But when, all of a sudden, they moved her somewhere else, it crushed me. They also changed zookeeper. I found myself alone with him,' she added, gesturing towards the source of the snoring. 'When he arrived, the slates were already on the table. So, he thinks I'm allowed to keep them. He doesn't know the Tenets well enough. He should know that they forbid a Congoid to practise the azbuki. Not that I care about the Tenets at all. They don't matter.'

Nobody had ever said in front of me that the Tenets didn't matter. I had been weaned on the Tenets, although I didn't recite them as often as Father did – I mostly pretended in front of him – but I hadn't expected to hear this blasphemy. I didn't reply: Daffodil's existence was too difficult not to try, at least, to listen to her carefully, without interrupting. And what I had already heard from Mozart the Heretic wasn't much better, after all.

I still thought about my last conversation with Daffodil. There was one thing she said, which I hadn't initially given much attention to, but which I was now mulling over inside the shelter. According to her mother's calculations, Daffodil's ancestors had left Without ten generations earlier. Generations is the only manner of measuring time that the Tenets allow, and Piko always repeated that men got inside these walls around twenty generations ago, when life in the Land of Without ended. Daffodil was clever and precise, and her mother must have been like her, I guessed, but their estimation about when humankind had arrived here conflicted with the truth Piko had shared with me. Like someone lost among millions of slates in the byzantius, I felt disoriented, wracked with doubt about whom I should believe, and ashamed, too, for questioning even a tiny fragment of Piko's knowledge.

After one lights-out of mounting cries, the pregnant woman gave birth to a girl. The mothers cuddled the baby, carefully bundled up in a cloth, and showed her around with pride. Once out of the shelter, mother and daughter would be deported to another perimeter. But what if we never left the shelter? The newborn girl would live her whole existence walled up in a room, and her own offspring, conceived and born in the shelter, would be told that the shelter was the only place they could live. Was I in a similar situation by believing that humans could only survive inside, just because I had always lived in the corridors, and by not being open to the idea that life continued beyond these walls?

I was thinking too much. I slapped my head to quit.

I decided to go back to the kids, and insist on joining their game to keep me occupied.

'No – beat it!' Tiruyte spurned me again.

'He's not giving up, Tiruyte!' a kid told him.

They all sneered at me.

I felt like an idiot.

But Tiruyte was nòt Bruttho. I didn't fear him.

'Let's fight!' I told him, glad that my voice didn't break in that instance.

I felt his inner sigh; he hadn't seen that coming. The kids shouted excitedly. Their genitors turned to see what was going on.

I drew close to him.

Facing each other, we began moving in a circle, slowly, our arms held high, our motions reminding me of what Flox had said about her father in his duels. The harmless circling went on for a while, and the impatient kids, craving violence, started booing us. But I wanted Tiruyte to make the first move. And he did. His pride hurt by the boos, Tiruyte suddenly jumped at me. He tried to punch my face, but I avoided his fist, and then grabbed him, my arms soon tight around his back. He tried to hit me on both sides, but failed, before releasing himself from my grasp. We resumed circling each other. I noticed that more genitors had gathered around us. Normally, grown-ups would have stopped our fight, but their own need for entertainment was now so pressing that they just watched us.

When Tiruyte, soaked in sweat, charged at me again, I did more than just grab him. Biting down on his right ear, I clenched my teeth so hard that my eyes felt as if they would come out of their sockets, and I only eased off when a piece of

lobe finally broke away. Blood dripped everywhere. His right
ear covered with one hand, Tiruyte stared at the floor, then at
his bloody hand, and finally at me as I spat the bit of lobe on
to the ground.

I had gone too far this time. All the bailiffs would lash me
in turn, of this I was sure. Father might even join them. And
my Juice would certainly end soon. My existence would cease.
I had no explanation for what I had done, other than something had simply taken over: a refusal to be excluded.

But it turned out differently.

After a short silence, the kids began to yell: 'Boz, Boz, Boz!'

I turned left and right to take in their shouts of celebration, and their genitors smiling at me. They had all liked it.
I was enjoying being liked. For the first – and last – time
Father approached me to pat my shoulders in what seemed
like approval.

From the trail of blood, I could see that Tiruyte had gone
to find his genitors by their bedrolls. He never came back to
that corner of the shelter, where, from then on, I was allowed
to stay with the other kids. Life inside the shelter became easier
for me. We engaged in tug of war, hide and seek, or hitting
another kid's knuckles until he flinched. Running around
pleased me. I really needed it. Like drawing on the slates; but
I would need to leave the shelter in order to resume drawing.

The other boys wanted to hear more about the thespians.
I was the only one who had ever been with a troupe and, now
that their genitors approved of me, the kids felt free to show
their curiosity. They asked questions.

'How far have you gone with them?'

I made it up: 'Perimeter ᗡᑌᕼᕼᗷ.'

It was at least ten thousand steps away.

The kids looked at me in awe. I enjoyed teasing them and, also, being admired.

'Is it true that each thespian has at least twenty women … ?'

I thought of Flox. Mother and Father couldn't hear me, so I replied: 'I've already chosen my woman.'

The kids looked at me in wonder. Under Tenet ⱻ⧻⧹, genitors chose a woman for their son; but thespians didn't appear to follow that rule. No one had paired Cardenio and Bologna. This made me think: so many lived with complete disregard for the Tenets. Bruttho, Mozart, Flox, Bebro. I, myself, had breached the Tenets by walking in the dark. I had been punished with the loss of Juice, Bruttho with the loss of his life, Mozart with the loss of his face. Only Bebro was still intact (his wrist scar not counting) and, apparently, cheerful. I hoped the same would be true for Flox.

'Where's your woman?' the kid asked.

'She's with the other thespians.'

'When will you see her again?'

His question annoyed me. I didn't know when we would finally leave the damned shelter, and how to reunite with Flox once out. I would have to rely on Mozart to find her, something I wasn't keen on. And it bothered me that, while the outside banging on the gate still persisted, fewer idlers were now doing it from the inside. They were getting used to the shelter.

VIII

MISDEED

Barely had the lights returned when Mother did a thing she shouldn't have: she coughed, loud, thrice. The idlers turned to us. Earlier on, the bailiffs had locked a coughing man inside the dungeon with others suspected of plague. The dungeon was almost full, I had been told. Seeing the first coughers dragged in by force, everybody had rapidly learned how to resist the temptation to empty their lungs. Panicked eyes in a reddened face meant that one was holding breath until the urge had passed. Others pressed their mouth and nose against their bedroll to make it go away, at times for so long as to almost suffocate themselves. Those around observed aghast, unsure whether to sympathise or call the bailiffs. But coughs, although rare, still occurred.

The bailiff who had violated a woman in the latrines came close to our sacks, though still keeping himself at a distance.

'What's gaun oan 'ere?' he asked.

'That woman coughed,' a man said, pointing at Mother.

The others nodded, fretting yet relieved that the bailiff was picking on someone else.

'Staun' up. Come wi' me,' the bailiff ordered Mother.

She glanced terrified at Father, then at me, as if she hoped that either of us would tell her not to follow the bailiff. Ending up in the dungeon was certain death, if not because of the plague, then from starvation – I hadn't seen any nutrients taken into the dungeon since the first cougher had been locked inside. I was no less terrified than Mother, for I knew she would never survive the dungeon in her condition.

Father stood up. I hoped that with him being a keeper and having helped to distribute food, the bailiffs would show mercy for his woman.

'She's not sick,' Father said. 'Look at her. She's fine.'

'Ah dinnae care,' the bailiff answered. 'We cannae wait fur her tae shaw th' plague.'

He didn't care. He wouldn't wait for symptoms to appear.

'Tell him you're well,' Father begged Mother.

Worn out by the long stay in the shelter and still weak after gipokaltsiyemiya, Mother raised her pleading eyes towards the bailiff, who in return stared at her long enough to render me uncomfortable.

The bailiff said to Father: 'Come wi' me.'

They walked together to a rare clear area among the thick crowd, next to the closest wall, where I witnessed a heated exchange – Father in particular. He kept putting his hands to his head, looking at the bailiff in anger, but nothing of what they said could be heard. When Father spoke, he went on for long, raising his voice, but the bailiff's answers were short, his voice was low, and I couldn't make out anything of his face. Mother looked at them with quivering eyes. Only after a while, and with growing intervals of silence, did I see Father nodding reluctantly at the bailiff. They parted ways, one heading for a group of other bailiffs, the other coming back to our bedrolls.

Father strove with all his will not to cry. As soon as Mother understood what had been agreed with the bailiff, she collapsed. 'We've no choice,' Father whispered to her, his hand caressing her back, while he looked around mortified, fearful that others might already suspect the terms of his agreement with the bailiff. Mother cried, and cried, but she didn't fight back. Neither of them seemed to care about me being there, or perhaps they thought I couldn't understand what was going on. Silence fell between the three of us, a quiet so unbearable that, barely noticed, I left them to go to the other kids; but the games didn't stop my mind from going back, again and again, to the bailiff laying his eyes on Mother, and to her desperate reaction after Father's return to the bedrolls.

When the lights were about to switch off, the bailiff reappeared. Standing between us and the latrines, he beckoned Mother with a hitch of his head. She stood up, slowly, then paused to turn to Father, perhaps hoping he would tell her not to move. But Father, covered in humiliation, just stared at her. Mother reached the bailiff, and they walked together into the emptying latrines. The lights went out. Inside the bedroll my body ached, and the pain I had felt when that same bailiff did those things to the other woman now appeared insignificant compared to the agony I was suffering for Mother. I fought with every fibre of my being not to stand up and go searching for her in the latrines. It would have been useless, anyway: even if I had found them in the dark, there was nothing I could do, and the bailiff would have severely punished me.

Apart from my wanderings with the thespians, I had never endured the dark for so long without Mother. I felt bad, and my wait for the blindness to end was interminable. Father's teeth gnashed throughout the entire lights-out, accompanied by a growling sound that I had never heard coming from him before. I wanted to whisper something of consolation, but I didn't because anything I said would have just increased his guilt. For the first time, I felt a sense of pity for Father.

When the shelter was illuminated again, and the racket of the awakened crowd had resumed, Mother came back from the latrines, limping. The idlers stared at her, then naturally glanced at Father, only deepening his shame for his failure to protect his woman. He knew the others knew.

As she walked towards us, reluctant to merge with the prying crowd, Mother stroked her robe in an attempt to smooth out creases that didn't actually exist, and looked at the floor as if to conceal some inner dirt from the others. I, too, gazed at the floor to ease my humiliation. Without speaking, Father hugged Mother, but she did not reciprocate, lacking the courage to look at him. I remembered when Flox had told me how playing with the toad had immediately turned her into another person. The same must have been true for Mother. She returned from the latrines a different woman. Having suddenly lost all the curiosity and hunger for life that her recovery from gipokaltsiyemiya had sparked, she seldom spoke and stayed in her bedroll, detached from us. If not for the fact her eyes were open, I would've thought that the disease had repossessed her.

We paid for Mother's coughs in another respect, too. Eager to see if she would cough again, the attention of the idlers was now upon her, even when they didn't openly stare in our direction. So, I should have guessed that someone would eventually find out what Father was up to.

'Hey … what urr ye daein' thare?' the bailiff who had gone to the latrines with Mother shouted.

Father paused, poorly disguising his fear and shame.

'What's gaun oan … ?' The bailiff searched Father's robe frantically, longing to find anything to compromise him.

Mother looked up, a jolt of fear breaking her aloofness.

'He wis hiding this,' the delighted bailiff said after taking a bluebottle out of Father's robe, holding it high for the whole shelter to see.

'Shame on you!' a woman yelled from three sacks away.

Stealing nutrients from the shelter was a violation of the Tenets, although I still didn't know what the sanction was. Glad to have found some way to occupy time, and prepared to lynch him, a throng of men moved towards Father, yelling: 'Thief! Thief!'

The group had almost reached our bedrolls when the bailiff, raising his stick, persuaded them to stay away. I think he did that more to retain for himself the privilege of punishing Father rather than to protect him. Other bailiffs arrived, and he hastened to tell them what he had found. Upon hearing of the smuggled bluebottle, a bailiff clubbed Father's leg with his stick. 'Dry ycr eyes! Y'll git at least ither five or ten o' thae,' he said, waving his stick in the air threateningly. The bailiffs laughed at Father groaning with the pain.

'Whit dae th' Tenets say 'n this trial?' one of them asked.

The five bailiffs looked at each other questioningly. In normal times, outside of the shelter, they would have consulted the Crier.

'Ten mair blows in th' legs,' the bailiff who had hit Father said, even though he sounded far from certain about his answer.

'Nae sure,' intervened another bailiff. 'Ah hawp that Tenet ⱁⱈⱂ commands that whoever steals anythin' shuid be gubbed two times oan th' palm o' his richt haun.'

A mere two blows on the palm of his right hand. I saw hope in Father. It didn't last, though. A third bailiff reached out for the red star of keepers sewn on his robe and, despite Father's instinctive, short-lived attempt to block him, jerked it away from the robe. He then dropped the star – the very same star I had seen Father wearing with pride since I was born – on the dirty floor.

'That's tae stairt wi'!' the bailiff said, prompting another laugh from the group.

Mother gasped. She knew the removal of his red star was for Father a sanction much worse than any conceivable amount of blows, and that, even if they spared his life, from now on he would be condemned to live an empty one.

'It's nae enough.' Another bailiff stepped forward. Father couldn't get away with it that easily, he said.

The others looked at him approvingly. After a brief silence in the group, a bailiff intervened: 'Noo that ah mind: Tenet ⱁⱄⱚⱅ commands th' removal o' nails fur fairn stealers.'

I shuddered. Father was sweating heavily. However, none of the bailiffs seemed keen to begin the horrifying torture on him. Even though I shouldn't, I spoke in his defence. 'Father took the calciferol for Mother,' I said. 'She hasn't been well. Father took it for her.' But I really shouldn't have interfered because the bailiff who had gone to the latrines with Mother responded: 'She is peely-wally, then. She shuid pack tae th' dungeon!'

'No, no, I'm well! Not the dungeon!' yelled Mother.

Curious to learn the punishment reserved for Father, the shelter had fallen into dead calm. All eyes were set on us, until a sudden screaking cut the stillness of the large room. The gate was being opened from outside. One after another, men turned in anticipation towards the entrance, forgetting Father immediately.

A bailiff walked in. He stared slowly left and right at the whole shelter, then said: 'Shift oot!'

The idlers rose from their bedrolls, and, fearing that the bailiff might close the gate, hurried to the exit in disorderly lines. Father, too, walked towards the gate in the insane hope that they would let him go as if nothing had happened, but a bailiff stopped him after five steps.

As the place emptied, the three of us remained there alone with the bailiffs. I had long yearned for the gate to open, but now, despite my glances towards the brimming corridor, I wasn't keen to walk out. Father's destiny mattered to me more. The bailiffs were still debating which sanction the Tenets prescribed for his wrong. 'We shuid choap his richt haun aff,' said one, quoting a Tenet I had never heard of – which, he argued, mandated the amputation of the thief's right hand for the stealing of nutrients from a shelter.

He was still speaking when a mounting hum from the corridor reached us. I turned around, and saw him. Much sturdier in build than I had imagined, he stooped to enter through the gate, and clutched in his hand was the same whip whose cruel use had been described to me in so many accounts.

'The Crier …' a bailiff whispered to us in a reverent tone, as if we were all equals in power and ruthlessness before him. The other bailiffs, certain that his coming was no accident, ceased to wrangle over the prescriptions of the Tenets the very moment they saw him.

The Crier walked at a slow but steady pace in our direction.

'This keeper stole fairn,' a bailiff told him as soon as he had reached us.

The Crier looked at Father, then at Mother, then at me.

'A thousand floggings,' he said with no discernible emotion in his voice.

Father threw himself down and began hitting the floor with his hands, desperate, wailing and weeping. Knelt before the Crier, Mother begged him for mercy, but the Crier, nodding to the bailiffs that they should carry out the punishment, didn't acknowledge her. Mother continued. 'If he can't be saved, I want to be with him,' she wailed. 'If he must die, I should die with him.'

The bailiffs looked at Mother, bewildered, like me, by her desire to follow Father in a meaningless sacrifice. But the Crier, expressionless, granted her the punishment she had asked of him: 'A thousand floggings.'

A bailiff, wishing to spare a son the sight of his genitors' execution, bawled at me to leave, to go to my unit. I went away, not just because of his order, but also because my pain for Father, and the anger at Mother's shameful desire to leave me behind, were unbearable.

They all watched as I hurried towards the gate.

'Boz … !' Mother called me.

I turned, and took ten steps back.

As I drew near, she slid her hand under my sleeve to gently grip my forearm. 'I must follow your father, Boz,' she said, maybe hoping that I wouldn't resent her for the rest of my existence.

'Why?' I asked in a broken voice.

'The Tenets say so,' she answered. I was immediately no less angry with the Tenets. because nothing could ever justify what she was being ordered to do.

'Go home, Boz. Go home,' said Father, a forlorn look in his eyes. We looked at one another for long, and I could sense his deep concern for the hard times that were coming my way. Unused to seeing Father so powerless, a swift flutter invaded my chest, promptly erased by the awareness that I would never see him again.

I left in tears.

To this day, I still don't know why they locked us inside the shelter, but only that it changed the course of my life.

Once out, I wandered aimlessly through the corridors, because I didn't want to go to our unit, where I knew I would feel even lonelier without Mother and Father. My mind was in such a muddle that I lack a clear recollection of my mean-derings: I just remember seeing idlers who glanced at me with suspicion, and swapped sides of the corridor so as not to cross paths with me, but also that I didn't care, fearing only that Mother and Father might already be dead. Then the lights went off, and I sat down on the floor, my back against the wall of the corridor, so that if somebody – or something – ambushed me in the dark, a narrower part of my body would be vulnerable to the attack. I tried not to breathe too loud. Eventually, nothing and nobody attacked me in the dark, and, when I woke up under the light, my fear of the dark was gone.

I wanted to go home. I needed food. Hopefully, some nutrients had been dropped in the hatch before the last darkness. I was starving, only adding to my desolation. To reach our unit – *my unit*, I should probably have said by then – I had to pass next to the shelter. There was no way around it. I feared I might see two corpses, wrapped in tarps, pushed out by the bailiffs. But the corridor was empty, and if not for the marks on the gate made by the desperate thrashing of the excluded, nobody would've known anything had happened there. I placed my ear, awkwardly, against the cold iron to see if anyone was inside, but nothing. I still wonder if the bailiffs ever bothered to open the dungeon inside the shelter to release those imprisoned.

Walking by his unit on my way home, I went to look in on Piko. I needed his support. Moreover, I hadn't forgotten that our next class would bring the azbuki to me, finally. But when I raised the canvas curtain, and he cocked his head with a slight frown, I realised that I wasn't welcome.

'The Juice may nourish you, Piko,' I said.

He nodded at me, but failed to reciprocate the salutation. He wasn't preparing to test his Juice, so I wondered how my visit had disturbed him.

'We've been inside the shelter, for a while,' I said.

'I know,' he answered, his lips pursed, as he placed a set of slates on one shelf.

'And you?'

'I was here,' he replied drily, as if he couldn't possibly have been anywhere else.

'What happened in the perimeter?'

'Nothing that I'm aware of.'

'So why did they lock us inside the shelter?'

'I don't know.'

Coming from such an eloquent man, his short answers bugged me, and not knowing why they had locked us inside the shelter for so long angered me even more.

'Are we starting the azbuki?' I asked, trying to forget the shelter.

He looked away and continued to arrange the slates; then said something I wasn't expecting.

'Boz ... we shouldn't meet.'

'What do you mean?' I asked, trembling.

'Your father has been disfellowshipped,' he said. 'I am not allowed to educate the son of a disfellowshipped man. And I wouldn't do it, in any case. He was a thief.'

His unforeseen hostility dazed me. The prospect of conquering the azbuki under Piko's guidance had punctuated with occasional joy the never-ending periods of boredom inside the shelter, helping me to keep going. But all seemed lost, now. Without the azbuki, I would remain an incomplete man, like all those damned idlers in the corridor, and the gates of knowledge would never really open to me.

'But he took the calciferol to cure Mother, for her gipokaltsiyemiya ...' I tried to justify Father's wrong.

'She wasn't alone in developing gipokaltsiyemiya. What made her so important?' he retorted, looking away. 'He was no different to those kids from Breathitt who looted the perimeter.'

I had no rejoinder, and arguing with him would be useless anyway: the many conversations with Piko had taught me that he seldom changed his mind, and he never disobeyed the Tenets.

After Mother, he, too, was abandoning me.

I left his unit, resuming the walk home, but a gnawing emptiness grew inside me: I had lost everything – Mother and Father, Piko, the respect of the people, the azbuki ... and perhaps even Flox. At that moment, I felt I would rather begin my Descent than carry on in an existence of desolation.

I arrived in my corridor. Even though the lights weren't due to go off yet, there were fewer idlers around than there used to be. I wondered if the long period in the shelter had changed them, so that they now preferred lazing around in their units rather than outside in the corridor. Not that I minded; I wanted to avoid suspicious glances or foolish questions. But I wasn't prepared for what I found when I pulled up the canvas curtain of my unit.

Bruttho.

A fist reached my face.

He had been waiting for me, just inside the door. Mozart the Heretic had spared his life.

Though I didn't fall to the floor, his punch still made me hobble around in confusion. He pushed me outside of the unit, where he delivered several more blows to my stomach.

'Where is Flox?' he shouted.

Bent double, I didn't answer. He tried to hit me again, but I shot back into my unit. An unwise decision, in hindsight, as there was no way to escape from Bruttho now, and I would have been trapped, if not for the aid of a precious tool on the floor: the stone ball. I picked it up, and despite its weight feeling unbearably heavy from my hunger and exhaustion, I summoned enough anger to carry the ball out of the unit – and, when Bruttho was right in front of me, hurl it at him.

Had it not encountered Bruttho's massive chest on the way, I reckon the ball could have travelled for over a hundred steps, proving I hadn't lost my hard-earned ability with the throws. Bruttho was pushed back with such force, and he hit the wall behind so violently, that the whole corridor might have collapsed; but, after shedding a generous patch of black varnish, the wall withstood. Two men, peeping at us through their canvas curtains, speedily retreated. We were alone in the corridor, or at least so I thought. Bruttho panted, holding his chest in pain, cursing at me.

'You took my woman. I own her,' Bruttho muttered. 'You and that damned monster took Flox.'

I didn't say anything, and it was indeed during my silence that, from one end of the corridor, we heard a voice saying: 'The Tenets prohibit duels.'

Bruttho looked at the Crier with no less dread than when he had first seen Mozart by the door of his den. The Crier moved towards us. I flattened against the wall, which I knew wouldn't be much help, but Bruttho was too scared even to move. Stalking past me, the Crier reached him and, having unfolded the whip, callously performed on Bruttho what he had done to Flox's father. I should have run away, but for some reason I couldn't tear my eyes from the gruesome execution. When he had lashed Bruttho so much that he was nothing more than an idle mound of flesh and blood, the Crier turned to me.

'You're the son of that thief, right?'

His comment stung, but I said nothing because, unlike Bruttho, I ran off. After no more than five steps, though, the corridor echoed with the crack of a whip. Grazing my back, the whiplash left a diagonal cut on my skin that reached up to my shoulders. My fear being greater than any pain, I kept running as fast as I could, corridor after corridor, even when it had become clear that the Crier wasn't pursuing me. My back ached, and I was exhausted, but I couldn't possibly go back to my unit to rest. And I still hadn't eaten; so, I took myself to the only place where, I hoped, nutrients and companionship would still be available.

Her run accompanied by the zookeeper's distant snoring, Daffodil was on the wheel. She understood immediately that something was wrong and, when I opened the glass cage in a wobbly manner, she rushed to help me. I told her everything, frantically. She listened, and then took a dirty pail from one corner and fetched me a handful of stale nutrients, which, given my severe hunger, I still welcomed. She gently took my robe off and, as I devoured the food, cleaned my fresh wound with patience and care, as I had done for her once.

'You need to leave … with me …' I mumbled, my mouth half full, as I looked around warily.

Her hand paused for a moment, as if she couldn't take in what I had just said while being engaged in something else, then resumed cleansing my back with the cloth, her movements slower than before.

'Are you still there?' I asked in response to her silence.

She had never considered leaving her cage, nor that it was possible, I guess, and so was going through the same emotions I had experienced after hearing Mozart say that life still continued in the Land of Without, and that a path to it existed.

'Where can we go?' she asked, dubious.

'Someone can help us,' I replied. 'More than one person, actually. I have friends.'

Daffodil looked at me, partly impressed, partly unconvinced. 'I've never been outside,' she objected.

'It doesn't matter. You're trained to walk,' I said, pointing at the wheel. I was tempted to tell her that our travels might even take us to the Land of Without, but I thought it better not to. One step at a time.

'Where will we get the nutrients?'

'Trust me,' I said.

'And if they catch us? My back cannot take any more scars …'

'Trust me,' I repeated. 'I'm sure you're curious to see what's outside of the zoo. It's all corridors and rooms, not much different from where we are now, but at least there is no cage waiting for you there. And no zookeeper … my friends will like you, and you'll be free to talk to them.'

Daffodil, I felt, was longing to do something else in her life other than running on the wheel or looking at the same slates over and over again, and she really wanted to open herself up to others. It was for these reasons that I finally persuaded her to join me.

'You'll have to wait, though,' she said.

'For what?'

'Wait,' she whispered again, and then stepped out of her cage for the first time ever. After padding across the floor repeatedly, and caressing the walls with her hands, treasuring these unprecedented acts, she walked alone to the zookeeper's room. I stood by the cage, unable to make much of the few muffled sounds that reached me from the other room. When Daffodil came back, she was wearing the zookeeper's large robe, hiding her dark face under his wide cape.

'And him?' I pointed at the zookeeper's room.

'He has been taken care of,' she just said.

IX

FAREWELL

'Wait here,' I whispered to Daffodil.

Having managed to reach Bruttho's old den unnoticed, we were now standing in front of the small room where, I hoped, the only man who might save our lives would be waiting for my return.

I walked in, and he was indeed there, standing where I had last seen him.

'Boz: I knew you would come back …'

'I'm ready for the mission, Mozart,' I said, well aware that there would be no coming back – much like when I first stepped out of our unit in the dark, against the Tenets. 'I want to reach Without. There's nothing left for me within these damned walls. And the Crier wants my skin.'

Mozart nodded in silence.

'But I first need to help a friend,' I said, unable to foresee his reaction to what I was about to say.

'A friend?' asked Mozart – though I suspected, from his tone, that he already knew.

'Daffodil. She's a Congoid. I helped her to escape. The zookeeper was torturing her. Daffodil needs a safe place to go.'

'You did right in helping her,' Mozart observed. 'My friend and his troupe will make good use of a new thespian. Bebro is staging a spectacle in perimeter ♀✛♉. Take Daffodil to him, and then come back to me.'

Mozart didn't say more. So, I left him, and walked with Daffodil towards perimeter ♀✛♉. It wasn't that far, and even if the journey had consisted of a million steps, my joy at meeting Flox again would have made it feel like a short walk. The plan was to leave Daffodil in the safe hands of Bebro, then reach Without under Mozart's guidance, so that if the outside was really hospitable as he claimed, and not the deadly expanse of smouldering earth described by Piko, I would eventually come back to take Flox out with me. Like Cardenio had done with Bologna.

Daffodil walked with her head down, allowing the large cape of the zookeeper's robe to hide her face, while I marched five steps behind with my head up straight. The bailiffs were searching for me, and someone would soon raise the alarm for Daffodil's escape, though though not before having the sight of the naked zookeeper inflicted on them. We had to walk rapidly, yet without drawing attention.

After reaching an empty corridor, where we felt safer, Daffodil slowed down to whisper in my ear.

'Boz ... that man with whom you just spoke in that room ...'
'Yes?'

'I recognised his voice. He's the kind man who used to bring new slates to my cage ...'

Mozart. He had shown real compassion for Daffodil, much more than Piko or any other man I knew of would have ever done. It heartened me, and I really needed reassurance about

Mozart in that moment: we were putting our lives, Daffodil's and mine, in his hands.

We had barely left the perimeter when the sight of two loaded tumbrels lifted my mood. The troupe had just ended the first act of a spectacle, punctually dispersed by the bailiffs, and was preparing to move to another perimeter, when Bebro saw me.

'Boz! The Juice may nourish you!' the spirited thespian cried out.

The others turned in our direction, including Flox, who stared at me from one of the tumbrels, a sudden joy igniting in her eyes. Eager to consider Daffodil's fate first, and only later my own emotions, I responded with a huge smile, so that she would know I felt the same.

'The Juice may nourish you, Bebro,' I said. 'This is my friend Daffodil.'

If Bebro felt any surprise at me being accompanied by a Congoid, it was very well hidden. 'The Juice may nourish you, Daffodil!' he said, hugging my travel companion, who was almost double his height, with sincere enthusiasm. Unaccustomed to being touched by a stranger, Daffodil stiffened a bit, but then smiled back.

'Mozart said you will be able to protect her ... as you have with Flox,' I told him.

'By all means!' Bebro exclaimed.

I was relieved, and Daffodil must have been too: I saw an unusual spark of hope in her dark, composed eyes.

Then Bebro added: 'But on one condition.'

'Yes?' I asked, slightly perturbed that he would put a condition on his help.

'You'll keep your promise: you'll be part of my next spectacle. And I have a part for Daffodil, too!'

I hadn't seen that coming. I laughed.

We shortly began moving. I sat alongside Flox and
Daffodil on the tumbrel, which, despite my offer to take over
the exacting task, was pulled by Bebro. Quite soon, Daffodil
pretended to doze off, so that Flox – of whom she had heard
so much during my soliloquies in the glass cage – and I
could finally be alone, reacquainting ourselves after such a
long separation. I told Flox how thinking of us together had
helped me to carry on during the period in the shelter, and of
my overwhelming fear of losing her. Flox stroked my head,
still wrapped in the cape. 'I knew we would see each other
again,' she whispered.

I glanced at the other tumbrel, and saw that the boy, Bebro's
alleged son, was looking at Flox and me with a hint of jealousy.
I felt a nascent hostility growing inside, but, conscious of what
a fool I would be to ruin this blissful moment with jealous
hatred, pushed it back immediately. I smiled at the boy, and
he reciprocated.

We stopped the tumbrels somewhere, and Bebro began
running with his cans to attract as many idlers as he could to
the next spectacle. I helped Cardenio to set up the stage, which
didn't consist of much more than a bundle of tubes, planks and
the multicoloured curtain, while groups of idlers, intrigued
by our unforeseen presence, were already hanging around us,
gawking at the preparation of the stage.

'Put this on,' Cardenio urged, placing a fuchsia wig on my
head, and rouging my lips and cheeks with a brush. 'We don't
want the bailiffs to recognise you.'

Meanwhile, as Bologna helped Daffodil try on her stage clothes, the two were getting to know each other. Daffodil, fulfilling her lifelong desire to talk to others in unconditional freedom, was telling her moving story to Bologna, who had only to hear the word *cage* to fall into a gigantic weeping bout.

'Boz, come here …' I heard a call from above.

'Yes, Bebro …' I said after raising my head.

'I want to share a secret with you …' he whispered. 'Come up here.'

I climbed on the stage and joined Bebro behind the closed curtains.

'Yes … ?' I said, hesitant, not wishing to appear too prying, nor too indifferent, over what he was about to tell me.

'After thousands and thousands of spectacles … Boz … this will be my last,' he said in the tone of someone who is well aware of the magnitude of a revelation.

'What do you mean?' My eyes widened. 'Why?'

'I wrote the next spectacle when my body had almost no wrinkles, and my cans ran much faster. To be honest, the last spectacle will be the first spectacle I ever wrote. But I have never put it on stage.'

'You don't like it enough?' I asked.

'No, on the contrary: I like it very much. But it's too danger-ous. It's my only spectacle where character is… a Congoid.'

He sensed my instant concern for Daffodil. 'You shouldn't be worried for her.' Bebro quashed my apprehension. 'They'll think she's wearing dark pigments on her face. Nobody will ever guess that Daffodil has escaped from a zoo.'

He then put a hand on my shoulder, as if it was him, always so keen to help others, who for once needed some understanding. 'The danger lies elsewhere,' he told me. 'If I dare to represent a Congoid in a spectacle, the bailiffs will never let me set foot on a stage ever again. The Tenets already forbid men from representing human life in the Land of Without, in any form, even though – I must say – the Crier has been quite tolerant with my representations of Caucasoids. But I'm sure he will never accept a thespian portraying a Congoid. Never.'

Bebro's eyes moistened, but he held everything back, continuing in a firmer tone: 'Still, my Boz, still ... I'll finally do this spectacle. I've been waiting too long, and when I saw Daffodil ... I thought ... who better than her? And we'll save some dark pigments, at least!'

I smiled and, despite the evident perils, didn't renege on my promise to help him stage the spectacle; because I owed Bebro, like everybody else.

Meanwhile, the troupe had joined us on the platform. Bebro explained the plot in detail, and told us what to say and what to do on stage. I could hear the crowd of idlers buzzing excitedly on the other side of the curtain, and their enthusiasm gave me a thrill.

When the curtains opened, Bebro and Cardenio stood alone on the stage. The large audience, which I could see also included a group of bailiffs, looked at them in silent awe.

'No, son, no ...' Bebro said, shaking his head, and upon it, a large violet wig.

'But Father ...' Cardenio, standing in front of him, complained.

'I will never accept that child,' Bebro interrupted, 'nor bequeath anything to you or to him or to ... her.'

'But he's the blood of your blood, Father.'

'A contaminated blood.'

'How can you say this?' Cardenio raised his arms in protest.

'His blood is contaminated … because this child is the offspring of a Congoid!' Bebro yelled.

The crowd of idlers murmured, and not in approval. Hiding behind a corner of the curtain, I realised they shared my incredulity in learning that a Caucasoid could sire children with a Congoid. Piko hadn't thought it appropriate to divulge this bit of his endless knowledge to me, apparently.

The tense murmuring rose when Daffodil walked on stage. She wore a large purple robe, whose cape only in part covered her face. The idlers, not suspecting anything, looked with a mixture of annoyance and admiration at the masterly disguise of a thespian portraying a Congoid.

Cardenio took Daffodil's hand, and she gently leaned her head on his shoulder. I wondered whether Bologna was jealous by now, but she wasn't around because Bebro had told her to wait by the tumbrels in case anything went amiss with the crowd.

Bebro turned his back so as not to watch his son and a Congoid standing so close together.

'Father, I really feel something for her,' Cardenio told him.

Still with his back to the forbidden couple, Bebro ignored what his son had just said. 'You can follow your whims … and play with whoever you want, son, even a Congoid. But a child? No … you shouldn't have. You have betrayed us, and lost our respect.'

Someone from the crowd shouted in approval.

'You'll both have to leave. There is no longer a place for you here. You must disappear. This child must not see the light in this house.'

Then, without even looking at Cardenio and Daffodil, Bebro left the stage.

Flox and I walked on.

'What happened, Brother?' I asked the desperate Cardenio.

'The worst, Brother,' he replied, gloomily. 'Father has denounced us, and our child. We must go.'

I glanced at the idlers: they didn't seem moved, at all, by the ordeals that Cardenio was suffering on stage because of his sincere passion for Daffodil.

He looked downcast, pretending to cry, but I told him not to. 'Wait, Brother, all is not lost yet. We will help you.'

An ominous hum rose from the crowd.

On hearing me, Cardenio raised his head in hope. 'You'll both hide in the secret hut,' I continued, pointing upwards at an imaginary spot. 'The one we built together on top of the hill, Brother, so that Father wouldn't know about it. We will bring you food, blankets, medicines, and your child will safely come to life there, Brother.'

Cardenio, overcome by my generosity, threw himself at me in a grateful embrace, during which the curtains slowly commenced to draw, dragging behind them not only the end of the first act, but also the incensed screams of the idlers, outraged by my sympathy for a man who consorted with Congoids. All of a sudden, unable to contain their anger, the crowd hurled insults, threw empty bluebottles on the stage, even tried to climb up. It was in that short while, when the rest of the troupe had already left the stage for the tumbrels, that Flox drew near. Among the encircling uproar, her fugitive kiss behind the curtains arrived unforeseen, and I now appreciate, in hindsight, that she did so because she was sure that no more suitable occasion would ever arise.

After staring at Flox in a daze, and incredulous at the situation I had found myself in, I took her hand, and started off towards the tumbrels, only to realise, when I felt a strong resistance, that a bailiff had grabbed her waist. Flox screamed, trying to break free, and I thwacked the bailiff in the face, regaining her hand, but only momentarily, because another bailiff's stick clubbed me in the neck. Most opportunely, Cardenio came to my rescue, shoving the bailiff off the stage with such force that I wondered how far this strong man could go with a stone ball. But when, still stunned by the blow received, I turned around, Flox had vanished. I looked around frantically, but Cardenio persuaded me to go with him to the tumbrels, because nothing could be done by then to save Flox in that moment, and other bailiffs were approaching the stage. Cardenio promised that Bebro would help me to find her.

Contrasted with the past blissful rides alongside Flox, the ensuing journey on the tumbrel was miserable. Not only I, but the whole troupe, looked forlorn: on account of Flox's disappearance, yes, but also because they suspected, in some way, I don't know how, the irrevocable decision to which Bebro had come. Nobody spoke until we reached a place to unfold the tent. I helped Cardenio and the boy to set it up, and then we all sat in a circle around the cans.

After eating in silence, Bebro addressed us all.

'My friends: your moment has come. After so many spectacles with me, you're now free to go it alone, without an old thespian standing in your way.'

The troupe muttered disapprovingly.

'It's true,' Bebro continued. 'You no longer need me. I've aged, and you've become independent. You've learned how to perform hundreds of spectacles, and you will create others on your own. From now on, Cardenio should take up the reins of the troupe.'

Cardenio nodded with pride.

'Where will you stay?' asked Bologna.

'I will stay with a dear friend, whom Boz and Flox were privileged enough to meet. And, finally, I will be able to practise some tricks I learned right after leaving the novitiate.'

Bebro took five little stone balls out of his robe and, having distanced himself a few steps from the troupe, began tossing and catching the balls in the air at such a speed that he seemed to have at least four hands available. At the height of his performance, he even managed to bounce the five balls in sequence off the tip of his nose. Despite being accustomed to his endless displays of talent, the entire troupe was yet mesmerised by such supreme skill.

'And the boy?' asked Bologna, a hint of nosiness ingrained in the question.

'The boy will stay with the troupe. Cardenio will teach him the craft, and will protect him, as if he were his own son,' a similarly equivocal Bebro answered.

Cardenio, relishing the newly acquired role of leader, hurried to reassure me: 'Boz, we will be glad to welcome Daffodil into the troupe.'

I smiled, and looked at Daffodil, who, judging from the twinkling in her eyes, was keen on the prospect.

'But …' Bebro spoke again, glancing at me with a half-smile. 'First, I need to help a young friend to find his woman.'

He then rummaged through one of the tumbrels, from which he took a satchel, and, having laid it on the floor, hugged each one of the members of the troupe, promising that they would meet again. Bologna sobbed, and the others, too, were deeply affected by Bebro's departure.

The two of us walked fast, not only due to the urgency of our task but also because – I suspected – Bebro wanted to escape the nostalgia of a lifetime of spectacles he was leaving behind.

I was curious to learn what plan he had devised to rescue Flox from the bailiffs. Once we had reached my perimeter, Bebro said, 'Wait for me there,' and he pointed at a vacant unit with no canvas curtain. I followed his order, went inside the unit, and occasionally peeped outside to see what he was doing in the corridor.

To my surprise, Bebro placed himself by a wall, took the five little stone balls out of his robe, and began tossing and catching them in the air at full speed. I was disappointed, almost enraged, because he was messing around instead of trying to save Flox.

I was wrong. Very soon, in fact, the prey arrived. A bailiff. Pacing through the empty corridor, the bailiff saw Bebro. He first looked suspiciously at this weird-looking man throwing balls in the air, and was clearly inclined to tell him to stop – but, drawn by Bebro's consummate juggling, he stood in front of the performer. The balls had made no more than five spectacular rounds in the air when Bebro, displaying no less coordination and without even needing to bend down, head-butted the bailiff in the stomach, making him drop silently to the floor. Bebro beckoned me. Together, we dragged the unconscious bailiff into a hidden corner of the nearby empty unit, where we took off his robe and gagged him. After fetching a long rope from his satchel, Bebro tied the bailiff's legs and arms from behind.

'You beat the living daylights out of him,' I said.

'So to speak?' he asked.

'So to speak,' I confirmed.

'He'll free himself, don't worry,' Bebro reassured me. 'But, when he raises the alarm, we'll already be far away.'

'Why aren't you killing him?' I asked. 'It'd be safer.'

'I don't deprive men, however loathsome, of their existence, unless for a greater cause,' he replied. Then he took a fine brush and some pigments from his satchel. 'You look a bit too young to be a bailiff. I need to age you,' he said, winking. I didn't know what he had in mind, but he seemed so sure of himself, and no one else could help me to rescue Flox. I had to trust him.

His brush grazing my face, Bebro slowly applied the pigments to my skin with the same accuracy with which Piko painted his precious slates. After a while, Bebro paused to examine the work done, and, not entirely content, patted my face with the wet brush a little more. 'You're perfect!' he exclaimed.

As he carefully put brush and pigments back into the satchel, he asked: 'Can you speak the language of the bailiffs?'

Having come to learn, despite my will, the awful language of the bailiffs inside the shelter, I nodded.

'Good, you'll need it.'

He then told me to put on the bailiff's robe and to walk alongside him through the corridor, where, having donned an orange and blue wig, he explained to me the most brilliant plan I had ever heard.

We soon reached our destination: a room teeming with noisy bailiffs, stationed to watch over a large group of girls bound for deportation to other perimeters. I counted twenty-three poor girls. Huddling together in the same way penguins once did to defend themselves against the icy winters, they looked disoriented, desperate, fearful of what their guardians might do to them.

The bailiffs suddenly hushed and turned around to see me clutching Bebro by one arm. I spoke: 'A've fun this thespian traivelin' in a corridor.'

One of the bailiffs, nodding slackly, took Bebro from me and pushed him to another corner of the room.

I frantically looked around, and saw Flox among the hapless girls. I winked a conspiratorial eye at her. In return, she gave me an intense stare.

Meanwhile, the bailiffs had resumed speaking, and I recognised immediately the unique opportunity that was emerging from their heated conversation.

'Amurnay aff tae Breathitt! Na wey!' one shouted. 'Ah'amnet mad. Ah dinnae wantae die!'

The other bailiffs murmured in agreement.

'Dinnae even think at me!' Another bailiff hurried to rule out, no less vigorously, the possibility that he would ever agree to take that girl to Breathitt.

'Ah kin pack thare. Fur whit?' I stepped forward.

All of the thirty-two bailiffs in the room turned around to look at the lunatic who had just offered to go to Breathitt.

Breaking the silence, a bailiff pointed at Flox: 'That yin haes tae be deported thare.'

'Ah kin dae it,' I said with no hesitation. 'Ah mist tek th' thespian tae Breathitt.'

I already had to take the thespian to Breathitt, in any case, I argued. The bailiffs looked at each other – puzzled, but also relieved that they might unexpectedly avoid the dangerous task. One of them approached me and, smiling, said: 'Bit noo tis late! Ye shuid bade 'ere fur th' mirk!'

For all my desire to leave the room together with Flox and Bebro as quickly as possible, not wanting to raise any suspicion among the bailiffs, I accepted his offer to remain there for the dark. Shortly after, I was sitting in circle for our meal. I hoped they wouldn't ask me questions, but our unforeseen arrival, and my apparent recklessness in offering to go to Breathitt, had made one of them, in particular, curious.

'Ah hae ne'er seen ye around ...' the bailiff asked, casually.

'Perimeter ᛒᛏᛯᛞ, nae far awa',' I replied to the predictable remark.

'N' whit brings ye aroond?'

'A clocked th' thespian. 'n' a bailiff tellt me tae bring him here.'

'Mmh ... why didnae thay let ye remain in yer perimeter ... streenge.'

The questions were becoming too many, and I wasn't so sure that I could maintain a conversation in his language for much longer.

I stuffed my mouth with nutrients, and simply replied: 'Dunno.'

'*Dunno?*' the bailiff asked, frowning at my mistake. I should indeed have answered *a dinnae ken*.

'A dinnae ken.' I corrected the mistake.

Too late. I had given myself away. After laying the nutrients on the floor, the bailiff began to slowly look around with evident suspicion in his bulging eyes, prepared to raise the alarm with the other bailiffs. They would torture me right in

front of Flox and the other girls; and, for all his resourcefulness, there was no way Bebro could save me, I feared. But, to
my surprise, the bailiff resumed gobbling the nutrients, not
before releasing an extremely loud fart, an act for which he had
needed his full concentration. He then yelled something like:
'Ye shuid shag th' lassie!'

I didn't know what what the word *shag* meant, but the
cackling of the other bailiffs annoyed me.

No other questions came, and I was feeling calmer, when
the arrival of a new bailiff in the room made me shudder again.
He was the one who had gone to the latrines with Mother. He
didn't look in my direction, and just took a seat in the circle,
taking some nutrients in his hands.

Had it not threatened Flox's rescue, I would've jumped at his
throat to kill him for what I considered a great cause: avenging
the deaths of Mother and Father. Instead, I recoiled, keeping
my sweating head almost level with the nutrients below me. If
he saw my face, he would surely recognise me, even with my
disguise. From that position, I could still look around, though,
and when I saw a bailiff whispering something in his ear I was
sure he was referring to me. Indeed, the newcomer looked in
my direction, but his lazy eyes weren't fast enough, and the
lights of the room extinguished before he could single me out.

The bailiffs muttered at the coming of the dark, but they
kept eating, burping and farting, while gasps of fear sprang out
from the girls.

When the nutrients had vanished from the floor, the bailiffs laid down to sleep. I did the same, but remained awake, so
that I would be ready to take Flox and Bebro away as soon as
the lights were back.

I should've predicted that thirty-three bailiffs in a dark room full of defenceless girls wouldn't stay still for long. I'm grateful that the first girl to yell was Flox, in a chain of strident, piercing, rebellious screams – she had suffered so much at the hands of men that she was no longer prepared to accept violence – because I couldn't have tolerated an entire lights-out without knowing what was happening to her. I stood up in the dark and, stumbling over more than one bailiff, rushed in the direction of her shouts. Soon enough, I was hitting the ravenous bailiff. He screamed, heaving his prey aside before he had even begun his violence, and rolled on the floor.

What happened next is difficult to describe – and even harder to believe. All I can say is that events didn't unfold as Bebro had intended; in fact, they turned out even better.

Nobody other than Flox and I knew what had really happened, but some of the bailiffs, probably believing that a pack from Breathitt had attacked the room, began thrusting their sticks at random in all directions. Soon, every bailiff was engaged in clubbing another bailiff in the dark, while the girls took wise refuge in a corner. Having managed to reach the entrance unscathed in a manner that still escapes me, Bebro, resourceful as he was, switched on a torch taken from his bindle and silently gestured to Flox, me, and the girls to leave. Half of the bailiffs were already out for the count, while the remainder were too busy fighting each other to notice us sliding away to join Bebro outside of the room. Soon, a long file of twenty-two incredulous girls was following the pied thespian and his light through the corridors, tailed by me – who, hand in hand with Flox, held my stick ready lest the bailiffs pursued us.

When the lights in the corridor came back, we decided to stop inside a vacant unit. Bebro hung a canvas curtain stolen from another unit across the door, so that nobody would see the girls. Although less intimidated than with the bailiffs, the girls still gravitated together in one protective throng at the centre of the room, finding evident strength in their closeness.

'Why were the bailiffs deporting them?' I asked Flox.

'For many reasons ...' she said. 'One girl was made pregnant by the wrong man ... he lived in front of her unit ... with his family. But, when her genitors were away, the man came into the girl's unit ... and played with her. When her belly began to grow, she told her family what had happened ... but they didn't believe her ... the man said she had seduced him. They cast her off, and called the bailiffs, while nothing was done to the man.'

Flox was forced to relive her own painful past, but didn't flinch.

'Another girl ended the Juice but ... she refused to commence the Descent. Because they couldn't fight her resistance, the undertakers simply pushed the girl inside the manhole and closed the lid. But she never walked down the stairs, she just stood there, under the manhole, in silence. So, when sometime later the undertakers came back to open the lid for another Descent ... she was still there! The undertakers gave up, and took the girl to the bailiffs. All these girls have sad stories behind them.'

'What can we do?' I whispered to Bebro, who had joined us.

'I will help them. They have nobody to rely on. With no more spectacles, I would feel useless, anyway. We must find food. And we must protect these girls from the Crier. He will not fold his hands and consume his own flesh.'

Then he looked at me: 'But now ... you must go, Boz. Mozart is waiting for you.'

'But I want to help you, and the girls ...'

'You will help us in the way that Mozart will tell you ...'

Flox intervened: 'Boz, I will stay with Bebro. There are too many girls here for him to do everything alone. And I don't want these girls to go through what I had to.'

I nodded, though I was sad to part ways with Flox once more, and back in my old robe, I left the room. But I kept the bailiff's stick.

X

AZBUKI

'You will complete your mission only on one condition,' Mozart said, gently caressing the scarabs on his necklace in little, circular motions.

I looked at him questioningly.

'You shall first learn the azbuki.'

He must have noticed my incredulity, and deemed it was fear, not excitement, that lay behind my instant sweating, because he hastened to assure me that I would learn the azbuki from none less than he himself. 'These belong to you,' he said, handing me the goggles that had become lost in the frenzy of our first encounter. 'You will need them when we leave. Don't drop them again.'

When the lights went off, we indeed left the dim room, and went through many corridors, where, to my initial amazement, Mozart, accustomed to walking in the darkness, needed no goggles. At the end of the last corridor was a door, which he opened to lead us inside a cramped room, barely fitting one pallet, a latrine, and a trigonal door on the left wall. As soon as we entered, Mozart warned me not to open the trigonal door – ever.

After taking two slates, a couple of brushes and some pigments from a satchel, Mozart exhorted me: 'The sooner we begin, the earlier you will reach the Land of Without.'

Still unprepared for the idea of acquiring what I had thought lost forever – the azbuki – I watched Mozart sketching two white lines on his slate, one with curved edges, crossing each other.

'*Az*,' he said. 'Repeat.'

'… *az* … ' I stammered, my feeble voice making its first giant leap into the azbuki.

'Repeat!'

'… *az* …'

'Correct. Now trace it,' he ordered, referring to my slate, so that on his command my brush swiftly filled the tablet with intersecting lines. Mozart had me scraping and redrawing the slate again and again, each time insisting that either the lines weren't straight enough, or they didn't intersect each other at the right height.

'The *az* opens the azbuki,' he said. 'Its shape replicates the body of the strongest and cleverest among all creatures – man. When all animals occupied their lives with a frantic search for food, men learned to farm, and to store the produce of their labour for long, freeing themselves to invest their powerful minds in other crafts. Tired of suffering in pain, men studied at length their own bodies, and in time learned how to treat many of their ailments. Then they created the azbuki, so that all the valuable knowledge acquired with great effort could be handed down to the children of their children. And, finally, men invented mathematics, a dimension existing first and foremost in their minds, and with which they erected buildings, created music, travelled long distances, studied the universe …'

Mozart paused, glancing at the trigonal door behind me, then resumed speaking with a touch of gloom in his eye. 'But man is also the greediest of all creatures, and was never sated,' he said. 'Voracious, always craving more. And to satisfy his greed, man tortured the other creatures, exhausted the land, emptied the waters of life, poisoned the air. Like a child unwilling to grow, man aimed at nothing else than the pursuit of his own pleasure, and the fleeing of pain, never considering that he wasn't alone.'

I had longed so deeply to learn the azbuki, but with the hope that it would grant me access to the gates of knowledge – not to Mozart's heresy, where he seemed determined to lead me. I needed to remain vigilant and guard against him manipulating my thoughts, just as Piko had warned he might try. Yet, if listening to Mozart's follies was the inescapable condition for learning the azbuki, I would accept it.

'But Earth rose up to avert man's complete destruction of life and tore down most of what we had been able to build over a long time.' He continued his ramblings. 'It was Earth, not Sun, that scourged the human race, shaking the ground with quakes, flooding villages with rains, sinking vessels with tempests, spreading epidemics, until we were made unable to inflict any more damage on the other creatures.'

As he traced a mark consisting of three joined stones on his slate, Mozart said: 'The *zemlja* embodies Earth.'

'If we keep behaving like superior beings, disrupting the cycle of life, acting like a virus to the other creatures, Earth will never forgive us, and will not allow our survival. We must restrain our hunger and live in harmony with the other animals. Earth gave to all the beasts of the land and to all the birds in the sky and to all the creatures that move along the ground, everything that has the breath of life in it, every green plant for food. There is no need to slaughter animals.'

I knew that before the apocalypse, men had devoured animal flesh, yes, but much like most other creatures: hadn't lions, in fact, hunted antelopes, crocodiles eaten tadpoles, and carnivorous plants swallowed insects? I didn't believe mankind was to blame, particularly because, before the apocalypse, they'd had to hunt for their own food to survive – they weren't given nutrients through hatches as we were.

'You must fill these many slates with *zemlja*s,' Mozart said, as he drew with one chalk a long succession of white strokes on the floor. 'Soon the lights will be on. I shall come back when the dark returns, and you must have ended by then.'

I frowned. It would be arduous to complete the task before the next lights-out. The room lacked a desk, so I laid on the floor, drawing, scraping and redrawing on the slate, helped in the exacting work by my scorching desire to reach Without, the only place where, I hoped, a life for Flox and me was still possible.

I had barely completed the assigned task when I drifted off, my head resting on the cold floor, the worn slate gripped in one hand. Sleep transported me to an empty corridor, and I recognised, as soon as I heard a child's moan nearby, that I had been there before. Without hesitation, I made my way into the room where the manhole, and the imprisoned child, ineludibly awaited me. 'Who's there?' I asked, having reached a distance of three or four steps from the cavity.

The echo of my voice resonated all around.

With no apparent reaction to my presence, the moans coming from the manhole persisted.

'Who's there?' I repeated.

The sound from below ceased.

Was the kid trapped inside the cavity scared of me?

I had reached the edge of the manhole, yet still lacked the courage to look inside, when a figeater crawled out of the cavity, sprinted between my feet, and vanished past me, taking away with him the shiny greenness I had so often admired on Piko's slates. My astonishment was interrupted by another scarab, featuring wings of a lively golden hue, who crept out of the manhole to dart through the room. Then came a third, and a fourth, followed by more. Soon, a multitude of scarabs erupted from the manhole, tumbling out in a stream of countless shapes and colours, dazzling like a carpet of precious gemstones, and their erratic movements left me entranced. I watched in awe as the iridescent creatures collided with one another, climbed up my legs, soared gracefully through the air, and the abundance of their colours obliterated the dark monotony in the room. I was still immersed in admiring their glowing vivacity when Mozart nudged me with his foot.

'Do you want to reach the Land of Without ... or not?' he warned.

Rubbing my sleepy eyes, I quickly took position, and after dropping some nutrients for me on the ground, Mozart drew on his slate.

Λየ

'*Cherv*,' he said. 'Trees. There was a time when the Land of Without was so abundant with trees of every kind that I once heard the remarkable tale of a boy who left his family to live an entire life in the canopy of a forest – leaping between oaks, elms and chestnuts, resting inside a massive sequoia, sustaining himself with fruits, seeds, roots and herbs. While, in real life, most people didn't climb trees, they still wandered through vast forests in search of food, shelter, or peace of mind, until every bone in their bodies ached. Trees aided animals, but animals, too, supported trees in every conceivable way, and they all lived in harmony – until man decided to destroy trees. First, to make fire, then to grow or build what he, and not the land, desired. Yet, eventually, man shattered the harmony, and from that moment, our downfall began.'

Mozart lowered his head, then, ceasing his painful reflection, gave me an exercise to practise the azbuki, one of the many assignments he ordered me to complete in the long period that followed. From then on, I worked strenuously with him in the dark, only to collapse into a deep sleep alone as the lights returned, until he came back to rouse me with a nudge of his foot, dropping some nutrients on the floor to share with him, before we resumed the exercises. Owing to our strenuous work, I learned to read and write all the signs of the azbuki, and to combine them so as to form meaningful words at first, and sentences of increasing complexity, later. Acquiring a deeper comprehension of the azbuki was so exacting, and Mozart's teaching so demanding, that there was little space in me to feel boredom or miss the presence of Flox and the thespians, while my increasing knowledge of the azbuki compensated me for the relentless work.

On one occasion, when I had already acquired some mastery of the azbuki, Mozart opened the trigonal door in front of me for the first time. He left the room alone and, after my futile attempt to peer through the partially open door, he came back with a slate, immediately handing it to me.

Prolonged body, black wing cases with amber-like dots, beaded antennae.

'Read it,' he ordered.

I squinted my eyes over the blurred language next to the painted image. I held my breath, then read its content with remarkable effort.

'The … charcoal … beetle … lays … eggs … under … the … bark … of … burned … wood … when … the … heat … has … just … subsided … so … as … to … avoid … predators … sensors … in … the … meso … sternum … allow … the … charcoal … beetle … to … detect … fire … smoke … even … from … long … distances … charcoal … beetles … are … known … to … attack … men … in … swarms.'

It was so long since I had seen a painted scarab that a surge of emotions grabbed me, growing even bolder when I recognised Piko's quaint brushstrokes on the worn slate. I wasn't sure how Mozart had obtained it. Perhaps he had received the tablet from Piko when they shared a cell, or maybe he had stolen it.

'Copy it!' Mozart commanded, and while I proceeded to bring the image of the charcoal beetle and the adjacent text to my slate, he silently left the room. It took me the rest of the darkness to complete the transcription and, as soon as the lights came back, I collapsed on the floor, the goggles still on. When I awoke, the room was dark again, and Mozart was there, holding a different slate in his hand.

'Read it,' he ordered. And so, I did.

'Copy it,' he then said. So, after scraping my slate clean, I replaced the charcoal beetle with a no less wonderful, glimmering jewel scarab.

From then on, I saw Mozart less and less. He stayed with me only to inspect my drawings or give me new slates, and would then leave until the next lights-out. We hardly spoke, and when I was alone, there was nothing available to me other than drawing in the dark or sleeping under the light. Even though Mozart never locked me in, I couldn't bring myself to leave the room, not even for a brief walk, as the bailiffs were still after me, and the Crier was known to patrol the empty corridors at lights-out.

It was around this time that the obsession for the trigonal door grew in me. It all started when, after I had copied a very intricate Goliath birdeater through a magnifying glass, I lay down for a rest. From my pallet, I gazed at the trigonal door and, before dozing off, wondered why Mozart had never allowed me to accompany him to fetch new slates. When I woke up, Mozart hadn't arrived yet, and my first bleary glance was directed at the trigonal door. A gentle push would be enough to reveal what lay behind it. The temptation grew into a habit: whenever I finished my drawing, and found myself idle in the room, not tired enough to sleep, I would fixate on the closed trigonal door. I once pressed my ear against its surface, but then withdrew in disgust after a sudden memory of the shelter's iron gate crossed my mind. I concluded, after some thinking, that the only solution to rid myself of this relentless curiosity was to walk through the damned door. But Mozart had warned me to keep it shut, and fear held me back for a while, until one day, after running my hands over the door in the hope of detecting any hidden danger, I overcame any resistance and simply pushed through.

I recognised instantly where the door led to: Piko's vault, and its smell of time. It was my fear of an encounter with him, more than the idea that prying into that vault might result in a breach of the Tenets, that almost made me rush back to my room. Yet, I stayed. After all, Piko was no longer my Master – he had renounced me – and I had already violated the Tenets irreparably by learning the azbuki from an expelled novice.

Two long parallel shelves teeming with slates surrounded me. I walked forward to reach the end of the shelves, only to realise that I was encircled by another four or five aisles to my left, and a further six or seven to my right. The collection of slates in Piko's vault was far larger than the stock held at his unit, seeming already vast to me. The sudden realisation that I could now, at my own will, read the text on all these slates, prompted an excited shiver through my body. Filled with curiosity, I knelt down to browse through the lowest level of one shelf. Plants. Under Piko's strict method, the hundreds of slates of that section systematically depicted and described the features of all young trees, vines, shrubs and herbs known to him. I took one slate that appeared less intimidating than the others – I had already examined that image with Piko during one class – and laid it gently on a nearby desk, careful not to scratch or break it.

The soapweed yucca. Woody stem topped by a crown of narrow, sharp leaves, and a vertical clump of white blossoms. Humankind used the substance in the stem, poisonous to swallow, to clean their skin – but, the slate added, they still ate the blossoms, faintly tasting of artichoke. I remembered Piko's class where he had spoken of this particular yucca.

My reading was still slow, and it took a while to reach the lower part of the slate, whose content, I recognised with surprise, was unknown to me. It said that moths took pollen from the stamen of one yucca flower and flew it to the stigma of another; then, after leaving the pollen in the style, where the flower reproduced, the moth lay her own eggs there, so that when they hatched, the larvae fed on yucca seeds. So, the moth and the yucca were necessary to propagate each other's species, and neither of them could survive alone. It was beautiful. But I was disappointed that Piko, for no apparent good cause, had chosen to keep this fascinating aspect of the soapweed yucca's existence from me.

A sudden awareness that light was about to return jolted me out of the yucca. I hastened to put the slate back and returned to my room, but struggled to fall asleep, as I couldn't help wondering if, on other occasions too, Piko had withheld some of his knowledge. It wasn't my last visit to his vault. Every darkness, after completing the tasks that Mozart had assigned me, I went back to the vault with my goggles, striving to memorise as much precious information from the slates as I could. I soon came to realise, with a twinge of regret, how greatly I had overestimated my own knowledge: each slate in Piko's vault, indeed, revealed far more than he had ever shared with me during our classes.

I had acquired the content of hundreds of slates, and my initial uncontrollable enthusiasm about Piko's archive was beginning to wane, when I suddenly remembered the small vault hidden behind one shelf. Nurturing an absurd hope that Piko might have left it open, I made quite an effort to locate it, only to find myself in front of a closed vault, and forced to admit to my own stupidity.

I was putting the slates back in front of the vault when the key began turning in the door's lock: twelve turns to the right and three to the left. I took my goggles off, and only then realised that the light had come back. Too invested in finding the secret vault, I had foolishly disregarded the passing of time. My room was too far away to rush back there. I could only flatten myself on the floor, taking cover behind a shelf.

A recurring sound throughout my upbringing, Piko's muffled footsteps resonated through the archive. There and then, a smarting heat of fear surged through my whole body. Aware of how Piko could see into me, I genuinely feared he might feel my presence in the room.

He reached a wide stone desk, quite a distance from me, yet from my hiding place I could still follow his weathered sandals pacing around. I breathed as quietly as I could, and tried not to move, even when the characteristic sound of little pots filled with pigments being placed on the desk made me shiver. Piko was indeed known for immersing himself in the painstaking copy of a slate until his eyes ached, and this would mean a very long period on the floor for me.

My fear was concrete: hunched over the two slates, Piko engaged in interminable work to transpose the content of the slate on to another. There were some pauses, when he laid his brush down to recover concentration and strength, before resuming working on the intricate features of some creature.

Quite unlike him, he emitted occasional sighs of impatience, and scraped the slate a couple of times to erase details that hadn't presumably turned out as he had intended. After a while, I recognised the light squeak that his iron ruler made when positioned on a slate: the image was complete, and Piko was beginning to draw the text next to it. He had soon to suspend his effort, though, and leave the archive, because dark was arriving. Once the desk was in order he hastened to the exit and, when outside, locked the door behind him. Three turns to the right and twelve to the left.

Though in dire need to use the latrine, I wanted to take a close look at his work before heading back to my room. After nearing the desk in a hesitant step mainly due to guilt over my resolute curiosity, I noticed that Piko had put up a suspended tarp over the slates to cover his work without smearing the pigments. I knew that the tangible act of removing the tarp, secured to heavy stones placed at the corners of the desk, would only worsen my guilt, and, thus, I lingered there for a while before deciding to uncover the slates. When I did so, I couldn't make any sense of what was revealed to me. Contrary to my guesses, in fact, Piko wasn't copying a plant or an animal; he was recreating the image drawn by Mozart that he had once shown me, an image we had both disapproved of for its heretical nature.

The two slates lay next to each other. Despite the sacrilege of the act, I couldn't help but admire the masterful work of his brush: were it not for the fresher pigments still drying on the copy, it would have been nearly impossible to tell one image from the other. Piko had resized the image to add some notes on the right side, the meaning of which remained, even after a third read, quite obscure to me:

It was a town of machinery and tall chimneys, out of which interminable serpents of smoke trailed themselves for ever and ever, and never got uncoiled. It had a black canal in it, and a river that ran purple with ill-smelling dye, and vast piles of building full of windows where there was a rattling and a trembling all day long, and where the piston of the steam-engine worked monotonously up and down, like the head of an elephant in a state of melancholy madness. Smoke lowering down from chimney-pots, making a soft black drizzle, with flakes of soot in it as big as full-grown snow-flakes, gone into mourning for the death of the sun. Fog everywhere. Fog up the river, where it flows among green aits and meadows; fog down the river, where it rolls defiled among the tiers of shipping, and the waterside pollutions of a great and dirty city.

The original slate held no text, so I couldn't say where the notes came from, but the more I read them, the more the language unsettled me – the description of men poisoning air and tainting water eerily recalling Mozart's heretic beliefs. I was utterly bewildered by all this, and sure that the Tenets would never permit anyone, even a Master of the Known, to write such a blasphemy on a slate. What baffled me even more was that he hadn't even locked the dangerous slates in his secret vault.

As I asked myself if Mozart had, in the end, manipulated Piko's mind, a clanky noise startled me. Someone was opening the door again. I tried to reposition the tarp, but that wasn't simple, as it needed to be fastened properly to the four corner stones, and my nervous hands offered little help. I managed to tie up three corners, but as soon as I positioned the last one, the tension of the tarp shifted two stones, forcing me to start all over again. After finally securing the tarp, I rushed behind a shelf. After twelve key turns to the right and three to the left, Piko entered the room again. Peering from behind the slates, I watched him approach the desk, remove the tarp, retrieve the heretical slates, and place them inside the vault. In that moment, I lost control, and the faint, trickling sound – along with a small patch on the floor – disturbed the room's silence. Piko stilled. Even though I couldn't see him, I felt his intent gaze sweeping the room for any sign of movement. But now Piko really had to leave, because the lights were to go out at any moment. So, after hastily locking the secret vault, he fled.

The dark arrived.

I put my goggles on, and went back to my room.

Mozart was there.

He stared at me – whether with with indifference or hostility, I couldn't tell. Still, I braced myself for him to scold me.

'You're ready to begin your mission,' he instead declared. 'You shall leave this cage.'

I was so relieved my confinement was ending, and so grateful that Mozart wasn't punishing me for the forbidden venture into Piko's vault, that for once his appearance seemed a bit less grisly.

'What's my mission … ?'

'You'll learn about your mission once in the Land of Without,' he replied, showing no particular display of emotion. 'Someone will be waiting for you outside.'

It was only then, when he spoke of the outside, that the whole of me really understood what I was about to do: assign my life to an outcast living in the dark, nourishing dangerous ideas no one else apparently believed in. There was no way back, anyway, no future life for me within those four walls. Yet, I found bliss in the perspective that Without might show me the wonderful creatures I had met through the slates, and found reassurance in the strength the learning of the azbuki had given me.

'But there is another condition,' Mozart said.

'What?'

'You must never question your mission, Boz,' he warned. 'Never. Even when its content does not please you.'

Having no other choice, I nodded. The alternatives were hiding in that cramped room until my Descent, or being whipped to death by the Crier.

I hadn't thought of him for a while – but obsessions, it's a known fact, return at whim, and unannounced – and suddenly I wondered if Thatem, the missing boy, had possibly gone to the Land of Without, and with Mozart's help.

'Have you ever met Thatem – a kid?' I bluntly asked.

Mozart lowered his eye in the nimblest of motions, then slowly raised it back. He seemed on the brink of answering my question, but he didn't. Then, after an awkward silence, he took something out of his robe. It was wrapped in a cloth. He gave the bundle to me, and I took it in uncertain hands.

'Open it,' he said, noting my hesitation.

I unfolded the cloth. Inside were two joined glass bulbs, identical in shape and size, one of which was half-filled with a fine purple powder.

'Don't lose it,' he warned. 'You will need it as much as the goggles for your journey to the Land of Without.'

"What is it for?' I asked.

He didn't answer, but took the object and placed it on the palm of his hand, allowing the purple powder to trickle down from one bulb to the other. Then he turned it, and the powder slowly began flowing once again. Finally, after wrapping the item back in the cloth, Mozart explained to me in great detail how to reach the Land of Without.

XI

BLACK

A woman had ended the Juice. She stared petrified into the open manhole, surrounded by three undertakers and a dozen idlers eager to watch her Descent. After commencing a hymn, she took a first reluctant step on the stairwell. Though her voice cracked slightly, she reminded herself that whoever walked in the darkness would soon meet the light of life – her conclusion met by a solemn murmur of assent.

As soon as she was no longer visible, I burst out of the throng collected round the manhole, and ran directly into the ground. Daffodil, still shrouded by the zookeeper's robe, followed me closely. Although I could feel their surprised eyes pursuing us from above, the listless undertakers didn't attempt to thwart our intrusion, and merely placed the wax-stained iron lid over the manhole, burying us underneath.

If not for the line of little candles that – one for each step – dotted the right side of the stairwell, the dark would have been complete. The woman looked at us but, too overcome by the abrupt truncation of her life, didn't seem questioning of our presence. We walked down, one after the other, in the suffused candlelight until the stairwell split into two even-narrower stairs. The candles lit the way only to the right, while the left path, immersed in black, was invisible to the bare eye.

'We shall take the right stair,' the woman suggested.

But I didn't. After putting my goggles on, in fact, I took Daffodil's hand, and the two of us set off through the darkness, as Mozart had instructed. The woman stood hesitant by the fork – the undertakers had told her never to depart from the trail of candles. When, after eight steps in the dark, I turned around, the woman was no longer there: she had chosen the light.

I took the clepsammia out of my robe. 'It must make one hundred and twelve complete turns,' Mozart had warned. 'Only then will you find the one path that leads to the Land of Without.'

I gave a first turn of the clepsammia, and began my journey with Daffodil. Sightless, she clutched my hand very tight, and I could feel the tense pulsing of her palm in mine as we trod the narrow steps that ran between two stifling walls. The stairs went up and down, so I couldn't judge if we were still descending or not, but I didn't mind: my main concern was to turn the clepsammia, without delay, whenever the last grain of quartz had left the upper bulb, and to keep Daffodil close to me.

After some five hundred steps, feeling herself dragged slightly to the right, Daffodil asked: 'Where are we going, Boz?'

'There's a hole, here,' I said, poking my head through an aperture in the wall. 'It's quite deep … maybe a tunnel …' My voice echoed slightly ahead of me. 'But it's too early for the path to the Land of Without; we've turned the clepsammia only four times.'

We continued straight ahead, and upon two hundred more steps, a second passage appeared on the left wall, soon followed by a third on the opposite side. The passageways began to appear more frequently, until each wall gave way to a passage roughly every fifty paces.

Fearing a bailiff's attack from one of the tunnels, I looked around in constant tension, yet remembered to turn the clepsammia when needed. Meanwhile, the goggles, without which we'd be lost, felt wobbly on my sweaty head. I felt vulnerable, lacking in control more than ever before.

Daffodil kept urging me to describe our surroundings, because my voice was a source of reassurance for her. But there was little to describe other than steps, walls, and holes in walls; and, most of all, there were no signs that anyone had ever walked that path. After the sixty-first turn of the clepsammia, we sat down to rest. Breathing had grown harder, and Daffodil was beginning to feel the strain of treading the narrow, invisible steps without losing her balance.

'Do you think we've enough of it for the full journey?' she asked after hearing me take a sip of calciferol.

I had two bluebottles in my robe. The other two were in her pockets. 'Yes. It should be enough. I trust Mozart,' I said, giving the clepsammia another turn.

Everything around us was so dauntingly narrow and cramped that, as we sat on the stairs, I didn't dare look ahead or behind, but kept my gaze fixed on Daffodil, and considered how she was better off without sight in these moments.

'What'll you do when we reach Without?' she asked. I had already posed that question for myself, more than once.

'I'll look for plants and animals. I truly hope some have survived. A snail – I want to see a snail. And millions of scarabs. I want to live with them in a jungle, if one still exists. I'm tired of men. You?'

'I want to meet others like me,' said Daffodil, already tired of mingling with Caucasoids. 'And stay out of a cage, if possible.'

We both understood, though neither of us could say it, that we were making our way along the cramped stairs more out of necessity than any real expectation of the Land of Without – which, we still feared, might be the deadly place that everybody, other than Mozart, had always told us it was. After deciding to undertake the journey, the feeling that I was engaging in an insane quest had indeed troubled me incessantly, giving me no rest, and I had even begun yelling in my sleep, soaked in sweat, flailing my arms and legs in fear. But, for some unknown reason, I still felt I had to do it.

When, after we had resumed walking, the upper bulb of the clepsammia emptied for the one hundred and twelfth time, we stopped again. To our precise right was a tunnel. We took it, Daffodil bending slightly to enter, for the path there was even more constricted than the stairs.

We had advanced three hundred steps through the straight tunnel when a wall, unexpected, interrupted our stride. Mozart hadn't said anything about a wall. Dropping Daffodil's hand, I looked frantically for some hidden opening in the wall. Nothing – the path ended there. I shouldn't have trusted Mozart, I thought, and my rage against him was still surging when I realised my silly mistake. One that could bring our lives to an end. I had kept turning the clepsammia even during our rest, when I should instead have stopped: Mozart had advised that the clepsammia should only be turned while we were in motion. This meant we had entered a wrong tunnel, not the one leading to the Without. My heart stopped, and I didn't know how to tell Daffodil. We had to go back to the fork where we had parted ways with the descending woman, and start all over again. There was no other option. I wasn't sure the calciferol would be sufficient for the whole journey, though.

I saw a tear running down her left cheek when she learned of my mistake, but Daffodil showed no anger. She was intelligent was intelligent, and knew it would be of no use. When we turned back, trying to walk as fast as we could, she no longer wanted me to describe the surroundings, and so we went back along the stairs in desolate silence.

Halfway through our journey, I noticed a feeble far light inside a tunnel to our right – the first sign of activity after the manhole had been sealed behind us. It could be the light of life, I guessed, or an alternative way to Without.

'Or the bailiffs,' Daffodil cautioned.

I had to go and see.

'Wait for me here,' I told her. 'I must check what's going on.'

'No,' she replied. 'Whatever happens … I don't want to stay here, alone in the dark.'

So, we moved together in small steps through the tunnel, making the least noise possible. As the light got closer, a humming sound grew audible. I soon realised that what lay ahead was neither the light of life nor the Land of Without, but a small, illuminated room with a high ceiling, from which long limestone spikes hung. As I poked my head around the entrance to see what was happening inside, Daffodil whispered in my ear: 'What is it?'

I hushed her, only to make even more noise in the process than she had.

Right ahead of us, on the other side of the room, I saw a large desk covered in bluebottles – at least one hundred, I guessed. It had to be some storeroom. But the walls were lined with square, bulky machines I had never seen before, from which the loud buzzing we had heard at distance originated.

Nobody was there.

'Bluebottles … plenty of them …' I said.

'Take them,' she urged.

We took two bluebottles from the desk, and with those filled the last available space in our pockets. I then approached one of the machines. I was curious. I touched the surface, and withdrew my scalded hands. That's why the room is so hot, I thought.

I couldn't fathom what purpose the machines served. When I turned sideways, I caught sight of a much larger adjoining room, accessible through an archway to our right. I whispered to Daffodil to wait for me, and to alert me if anyone was coming in.

She nodded, and so I entered the second room alone.

There were no machines there, just a long row of wide tables, each covered with lines of tarp sacks. I reached the first table, glancing left and right cautiously. I touched the closest sack. It was bulging. I unzipped the tarp. Sighing, I zipped it back up, and returned to Daffodil without saying anything.

'Let's go,' I told her.

'What was there?' she asked.

'Nothing, just provisions.'

I saw no good in telling her that the sack I had opened contained the lifeless body of the descending woman. We returned to the main stairs, and reached the junction where I had last seen her alive. From that point, we restarted our path to the Land of Without. I shivered when Daffodil guessed aloud where the woman might have ended up by then, but didn't comment.

No further rest was taken, and as soon as the full quartz had moved one hundred and twelve times through the clepsammia, we saw a tunnel to our immediate left. We entered it and – hoping Mozart's precious tool to count time hadn't betrayed us – I finally tucked the clepsammia back inside my robe. The tunnel was no different from the one that we had mistakenly taken before, and so I feared another error. But I swiftly willed my mind to go blank, and to reject any doubt. All the tunnels looked alike, in fact, and there was no reason to believe I was wrong again.

We had gone at least two thousand steps, or perhaps more, before reaching an unexpected widening in our path – the first since the start of our journey – where a desperate urge to rest took over both of us. We laid on the floor, one next to the other.

Daffodil asked to borrow the goggles.

I was now blind.

My heart beat faster and louder through the thick silence that only accentuated the suffocating darkness around us. For some reason, it occurred to me that if Daffodil wanted, she could easily run away with the goggles, leaving me there forever. That would mean certain death. Or, perhaps, I could still make it to Without by feeling my way forward – if the remaining path were really straight, with no more turns, as Mozart had said. He hadn't said how far our destination was, though. I tried not to panic, nor to ask Daffodil for the goggles back, because she too deserved to stay out of the blindness for a while. I thought of those idlers enduring a sightless life of desperation, like that kid in our corridor who had suddenly gone blind – Piko couldn't explain why – and had been taken away to another perimeter among the cries of his father and mother. A painful memory. So, I tried to imagine myself as a bat in a cave, used to living in the dark and unafraid of the absence of light, for it reassured me. But I then recalled how bats used to live close together in huge colonies, while Daffodil and I were alone, and the solace thus ended.

'A young man once came to the zoo.' Daffodil began speaking. 'He stared at me from behind the glass like everyone else. But this kid remained there for much longer, until I realised that only his eyes, and not him, were watching me. He was elsewhere. I pretended not to care. Other visitors arrived, but the kid was still there when they had long gone.'

I listened intently, grateful for this distraction from the endless black, though I couldn't quite tell where her story would be heading.

'A woman then entered the zoo,' Daffodil said. 'She marched to the glass of the cage, but didn't acknowledge the kid. She looked sad, even more than he. I kept glancing at them at my own risk. I wasn't allowed.'

Then Daffodil told me about the strange dialogue that had followed between the two.

'I shouldn't be here …' the woman had whispered.

Her words sounded unclear to Daffodil, who understood what the woman meant only when the kid, too, spoke: 'I wanted to see you once again before leaving.'

The woman sighed: 'So, you'll leave …'

'Yes, if you are tired of me.'

'I'm not tired of you … but we can't go on … if he finds out, he will lash us to death.'

'We can move to another perimeter together …'

'They'll find us … he's a bailiff … I have been paired with him: there's nothing I can do.'

'But you prefer my body …'

'Yes …'

'So, you will look for Without. Have you found the way?'

'My real father knows the path …' he had answered.

Daffodil told me she had been listening to all this from the cage, and had been forced to hide her surprise.

'Come with me,' the kid had exhorted the woman.

'I can't …'

'Why … ?'

'I'm with child.'

The kid began hitting the glass with his fists desperately, then he asked: '… is the child mine?'

'I don't know …'

The kid ceased hitting the glass, and began crying, softly.

'I can't bring the child growing inside me to die in the Land of Without …'

'There's life outside … a much better one than here.'

'Your real father believes so … but the Tenets say no … I'm scared …'

When a third visitor entered the zoo, Daffodil told me, the kid had left. 'I've never seen him again.'

'And the woman?'

'She came back with another man, and later on, she even held a lively child in her arms … the child resembled the kid … he had to be his …'

I was left moved by the sad story of this kid who, like me, had had to leave his woman within the walls, though was also comforted in knowing that other idlers had found the courage to search for Without. We weren't alone, Daffodil and I – Mozart had already said that.

We remained in the widening between the walls, and soon the deep silence was pierced by Daffodil's light snoring. I, too, fell asleep, and, when I awoke, she had already put the goggles back on my head.

'We shall move,' she said.

I stood up, and looked for her hand. By then, I had ceased counting the steps. It no longer made sense, especially since I didn't want to be constantly reminded of the mesmerising precision with which a new passageway appeared on either wall every fifty paces. I was sure Mozart had told me to walk straight, without taking any diversion, at that point. But what if I had misunderstood him, or if he had been wrong? I was tempted to peer into each side tunnel, just to see if there might be a shortcut to our destination; but, after a first attempt, Daffodil wisely advised against it. We should resist the urge to stray away from Mozart's instructions, she said, and just follow them. She was damned right – I would've driven myself insane by looking into each and every passageway.

When I spotted, right ahead of us, a rusted bluebottle on the floor, I interpreted it as an encouraging sign: at least we weren't the first ones to follow that path. But it also reminded me that only one bluebottle was left in our robes. We had to hope that the end of our journey was near.

I was starting to long for anything that might break the stillness around us: a movement, one sound, some light.

By now Daffodil and I were taking turns with the goggles. I really missed the alternation of light with darkness. We had resumed using the clepsammia for the purpose of making our rests as regular as possible, agreeing to sleep every two hundred turns. We also talked more than we really wanted, to quell the monotony. 'Scarabs used Sun, Moon and the stars as guides to walk in a straight line,' I said, glancing at the path ahead. 'Did you know?'

'We don't need them,' Daffodil responded. 'We're walking in a straight line anyway.'

'True,' I said.

'Did you know that the rainbow scarab favoured human dung?' I insisted. 'Because men ate more varied food than animals.'

'No, I didn't, Boz,' she replied with no apparent interest in her voice. 'After your time with Mozart, I believe your knowledge has far surpassed anything I could have learned from inside a cage.'

I suddenly felt undeservedly privileged for having lived my life outside of a cage, so I decided from that moment on to avoid sharing anything with her that might sound like I was boasting about my undeserved broader knowledge. And it wasn't the only reason for which I believed Daffodil might have cause to blame me. 'I was a fool in trusting Mozart,' I said, as we continued down through the unchanging dark supposed to usher us into a bright outside world. 'And in dragging you here ...'

'It's a fool's regret, Boz,' Daffodil warned. 'We can't go back. When I was trapped in that cage, I believed my life could never be anything more than it was. I glimpsed at what freedom was through the glass, yes, but I never imagined I could reach it

– or that I deserved it. But then you came into my life and encouraged me to strive for freedom. You freed me – first and foremost, from within. I will not give in … we'll not end our lives within these walls …'

Only in that moment did I realise how, despite everything the cage had taken from Daffodil, it had also given her something in return: an immense willpower, a thick skin to resist adversity, and an inner strength I was determined to draw inspiration from. We shared the last sip of calciferol, and I threw the empty bluebottle on the floor for the next lunatic traveller to find. Soon, even earlier than expected, we felt weaker and, pace after pace, our legs became heavier. We quit talking to save the little strength we had left. I no longer looked into the repeating tunnels, but just straight ahead, hoping to discern some hint that the Land of Without was close, but all I saw was an immovable dark. I don't want to die. I don't want to die, I kept telling myself, somehow hoping that my will might be enough to lead us outside.

An old memory surfaced in my blurred mind. I was in the latrine of our unit when, earlier than expected, the lights went out. Mother and Father were already lying on their pallets, no more than nine steps away, but to me – a child – the distance seemed scarily huge. I began crying, desperate.

'Boz, don't be scared … we're here …' Mother whispered.

'But I can't see you …' I shouted.

'It doesn't matter … imagine an invisible thread between us. You just have to pull the thread, and you'll reach me.'

'I can't! I'm too scared!'

I kept crying in the latrine.

'If you don't move, you'll never get to us ... and you'll always be alone ...'

For all my fear, I knew she was right. I had to move. So, imagining myself pulling a thread, I walked very slowly in what felt like an endless journey to Mother's pallet. When I reached her, she hugged me. She had never done so before.

I must do the same, I thought: walk through the black tunnel, and convince myself I'm pulling a thread bringing me to the Land of Without, where I would be fine, just as I had felt in Mother's arms. My legs carried me through the tunnel beyond my control, and I feared they might give out at any moment. Though she was right behind me, I couldn't say if Daffodil was possessed by the same fear, or if the strength developed inside the cage had come to her rescue. All I knew was that we had no choice but to keep moving forward.

'Can you hear it?' Daffodil startled me.

'No ... what ... ?'

Before she answered, I heard it: a whistling noise, entirely new to my ear, coming from ahead; loud and diffuse, a bit like the racket of the crowd inside the shelter, or a multitude of stone balls rolling on the floor. When, an instant later, a most threatening confusion invaded our path, I yelled 'Let's go in here!' and dragged Daffodil with me inside a tunnel to our right. We stood there, impassive, silent, as the frightening noise grew in power.

When the sound finally arrived, it wasn't alone. A harsh cold, too, filled the tunnel, and an unknown force began slapping my skin, though with a kind of gentleness in it. The force grew so powerful that I pressed myself low to the ground, clutching the floor with one hand to avoid being swept away, while the other pressed my goggles tightly to my face. I kept shouting, even though the deafening sound, blowing all over us, swallowed my screams.

I thought it was the end.

Whatever that was, it left us quickly. I lay on my stomach, coughing up dust, exhausted, yet heartened that my goggles were still intact. As I turned to search for Daffodil, my heart clenched at the sight of her lying motionless, ten or twelve steps from me; but, when I called her name, she tilted her head, and began crawling towards me. 'I'm still here,' she whispered. We lay on the ground for a while, hugging each other in amused silence, our resolve strengthened by the sheer joy of being alive. Then, our backs against the wall, we sat next to each other.

'What … was … that?' I asked, panting.

'Wind,' said Daffodil, not before a thoughtful silence.

She was possibly right. I remembered Piko's description of wind – a strong, noisy movement of air, invisible but mighty, harmonious yet willing to tear apart whatever stood in its way. It could very well have been that. Even without a preceptor to guide her, I had to admit Daffodil's mind had ventured much further than mine. If her intuition was correct, we were getting close to Without. There was no other explanation I could think of, nor did I want to.

Contrary to the hope our struggle against the wind had raised, however, nothing else punctuated the stillness of the tunnel; and, as our enthusiasm eventually waned, it didn't take much for weakness to seize us once again. I wasn't sure how much more our bodies could take. They needed calciferol, and repose. I wondered how the path we were on could be so long and monotonous. Had the kid of Daffodil's story really gone through the same way? Had he survived? And Thatem?

Only seeing a clear purpose ahead kept me from giving up: I was determined to reach Without and see all the animals I wanted, bathe in the water of rivers, perhaps even admire a chain of mountains.

'I need to rest,' Daffodil said abruptly.

'If you sit down when you think that you can no longer make it, you'll never stand up again,' Mozart had warned, before telling us to walk ten thousand steps with no rest in the dark corridors, and that had been our sole preparation for this long, painstaking journey. But Daffodil's feet ached so much that she had to take off the loose sandals borrowed from the zookeeper. She had lived her entire live barefoot, and large blisters had formed on both feet. We hadn't anything with us to cure them. I didn't think she could go much further. I didn't want to abandon her, as much as I didn't want to die in that tunnel. I sat down close, and told her an episode from my childhood that, I hoped, might take her mind off the pain as she regained some of her strength. Only then would we decide what to do.

'Two children chased me in the corridor,' I recounted. 'I ran, ran, but they were still behind me. I was terrified.'

I glanced at Daffodil. She struggled to listen, her quivering hands wrapped around her knees.

'I had just rounded a corner, resigned to being caught, when I heard someone hissing. I slowed down, and looked around. Behind the edge of a curtain, left ajar, I saw a woman staring at me. She hissed again, beckoning me inside her unit. I gave her a quick, searching look: she seemed benevolent, and worried for me. I hurried in, and she closed the curtain. Soon after, the two children appeared in the corridor. I heard them outside, rushing past the woman's curtain. "Don't worry, they've gone," she whispered when the corridor had fallen silent again.'

I glanced at Daffodil. Despite her fading strength, she was still listening. I stroked her right shoulder, but was met with a weak smile.

I told her of my conversation with the woman – the first of many.

'Why were they pursuing you?' the woman had asked.

I told her that the children had tried to take my robe off, and have me walking bare among the idlers.

The woman looked at me with amused pity.

'Do you want some nutrients? I don't eat much,' she said.

I accepted the nutrients so as not to disappoint her. As I ate the nutrients, a stone board lying on the floor caught my attention.

'What's that?' I asked.

'A game called senet,' she answered. 'Do you want to try it?'

I nodded with enthusiastic eyes.

'But not now. The lights are about to go off. Come back when you can. I'm always here. I never move.'

I went to my unit, and said nothing of her to Mother and Father. She had smiled at me, and idlers weren't supposed – under a Tenet I no longer remember – to smile at children who weren't their own. They would've disapproved it. But, after a lights-out without sleep, I went back to see the woman.

She was there, prepared to introduce me to the game of senet.

'That's where you learned how to play it so well,' Daffodil said, slowly turning her head towards me, even though she couldn't see me.

'Yes ... but not only that. We talked a lot. A bit like you and me at the zoo. I went to her unit very often.'

I once asked the woman why no man and child lived with her, and she replied that they had both gone. Where, she didn't say.

'Sometimes I feel alone, but I'm glad that I've found a friend,' the woman told me. I blushed. She made me feel important, more than Father and Mother did. 'I belonged to a troupe of thespians,' she said when I asked her where she had learned the game. 'We travelled on tumbrels to do spectacles for the idlers, even for long journeys, and that's when they taught me senet.'

Back then, I didn't know who the thespians were and what the spectacles were. 'We entertained the idlers by staging stories, or by singing them songs,' she said. 'They liked it so much. Have you ever heard anyone singing a song?'

'Just hymns with the other kids.'

'Do you want to hear me singing?'

I nodded, a bit awed, a bit excited.

I still remember the song she sung to me, and I liked it because of her sweet voice, even though I didn't understand the meaning of what she said.

When he takes me in his arms ... when he speaks to me in a low voice ... I see life through rose ... he tells me words of love ... and it does something to me.

'Is it a hymn?' I asked, even though there was no reference to Sun or the Crier.

'Kind of,' she replied. 'I usually don't sing. It makes me sad, thinking of when I was with the troupe. But I've made an exception for you. You're a special child. You're not like the others, you're different. I felt it immediately when I first saw you in the corridor, chased by those children: you're gifted.'

I couldn't resist the temptation, when I went back home, to tell Mother and Father that a thespian had called me a gifted child. It was a mistake, but at least I didn't hint at my many visits to her unit. Father became furious. The thespians were heretics who defied the Tenets, he claimed, and even a simple smile from one of them could drain me of all my Juice. I should allow no thespian to approach me in the corridor, ever – he ordered. I was still unaccustomed to questioning Father, so I took his order seriously, and ceased to go to the woman's unit. I never saw her again.

'Do you know what's strange?' I said to Daffodil. 'The woman never asked for my name, and I never asked hers.'

Now drowsy, Daffodil barely reacted. I shook her right arm, trying to rouse her, when a swift movement in the bottom right of my goggles disrupted the stillness around us. At first, I thought the wind had damaged the goggles. But the sighting persisted, and I suspected that what lay before us was simply a figment of my imagination, as had already happened: catching a glimpse of an imaginary scarab that would soon vanish. But, this time, apparently not intent on disappearing, the scarab was still there, crawling ahead, illuminated by the inner glow of my goggles.

'Daffodil … Daffodil!'

Daffodil rose her head.

'A scarab …'

I could see from the movement of her eyes that she thought I was just dreaming.

'Look,' I said, placing the goggles on her. 'What do you see?'

Silence ensued. 'A scarab,' she said in a most incredulous tone.

'Don't you understand ...' I murmured, '... that we must be incredibly close to the Land of Without? And there's life!'

Retreating from her drowsiness, Daffodil stood up.

'We shall follow the scarab outside,' I urged, and Daffodil gave me the goggles back.

The scarab was moving ahead. From its body shape, it could be a brown chafer, I guessed; but the goggles tended to neutralise most shades of colour, making it very hard to tell a species with certainty.

The crawling grew faster as our path grew narrower, until I realised we could no longer stretch our arms, even slightly, without touching the walls. Then, all of a sudden, a crack in the floor swallowed the scarab. We had lost our guide. Fear grabbed me, and I yelled at the scarab to come back, but it was of no use. I crouched on the floor, crying. I handed the goggles up to Daffodil, and begged her to forgive me for dragging her on this damned journey. Daffodil stood silent – I couldn't say whether out of rage or pure misery – until she said in a broken voice: 'Boz, look there ... take the goggles and look ...'

I put the goggles on and, from the floor, looked up at Daffodil pointing her arm towards the ceiling.

Right above us was a manhole.

'What ... ? Daffodil, we must open it!'

Nodding, Daffodil said: 'I will hold you up. I'm too heavy for you.'

So, I climbed on her shoulders with not inconsiderable difficulty and, dangling precariously in the air, tried to unhinge the manhole's grated cover with my bare hands. But the cover didn't want to be removed. We wobbled back and forth for quite a while, until Daffodil fell straight to the floor, and me with her.

I hit my head.

When the pain had receded enough to allow me to raise my head a little, I discovered in shock that the goggles hadn't survived our fall.

'Are you here, Daffodil?' I asked.

'Yes,' she whispered.

'The goggles are broken …'

Never had I seen Daffodil in tears, not even when the zookeeper, with all his brutality, had done what he had done to her. But now, alone with me in the black, confined inside an endless tunnel, lacking the strength even to stand up, Daffodil allowed herself to cry. Sharing her same fate, I too surrendered to desperation. And it was only when our moaning and whining had finally subsided that the clanky sound of a manhole cover being lifted reached our ears.

XII

WITHOUT

Squinting through the half-light, my hazy eyes discerned the scaly ceiling, and I frantically touched my face, chest and arms in search of reassurance that, despite the piercing headache, I was still whole. If not for the iron door to my right and a large window ahead, obscured by white varnish, the room wouldn't have differed much from my old unit. A peculiar smell, neither pleasant nor unpleasant, and unlike anything I had ever encountered, confirmed that this couldn't be home.

I was lying on a large pallet, my dark robe replaced by a thin tunic of a much lighter shade, but my thoughts were so blurred that I didn't even wonder who might have made the change. I looked around for Daffodil – unsuccessfully. I sharpened my ears, but no sound arrived. I shook my legs to rouse them from their numbness, though I was too feeble to move. It was hot, and I was sure that the heat wasn't coming from within, but was already in the air.

When I widened my eyes so as to dissuade them from closing, I first noticed it: the glass. A wall stood between me and the window ahead. Turning my head left and right, I realised that tall glass barriers, firmly joined to the wall behind me, had also been erected on all sides of the pallet. And there was glass over me, too.

I was inside a cage.

I didn't want to believe it – a roofed cage. As if chained to the pallet, my whole body rattled furiously, yet without changing position. My hands rapidly clenched into fists, prepared to crush the glass; but the frightening perspective of enduring a trapped life was too much to tolerate and, crossed by an inner yell of anguish, I collapsed.

When I reopened my eyes, a tall, bearded man was standing before the cage.

'The Crier!' I shouted.

'Not really. I'm Thatem,' he said.

My reaction was slow in coming: '*That* ... Thatem?'

'No. Just ... *Thatem.*'

I peered at him. He wasn't, in fact, the Crier. His hair wasn't even purple.

'I'm glad you made it,' Thatem said. 'Father's instructions aren't always as clear and precise as they should be.'

'Your father?' I asked.

'Yes,' he answered.

'Mozart ... is ... your father?'

'I've just said that,' he replied, slightly annoyed by my sluggishness.

I stared at him. He was thinner than most idlers living within the walls, and his complexion much darker. Of course, he couldn't possibly bear any resemblance to his disfigured parent.

'Where are we?'

'Welcome to the Land of Without,' he smiled. 'But mind: nobody here calls it that. We call it Earth.'

'Can you open the window and show me the creatures?' I gushed.

'Wait! Not so quick,' Thatem chuckled. 'It'll take some time for you to get acquainted to this place. That's why you're inside the oxygen chamber.'

'Ah ... it's not a cage ...'

'A cage? No ... !' Thatem guffawed. 'You saw yourself running on a wheel, stared at by a procession of Congoids? That's why you fainted? Phew ... too funny!'

Thatem laughed a lot, maybe too much, I could already see. But I was so glad to be alive that it didn't bother me.

'Speaking of Congoids: your friend is in another oxygen chamber,' he said. 'She's safe and sound.'

I couldn't wait to see Daffodil, hoping that she wasn't too upset with me for everything I had her go through to reach Earth.

'Have you told her that she's not back in a cage?' I asked.

'Yes. And do you know what she said? That at least her cage at the zoo had no ceiling.'

This time I was the one smiling. But not for long; I didn't want him to think I was content in my seclusion.

'When will I leave this ... chamber?'

'It'll take some time – I told you. Your organism must first get used to all the germs and bacteria frolicking around here. You need to stay inside. Thirty days, maybe.'

'What are *days*?' I asked.

'Ah ... true ... you've never counted time ...' Thatem said, and snapped his fingers in acknowledgement that he should've remembered. 'I'll teach you. No worries. You'll need it for the mission.'

'What is my mission? Mozart didn't say.'

'I've no idea. You'll receive instructions when it's time.'

Frustratingly, the moment of learning what my mission consisted of never seemed to arrive. But I had told Mozart that I would do it, as a condition of leaving the corridors, and I *would* do it.

Through a hatch in the chamber, Thatem left a fistful of lozenges inside a container fastened to the glassy wall. 'You'll have to swallow these ... and only these ... for a while. Slowly, slowly, you'll be able to eat real food,' he said. Then he pointed at a satchel next to my pallet. 'Tomes: food for your mind, and soul. They're precious, so treat their pages carefully; it takes a scribe's full lifetime to copy the text of a single tome. You must keep practising the azbuki. You'll need it for the mission ... whatever it'll be ...'

'What is a ... *soul?*' I asked.

'In time, Boz.'

He walked towards the exit. 'You must get used to days and nights, the earlier the better,' he said, putting out the two lanterns in the room and closing the iron door behind him. And, from then on, he would always turn the oil lanterns on and off in what he claimed were the start and end of day.

Having meanwhile regained some of my strength, I got up from the pallet and approached the glass to take a lozenge. I passed my hands over my new tunic, whose surface was much smoother and fresher than the robes I wore in the corridors. I touched my cheeks, and felt the abundant hair growth. Perhaps they don't pull their hair out here, I mused, thinking of Thatem's huge beard. I paced inside the chamber for a while, my thoughts growing sharper accordingly. I then let my eyes fall on the satchel, from which I took one of Thatem's precious tomes.

Piko had told me that tomes were like slates, only with far more azbuki inside, but that they didn't last as long as the slates – which was why there were no more tomes in circulation. He was wrong, apparently.

I thumbed through the thick tome with extreme care, for its pages seemed so delicate, and the binding rather slack. Each page contained a mesmerising length of text, much more than any slate might ever include, and the content felt even more valuable when I considered that its copying had taken a scribe's lifetime. The orderly, almost geometric, writing was so minute that, as I tensed my eyes to make out the azbuki inked on the feathery pages, I wondered if a scribe had lost his eyesight in the exacting process of transcription. That tome occupied the space of seven or eight slates, not more, but it seemed to contain the knowledge of seven hundred slates.

The first pages, whose sticky corners called for some effort to pull apart, told of two creatures meeting by a pond in the middle of a dry and sandy plain.

'Finally …' said the first creature, nearing the pond with her webbed feet, and then slowly breaking the water with her orange beak.

Meanwhile, the other creature glided through the air before landing gently at the watering hole.

'What's your name?' she asked.

'Penguin,' answered the first, her beak still wet. 'And yours?'

'Seagull.'

'I thought you always travelled in groups,' Penguin observed.

'We used to – but not many of us have survived,' Seagull commented wistfully.

'What happened?'

'The fish in the sea ended,' Seagull answered. 'My friends starved to death, and so I chose to leave.'

'Oh,' Penguin commented, lowering her eyes.

'Man?' she suggested.

Seagull nodded glumly. 'And you: what brings you here, Penguin?' she asked.

'I lived on the iced sea, and like you, had many friends,' answered Penguin. 'We lived in peace, helping each other to survive through the cold season. Then, the ice slowly began to disappear. We barely noticed what was happening, initially, because of all the mountains of ice still around. But, season after season, the ice shrank more and more, until eventually there was not enough for all of us to lay our eggs or breed our chicks on it. So, many eggs never hatched, and many chicks drowned. I am the only one left.'

'Man?' asked Seagull.

Penguin nodded.

A low persistent buzz heralded the arrival of three other creatures to the pond. They flew in a group over the water, under the attentive eyes of Penguin and Seagull, then landed together on a flat stone next to the pond.

'What are you?' Penguin asked.

'We're Bumblebees,' they answered in unison. 'We've been inseparable since birth.'

'Shouldn't you be flying over lavender, foxgloves and sunflowers?' enquired Penguin, a curious creature.

'Have you seen any lavender, foxgloves or sunflowers, of late?' Bumblebees observed, slightly rattled by the question.

Penguin and Seagull sighed. But their forlornness didn't last long, and the animals, well aware of the privilege of life, treasured standing within the beauty of the little pond, surrounded by a calm swathe of sand and under the bluest of all skies.

After a while, along came another creature. It paced around, then immersed itself in the water, laying its head on the edge of the pond.

'What's your name?' Penguin asked.

Concentrated on admiring with utmost pleasure its own image on the water, the creature said, rather inattentively: 'I don't know.'

The others looked at each other, puzzled.

'How can you possibly ... not know your name?' Penguin asked.

'I've forgotten it ...' it said.

After the mysterious creature had drunk abundant water, and emitted numerous sighs of pleasure, a yellowish patch began to radiate through the pond.

'But why are you peeing in the water?' Seagull asked. 'We need it.'

'I'm leaving at any moment ... I will not drink this filthy water, anyway,' it retorted.

The other animals looked at it in disdain for its arrogance, but the creature didn't seem to care, and simply closed its eyes to rest.

Outraged, Penguin raised her voice: 'I now know, from your behaviour, who you are ...'

Eager to learn who this creature was, Seagull bobbed her head towards Penguin as the latter shouted: "You're Man!'

At hearing his name called, he opened his eyes: 'Yes! And I'm hungry ...'

Man rose from the water to run towards Penguin. 'Your flesh is what I need! I'm starving ...' he shouted, and despite her attempt to escape, he quickly reached Penguin.

'Leave me alone!' yelled Penguin, trembling under his firm hold.

Seagull was flying around, trying to hit Man with her beak, but he kept her away rather easily by waving his strong arms in the air. When Man raised a fist to hit Penguin, Bumblebees, who so far had only watched the events, took off from their stone and, after twirling fast in the air, swooped down towards Man. One of them darted her sting into his bearded neck, causing his fist to drop down just before he managed to hit Penguin. Man jerked back, losing hold of his prey. Meanwhile, Bumblebees kept spinning and vaulting in the air, their buzz becoming more intense. Penguin was free, but just briefly, because, in spite of his aching neck, Man came back. He had almost recaptured Penguin when Bumblebees, swiftly changing the trajectory of their flight, took aim against him. Man tried to stave them off, but to no effect, and Bumblebees stung him for the second time and then, again, for a third, last time. Man could no longer bear it, and ran away screaming, cursing all those creatures at the idyllic pond.

'How are you?' Seagull asked Penguin.

'I'm shaken, but fine,' she answered, still panting, frightened. 'But where are Bumblebees?'

Seagull and Penguin looked around, and saw that Bumblebees were lying on their stone, writhing almost imperceptibly.

'What happened?' Penguin asked them.

'Our lives are ending ...' Bumblebees answered together.

'Has Man hurt you?' Penguin asked.

'No ... but our lives were the sacrifice necessary to save yours ...'

'No! No!' Penguin cried out, a tear running down the white of her face. 'You shouldn't have ...'

'All creatures should help each other ... and not be selfish ... you would've done the same for us ... we're sure ...' Bumblebees whispered, before closing all their fifteen eyes forever.

I closed the tome, careful not to press the cover too hard, and reflected on what I had just read. Neither Piko nor Mozart had ever mentioned that animals could speak. I decided I should ask Thatem, who had actually seen real animals, not just those painted on slates, what the truth was.

I then recalled Piko saying that each species had its own unique value that set it apart from the others: ants stood out for their preparation, badgers excelled in protection, locusts had the strongest sense of camaraderie, and lizards mastered resilience better than any other living being. Bumblebees were definitely gifted with courage. But what about men: what lesson could we teach to all other creatures?

Thatem entered the room in that moment.

'How're you doing, young man?'

Thatem let out a laugh – noisy, as always – when I asked him to confirm that animals could speak. 'No! It's just a story ... a fable ... like those that Bebro puts on stage. He keeps everything in his mind, but others wrote their stories down so as not to forget them ...'

I sighed in relief: the opposite answer would've caused me to seriously question all my knowledge.

'You weren't ready to chat with a donkey, right? Imagine the breath!' He laughed and, winking at me, added: 'Bebro, Piko, my dad … what a gang … eh?'

I stared at him, blankly.

Then he added to my confusion by pointing at the tomes, and saying: 'Some of the stories there are true, though …'

The room had become much cooler. I assumed night had fallen outside. Temperature never varied so drastically within the walls. I put a blanket over my shoulder.

'Shall we take a quick look outside?' Thatem said, approaching the closed window. I widened my eyes in approval, and let out a smile that, judging from the slightly condescending look he gave me afterwards, must have seemed rather dumb. The shutters were stuck, and it took quite a while for him to open the window, his struggle only making me crave the outside more, but he finally made it.

Past the open window, though, was complete darkness.

The blackest of all blacks.

'I can't see a thing …' I lamented, though not really in the position to complain about anything from behind a glassy cage, whatever he liked to call it.

'It's normal … at night-time …' he said, quite perversely, before shutting the window with much more ease than the opposite process. In that moment, the suspicion that I had not really arrived in the Land of Without hit me.

Alone once again, I went through the tomes in the satchel: my only companions, at least for now. Their stories didn't just ease my loneliness, but also gave me some glimpse of Earth as I waited to leave that room.

From the tomes, I learned that, whenever they really desired it, the outside people could make decisions regarding their future. People moved from one place to another, and enjoyed meeting people they had never met before. Where I came from, by contrast, men stood where they were told to, unless they wanted to be flogged by the bailiffs. Outside people found happiness by honing a craft, or by helping other men, or by feeling powerful. It took me quite some reading to understand what being powerful truly meant: controlling other men, punishing them, changing their lives. You couldn't be powerful where I came from; only the Crier was powerful. Bruttho had tried to be powerful, but I had seen first-hand how that ended for him. I also learned that the outside people could bear more than one child, that boys and girls didn't live in separate perimeters – the outside wasn't divided into perimeters to start with: how could you, in fact, partition the sky? – and that they weren't paired one with the other by their genitors. I finally understood what *money* was. And the troubles that it generated. I read with incredulity how it stood at the centre of people's lives, even worse than the Juice within the walls, and what people did to have more of it. I couldn't find the Tenets mentioned anywhere. The outside men had rules, yes, but they changed from place to place, shifting rather opportunistically.

Much like his father had done with the slates for Daffodil, Thatem came to see me every day to talk and to give me new tomes, making it even harder for me to tell my oxygen chamber from a cage. Though – I must admit – Thatem was a much better host than the zookeeper.

At times, the tomes could prove quite confusing. Not only did I find it difficult to determine whether a story was true or not, but I also encountered contradictions across many parts. Love, for example, was often mentioned. I recalled when

Cardenio had whispered to Bologna, 'Whoever loved, that loved not at first sight?' or when the sweet lady had sung to me, 'He tells me words of love … and it does something to me …' Yet the true meaning of love eluded me, especially since the Tenets had never addressed it.

I asked Thatem. 'Love is when you would do anything for someone, even giving your life away, because without them you wouldn't survive anyway,' he answered. At once, my thoughts went to Flox, and I was certain that what I felt for her was love. But love had to mean something more, because the tomes also spoke of loving one's enemies and doing good to those who hated us, and it wasn't evidently to Flox that they were referring.

The outside people seemed obsessed with love, almost as much as with money, but despite writing much about it, and preaching about its relentless pursuit, they didn't really embody love, and were quick to harm others in order to get what they desired. However, the passage in the tomes that disturbed me the most was one that, in vivid detail, described how humans had sacrificed animals and plants out of pure selfishness, merely to enhance their own pleasure.

It all began when men invented a machine that allowed them to travel faster than with horses and donkeys, by burning vast amounts of rock or wood. Before long, countless of these machines were in motion everywhere – across flatlands, up steep mountains, over water, and even in the air. Quickly, a large cloud of filthy smoke began to encircle animals and plants, harming them. Still, men didn't care, and created more machines for other purposes, so that the mass of filthy smoke became larger and larger, until it was even capable of blocking the light of Sun. When darkness fell over Earth, the blinded men started crying out in fear, and begged Sun to increase the strength of its light, so that the rays could penetrate the thick mass of smoke that men had foolishly created. Sun listened to their pleading, and the sunlight came back, but with such force that, while saving humans, it nonetheless killed most other creatures, melted the ice of the seas, and dried lakes and rivers almost to their bottom.

'But why did men have to burn rock and wood?' I asked Thatem.

'To nourish the machines,' he said. 'It's like when you eat the nutrients, and feel stronger. You need it. It's the same with them: the machines couldn't survive without burning the rock and wood. It's called *energy*.'

And, indeed, energy was mentioned even more often than love and money within the tomes. Machines had made the lives of men easier in exchange for energy, but had also made the existence of most animals and plants intolerable, if not depriving them of life altogether. It was men who had given Sun no other solution than to slaughter all the flora and fauna, and to enable men to pursue a solitary, greedy existence. I loathed the human race, and was disappointed by Piko, who hadn't shared the real truth with me. But the tomes didn't say whether life still existed outside the walls, and this omission contributed to my doubt over whether I had really reached Earth or not.

But then, something happened.

The lanterns in the room were flickering when I awakened and, for the first time, saw the oxygen chamber open. I sprang to my feet in delighted incredulity, and set off towards the exit, before stopping abruptly by the chamber's threshold due to my sudden recollection of the dangerous germs circulating outside.

'Come outside, young man!' Thatem yelled from the adjacent room, whose iron door had likewise been left open. 'You must meet a new friend.'

Perhaps due to his relentlessly cheery tones, Thatem had by now gained my trust; moreover, remaining a prisoner of the glass didn't seem like an ideal prospect, so I resolved to step out of the chamber. Despite mild shivers of fear coursing through my body at every step taken in the direction of his voice, I reached the other room.

Thatem was sitting at a rectangular table, and there was also a second man, his back turned to me, with long white hair reaching past his shoulders.

'Join us,' Thatem said, pointing to a chair on the opposite side. For once, his voice was solemn, as if this was a moment whose gravity needed to be appreciated. When the other man turned, I could barely contain my surprise at seeing the multitude of long furrows pitting the whole of his face. For some reason, they were fewer and deeper on the brow, while more diffuse but thinner on the cheeks. Never had I seen anything like it, and so for some time I thought the man had received the same punishment as Mozart.

He remained silent, but sketched out a tight smile for me.

'You've never met anyone that old, right, Boz?' Thatem asked, reprising his usual teasing. 'There's no Juice here to end the people's lives at the Crier's will. But don't allow his wrinkles to trick you, Boz. Our friend Bela has enough energy inside to make the largest of the machines jealous,' Thatem continued. 'Right, Bela?'

Bela took a half-bow and, looking downwards, let out another smile, this time slightly less constrained. I looked at his body, and noticed that it was little more than bones. I then looked around the room, longing to see an open window, or an animal, or even better, an insect – my too-short encounter with a scarab in the tunnel had left me wanting more – but failed to see any indication of life outside. To my right, laid against a wall, stood a large stone board, on which rested a group of tools whose functions were unknown to me back then. The only window in the room had again been covered in varnish, while the greyish walls were so dirty and flaky that I guessed no blackwashing had ever gone on there.

'Where are we?' I asked.

'In the kitchen …' Thatem answered.

A kitchen: where the outside people prepared food, I remembered from *Dead of Night, Life of Men*.

'Do you want to eat with us?' Thatem asked.

I stood up to go and get a lozenge, but when Thatem grasped my intention, he slowly raised his hand in the air to stop me. 'We've prepared something better for you,' he said.

Bela was stirring the contents of a metal vessel that, I would later learn, the outside people called a *pot*.

'… lamb? …' I asked, visibly recoiling: I would never eat the flesh of an animal.

'We wish …' Thatem commented wistfully, yet without losing his eyes' lively twinkle. 'But what Bela has prepared is good, too.'

Bela put a bowl in front of me, in which he carefully poured a yellowish hot liquid.

I stared with suspicion at the steaming basin.

'Tumbleweed soup,' Thatem revealed. 'It took Bela hours to prepare it for you, right?'

Bela nodded, while his eyes, perfectly encapsulated in the wall of wrinkles, examined my behaviour and me.

'Wait: otherwise, you'll burn your tongue,' Thatem warned, as Bela served him a bowl of soup too, and then one for himself.

As the steam subsided, I brought the bowl closer to my nose, unaccustomed to being so near a source of warmth. The soup had a smell. Not strong, but still a smell, completely unknown to me, and nothing that I had ever experienced inside the corridors.

'Try it! It won't kill you!' Thatem urged.

Bela smiled, even revealing part of his lower teeth.

I sipped the tumbleweed soup. And spat it on the table. The flavour wasn't unpleasant, but my mouth had instinctively rejected its pungency.

Thatem broke into noisy laughter. 'I did the same … !' he said. 'You're just not used to it. Try some more …'

As he cleaned the table with a weathered cloth, Bela nodded at me, so as to confirm that I should heed Thatem's encouragement. So, the bowl wobbling in my sweaty hands, I tried the tumbleweed soup once more. This time, it went down with less difficulty. Focused on feeling the unprecedented experience of a hot liquid gliding down my throat, I couldn't say whether I liked it or not. And, used as I was to ingesting nutrients on the floor, doing so while seated in a chair felt awkward.

'Do you like the soup?' Bela finally spoke in a tender voice, not much more than a whisper. I nodded, striving to look as convincing as possible, while I rubbed my tongue against the roof of my mouth, partly to ensure the heat hadn't harmed it, partly to capture the fading taste of the soup.

'I hadn't seen anyone come out of the manhole for a long time,' Bela said, clutching his own bowl in his hands, while looking around pensively. 'Thatem was the last. He was a kid like you, back then.'

With the bowl covering his face, I couldn't see Thatem's reaction to the comment. I wondered under what circumstances he had left the corridors and whether he had endured misgivings similar to mine there.

'Which perimeter are you from?' I asked Bela.

He glanced at Thatem knowingly.

'I'm not from the same place as you,' he admitted. 'I was born outside. Father escaped the corridors, and met Mother once here.'

It was possible. I had never seen a man looking so old in the corridors, and he spoke with an undulating accent that was entirely unknown to me.

'I grew up in a house like this,' he added, looking left and right. 'I was a child when, once a year, I helped Mother cook pigeons' eggs with my brothers.'

I had just met my first person born in the Land of Without. I stared at him intently, trying to discern whether, apart from his thinness and the aged skin, his body differed from mine in any other aspect. Assuming that we were really outside.

'Bela will accompany you on your mission, Boz,' Thatem interjected, as if leaving room for memories was inappropriate in the circumstances. 'He's actually the only one who knows what it is about. But don't try to ask him now; he won't answer.'

'Can I see the outside?' I asked instead.

'Tomorrow at dawn,' was Bela's answer: short as my question had been.

'Come with me, Boz,' Thatem said, lifting himself from his chair and beckoning me with a smile.

Ten steps later, he opened a door.

'Daffodil!' I shouted.

My friend was hunched on a chair next to a huge mass of spiky plants that almost filled the room. She stood up, smiled, and hugged me tightly. She had already cried inside the tunnels, and wouldn't allow herself to do so again – I knew that – but I could feel her overwhelming joy at seeing me.

'What are you doing?' I asked after seeing a fistful of tumbleweed in her hand.

'Working,' Daffodil replied, sounding unaccustomed to the response.

'Yes,' Thatem intervened. 'Everybody here contributes in some way. I find the food, Daffodil helps prepare it, Bela cooks it, and you will help us. You have to earn your bread, clear, Boz? It's not like where we come from: ain't no *communism*, here.'

I helped Daffodil to separate the tumbleweed shoots from the rest of the plant – monotonous, but at least we could stay together.

'Have you been outside yet?' I asked her.

'No ... tomorrow at dawn ... can't wait for it ... and you?'

'Same as you ... but are you sure you want to do it?' I asked.

'Why?'

'I mean ... what if it's dangerous? What if they capture us?'

Although I considered myself brave, I experienced moments of doubt, whereas Daffodil, despite having only just broken free from her cage and narrowly escaped death with me in the tunnels, showed no fear. 'We've gone through what we've gone through just to see that sky, Boz,' she told me, pointing at the ceiling with a steady gaze. 'And I will not allow anyone to capture you …'

I nodded, and we hugged again.

I looked around. There was a small square window next to the ceiling. 'Why are all the windows shut, and covered in paint?' I asked.

'Thatem says it's to keep the light of Sun away. It can get quite hot here. But we can keep them open at night-time, as long as the lanterns are doused,' she answered with an air of doubt, before adding: 'I think they just don't want us to be seen here – that's the truth.'

Her comment cast a heavy silence over the room. I found myself wondering – and I suspected Daffodil did too – what would happen if they caught us. They'd either kill us outright or drag us back to the perimeter after giving us a proper beating. But I doubted the bailiffs patrolled beyond the perimeters; which meant someone else was after us. For the first time, moreover, since arriving in Without, I felt the distance from those I'd left behind, the ones who mattered to me: Flox, Bebro, Cardenio and his troupe, Mozart with his madness. I even missed Piko, the man who had built me, as he'd once rightly said, though he'd never have approved of my choice to leave the perimeter – or perhaps yes, thinking of the heretic image I had caught him copying.

XIII

OUTSIDE

My gaze was fixed on the ceiling when Thatem stormed into the room. 'Wake up! Time for some hunting!' he yelled, though no doubt aware that I had been unable to sleep in anticipation of dawn. I was excited, but also feared that the outside might be a disappointment – or, worse still, that Sun might harm us.

We sat with Daffodil at the kitchen table, while Bela prepared the tumbleweed soup, feeding the kitchen fire with the roots that Daffodil and I had separated from the plant's shoots.

'If all goes well, this evening we'll eat something even better than tumbleweed soup,' Thatem declared, as Bela placed four steaming bowls in front of us.

Nobody spoke during the meal. I sweated a lot, and not from the soup's heat, while Daffodil, usually very composed, couldn't keep her feet still under the table. After escaping one cage following a lifetime of imprisonment, she was now about to leave with me a secluded life within walls. The tumbleweed soup was evidence that the outside existed, and was habitable, it would seem, but our forthcoming exit into the unknown frightened both of us.

After emptying our bowls, we followed Thatem to the hall twenty steps away. From there, without much preamble,

Mozart's son opened the rusty door that would finally bring us to our coveted destination.

As the door widened, a blend of bronze, orange and yellow light filled the hall. Though the brightness wasn't blinding, I hastened to cover my face with both hands – perhaps in recollection of Mozart's disfigurement. I turned, and saw through my fingers that, behind me, Daffodil was staring past the door in utter awe.

Thatem led us outside. Glancing down through my squinting eyes, I realised that we were treading on a brittle, dusty surface scattered with fine sand. Although I couldn't see the horizon, I somehow felt the absence of walls around us, and the wide space to which it gave way, and the warmth of Sun pinching my pale skin in our first encounter ever.

For the initial thirty steps, I feared that the heat might suddenly intensify and burn us when it was too late to rush back into the house; but, eventually, I realised there was nothing to fear from Sun, at least for the time being. And when I uncovered my face, my first proper view of the outside was the immense plain of land around us. The unfurling horizon was so wide that my eyes, already strained by the unusual light, struggled to reach its edge. I – a kid who'd lived his entire life hemmed in by the close walls of rooms and corridors, with no possible access to open air – was now standing in an endless prairie with no apparent boundaries. A dizzy spell hit me, and I had to look down at my feet to maintain my balance.

'Hold on to me, Boz,' suggested Thatem, who had experienced his first encounter with Sun thousands of days earlier. I did what I was told, and when, not much later, the sense of overwhelm receded, I even dared to look up. Scattered, ragged clouds, less dense than those in the museum's ferrotype, only in part covered the entrancing light blue sky, filtering the mild daybreak's colours in a wondrous effect that turned my unease into rapture. I stilled, wanting nothing more than to gaze upward, and feed my new bliss with further contemplation of the outside. It felt right to be there, unconfined, even though my heartbeat sounded so loud that I feared it might ruin the experience.

'Wonderful, eh?' said Thatem.

We met his remark with silence: neither Daffodil nor I were in a state to speak. I glanced around. Apart from sparse straggly bushes, the visible landscape consisted only of rock and sand, with a cluster of low hills in the distance. I crouched to gather a handful of sand. I let the warm grains brush against my palm, then trickle through my fingers, and, in those brief moments, sensed more life inside me than ever before. But I couldn't forget all the friends I had left behind and, knowing they would probably never experience this wonderful sensation, I restrained my joy.

'We must move,' Thatem urged us. 'Once Sun is too high, they'll be gone.'

I found it difficult to concentrate on anything other than capturing the details around me, so as to preserve some recollection of the landscape in case I never walked outside again. I noticed occasional blurred footsteps on the ground, but couldn't determine, in all my agitation and excitement, whether they belonged to a man or some other creature. I threw intermittent glances upwards, too, and remembered, for some reason, the heretic's belief that whoever ended the Juice ascended to the realm of the skies.

We walked for a while, then Thatem stopped by a huge rock. After inspecting the ground around the base, he whispered to himself: 'It's here.'

He had brought a wire cage with him and, as he climbed up the rock, told us to keep the opening of the cage pressed against the lower edge, covered by a large patch of thick weed. When Thatem began jumping on the rock, shouting at us not to move, Daffodil and I exchanged confused glances. The curious spectacle continued for quite some time, and our perplexity grew accordingly, until, around Thatem's twentieth leap, a tiny, furred animal darted out of the undergrowth, ending up inside the cage.

'The mouse is ours! Close the cage!' Thatem yelled, all excited, and so we did.

I initially believed that Thatem had us catch the mouse to observe it more closely, but I realised my mistake when, after the mouse had tired from running and wriggling within the wire cage, Thatem opened the hatch and strangled the frightened, exhausted creature with his bare hands. While Thatem, smiling in satisfaction, put the lifeless mouse inside a cloth bag loosely fastened to his tunic, I suffered for the pain inflicted to the first animal I had ever seen. Despite my reluctance, we repeated this process several times until four carcasses shared the cloth bag. At that moment, Thatem warned: 'Let's go back inside, before Sun gets too strong ... you don't want to burn your pale skin ...'

I still vividly recall our first hunting expedition, not least because, once inside the house, Daffodil and I went over the events of that dawn again and again, to ensure we wouldn't forget them. Our recollections didn't entirely align, though.

Daffodil insisted that, on our way to the rock, she had glimpsed two tiny birds swaying in the far distance. But I was certain that, had that been the case, I would have seen them. The emerging light of dawn, or her intense desire to see a bird, had likely tricked my friend. For her part, she didn't remember the gentle, sandy breeze that I had felt as we approached the rock. But, in the end, it didn't really matter.

When we gathered round the table for the next meal, I told Bela I could not bear to eat the mouse. 'It will taste good with the lupins,' he, retaining a soft voice, nonetheless objected. 'We're privileged. Thatem is a great hunter of mice. The best in all the plain – I should say.'

'Are there many other houses like this around?' I asked.

'The closest is two days away by donkey,' Bela replied. Thatem had by then taught me how to count time, and I knew that two days meant quite a journey.

'Who lives there?'

'A family of eight. We call them *the rabbits*,' Thatem intervened.

'Rabbits?' I asked, excited.

'Yes, they're very fertile. Three sons and three daughters,' Thatem pointed out, thwarting my notion of meeting other animals, even though I would have been curious to see the daughters.

Bela served the now unrecognisable mice, baked without limbs and tails, which – I was told – had been combined with the lupins to create the accompanying brownish sauce.

'Boz, you need to eat the mice,' Bela almost pleaded. 'Nobody can live on tumbleweed soup alone, and we cannot give you any more lozenges. We need them…'

'For the next person coming up through the manhole,' interrupted Thatem, winking his right eye.

I reluctantly consumed the one mouse allotted to me, trying to ignore the fact that my teeth were sinking into the meat of a formerly living creature. 'Be careful with the bones. You don't want to choke just after your first trip outside ...' warned Thatem. The mouse sated me more than the soup, I had to admit, but I didn't follow Bela when he said that the taste of a properly cooked mouse was *bittersweet*. Too many concerns, in fact, prevented me from savouring the dish: primarily, a fear that the mouse's flesh might revive once squeezed between my teeth, which prompted me to swallow every new morsel as fast as possible. Moreover, I couldn't help but wonder if, by eating an animal, I was ingesting its emotions – particularly the fear and desolation experienced at the moment of death – and whether these feelings would be painfully transmitted to me. Finally, I also worried that our killing of an animal might have violated the Tenets, even though I had long ceased believing in them.

'I may be a great hunter,' Thatem said. 'But you're the greatest of all cooks, my Bela.'

Much like he always did when praised, Bela bowed his head, and issued a timid smile.

He put an iron cup on the table, right in front of me.

'Where did you get that?' I asked.

'There's a well not far away. We can go there together next dawn,' Thatem intervened. 'But now, drink it.'

I swallowed the drops of water from the cup, and their stony flavour reminded me of my old unit's floor. Daffodil also drank the water, and together we went back to the sorting of tumbleweed in the other room.

'Thatem says there's a village of Congoids not too far from here,' Daffodil told me while dropping the seeds into a bucket that Bela would later grind into flour. 'He's promised he will take me there.'

'When?' I asked, pausing my work abruptly. I didn't want to part ways with her, at least not yet.

'Soon,' she answered, pleased with my concern over her coming departure. 'He says the village will welcome me. I can work, and help them. Thatem has traded with their chief in the past. It takes three days by donkey to reach the village. I want to live there ... have a child ... that's what I always wanted inside the cage ... but I never thought it would be possible.'

We worked in silence, looking down from our chairs at the heap of tumbleweed.

Daffodil broke the lull in the conversation: 'I owe it all to you, Boz.'

I wasn't ready. Apart from Flox, no one had ever expressed gratitude to me before.

'I'll miss you, Daffodil ... still, I will be happy for you ...' I thought was the easiest reply.

At least Daffodil knew what her future might hold. But what about me? I still didn't know anything about my mission, or when it would start, and all this secrecy made me feel even more vulnerable.

I had finished sorting my first heap of tumbleweed when sudden cramps took hold in my stomach. I rushed to the latrine, but wasn't quick enough: I puked on the floor, and dirtied my robe. What my body was going through was even worse than the nausea from the varnish, and I soon found myself lying, as if lifeless, on the floor. As I writhed in pain,

I could hear Daffodil suffering the same torment in the next room, while from the kitchen came Thatem's laughter. *He has poisoned us*, I feared; but the truth was that he simply enjoyed seeing others suffering what the bacteria in the water had first done to him on his arrival. For what must have been two or three days, I lay in bed, or ran to the latrine, before gradually regaining my strength. And, when, for the first time since the infection, I stepped into the kitchen, and Thatem asked, 'Are you coming to help me fetch some water from the well?' his reference to water caused a bout of nausea in me.

'You'll get used to drinking water,' Thatem said reassuringly, noticing my reaction. 'You won't feel bad again. The worst is over.'

He was right: I never felt bad again, apart from the time he insinuated that the calciferol of the corridors was made with the ash of burned corpses.

By the time Sun had shrunk to a glowing orange ball in the far distance, we left the house, carrying two empty buckets each. Daffodil remained inside to help Bela. I was keen to see the outside again, and to compare this new experience with the preceding one, confident that I would notice details of the surroundings that had eluded me during our first walk. And, indeed, there was a group of low hills to our left that I had missed before. Thatem was taking us there. After roughly forty hundred steps, we had grown close enough to the hills for me to make out something atop one of them. Excited, I dashed forward, leaving Thatem behind. 'Be careful, Boz. You don't need to rush. The mulgas will not flee!' he warned.

When I had climbed the hill, I stood before one of the four trees at the top. I hesitated to touch its thin trunk, not only as

I was unsure how I might react, but also because, in hindsight, I didn't quite feel allowed to do so. I stood there for some time observing the tree, and realising how Piko's mulgas had in fact betrayed me: nature alone, indeed, could breathe life into a creature – not a brush and some pigments.

When I sensed the wood scratching my hand, I became instantly aware that, if not for Flox, I would never consider going back to the corridors. At last, I was touching life. The marvellous surface of the tree was tender and rough all at once and, though I knew it couldn't be possible, seemed to pulse under my trembling fingertips. I was captivated. Thatem didn't interrupt my ecstasy but, as I stroked the wood repeatedly, I could hear him doing something behind me. When I turned, he was collecting tiny stones from the ground.

'What are you doing?' I asked.

'Mulga seeds,' he said. 'They make for great seedcakes. Bela will be glad.'

I helped him.

'We must go to fetch the water now. It's safer if we get back to the house before the full dark comes,' he said shortly after.

We walked another five hundred steps past the hill, and reached a group of bulky stones that someone – I guessed Thatem – had placed in a circle to mark the presence of a shallow water-hole. I would have expected to see animals by the water: maybe even Penguin, Seagull and Bumblebees. But, to my disappointment, there were none; perhaps unsurprisingly, I should add, because the little water in the pool was unattractively brownish.

'Artificial intelligence sucked it all up,' Thatem said.

We filled the buckets with the remaining water, and made our way back to the house. The sunlight had turned considerably dimmer, and the air cooler. I felt a warm breeze caressing my skin – a pleasant new sensation – and I was amused to notice how, despite being so different, the trunk of a tree and a gentle wind were both so pleasing to my senses. The Land of Without had much to give.

'Tomorrow, you'll help me to prepare some tools to barter at the marketplace,' Thatem said. 'We need oil for our lamps.'

A corner at the back of the house served as a workshop. Its largest part was occupied by a long table, under which stood a crater filled with some objects, while the wall hosted many rows of tools resting on nails.

Thatem saw me running a gentle hand over the table. 'It's plastic,' he said, causing my hand to withdraw in fear. His books had taught me in great detail how plastic caused the deaths of so many animals and fish.

'It must be very old,' Thatem added. 'Four or five hundred years, I believe.' I wouldn't have guessed: the plastic looked unscathed. 'Whittle this,' he then instructed, handing me a tiny piece of wood and a carving knife. But when I remained still, hesitant, he snatched the tools back. 'Aren't you the son of a keeper?' he scoffed, shaking his head in contempt. Only when he remembered that there was no wood where I came from did his expression soften, and he showed me with slow movements how to whittle. I caught on quickly, my hands adapting with surprising ease. Before long, he was watching my deft handling of the knife with quiet approval.

'Your skin needs to get a bit more tanned or, pale as you are, they'll work out where you come from,' Thatem said, keeping his eyes glued to a large blade he was grinding.

'Who knows about us?' I asked him the question that had been nagging me for a while. Did the outside people know of us – those who came from the corridors?

'The residents of the palace know about us,' he answered.

'The palace?'

'Yes. One week by donkey from here stands a tall mountain. A river flows through its flank, bearing the clearest imaginable water, and sustaining a large garden laden with greens and fruits of all sorts, at the centre of which stands a magnificent palace. The palace know about us.'

I struggled to follow. 'What do you mean? Why?'

'In time, Boz,' Thatem quashed my curiosity. 'Now you have to carry out your work.'

It wasn't an imposition for me; I enjoyed working with the wood. Perhaps Thatem and I could craft an engraved cathedra, like the one Bruttho had stolen from the choir room, and trade it at the marketplace.

I asked Thatem what he was sharpening the blade for.

'In case somebody tries to steal something from us …'

That night, I – a kid released from a place of mandatory artificial light or dark – stared in awe at the battling of moonlight with darkness outside the window, which we were allowed to keep open when Sun was down. It was no doubt the enormity of the sky, and the sense of power that I derived from such a wondrous sight that drew me to it. But not just that: I believed that the more I stared, the more I could understand. Much like my past yearning to discover what the museum's clouded sky concealed, I now wondered what lay behind the luminous veil of stars above me. Piko had claimed there was nothing other than emptiness behind the sky; but I was no longer sure he deserved my trust.

This wasn't the only source of concern. Thatem had roused my curiosity with his story of a palace nestled in a marvellous garden atop a distant mountain. I wanted to see it for myself. I was growing restless at the house: that was the truth. Since arriving outside, Thatem and Bela had been my only encounters, and a painstaking sense of isolation, almost unbearable for someone brought up in a corridor full of idlers, was creeping in. But, when, worn out by all the thinking, I was on the verge of dozing off, a swift motion by the window made me flinch.

In the faint moonlight, a flattened shape had reached the ledge.

I was certain, for some reason, that no dangerous creature – aside from humans – could possibly come near the house, and so I crawled with some confidence towards the window, making the least possible noise. I stopped ten steps from the wall, close enough for my eyes to carefully examine the unexpected visitor. But, despite staring at her whole shape for quite a while, I couldn't ascribe the pointed nose and long, furry tail to any animal I knew of. The shape was longer than a rat's, and the ears not as pointy. It couldn't be a sable either – not in this heat – nor a ferret, which had a much smaller frame. Her fur was too short to belong to a rabbit, and her tail was shaped differently from a squirrel's. When, upset by my failure to identify the furry animal on the ledge, I got a bit closer to look better, the creature rushed away with a squeaking sound, which no slate could possibly ever help me to identify.

The morning after, I told Thatem.

'A mongoose,' he stated.

'What? Impossible!'

I had instantly excluded the mongoose. 'They have striped tails. She didn't.'

'Mongooses don't have striped tails. Raccoons do,' he argued.

'Impossible,' I insisted, having seen so many slates portraying mongooses. 'Their tail is striped.'

Thatem burst into a long-lasting, mocking laughter that annoyed me, because I didn't initially understand the reason behind it.

'Do you still believe in the slates?' he teased. 'They're inaccurate. Generation after generation, too much copying has gone on, I daresay …'

It took me a while to respond. 'How do you know it was a mongoose … if the slates are inaccurate?' I asked. Bela and Daffodil were both looking at me, and I could tell from their eyes they understood my dismay.

'I see mongooses every other day. We don't need the slates out here,' Thatem countered. 'And the slates are useless – at least most of them – even inside.'

I flinched. Not obviously, but I flinched. Seeing the credibility of the Tenets slowly crumble before my eyes had caused little turmoil in me, but Thatem's casual dismissal of the slates was a painful one. The content of the slates had been my only truth for a long time, and he was plainly questioning its veracity. But I told myself not to react as wildly as I had seen Piko doing in front of every unreliable slate. Not least because it was unlikely I would ever see a slate again.

'Stop brooding, Boz. We must go to the marketplace,' Thatem ordered, patting my shoulder. 'It's not a short journey.'

We went behind the house, a place I had never ventured, and where – I discovered – stood a shack.

'What's it for?' I asked.

'The stable. We keep our donkeys there.'

A pang of excitement hit me in the gut.

Donkeys to see and touch!

The mongoose was almost forgotten – almost.

Thatem opened the door of the stable. I could never have foreseen the stench coming out of it; even worse than the shelter's latrines. I hastened to cover my nose, but it was too late, and I puked next to the entrance. Unimpressed, Thatem handed me a cloth to clean my mouth.

Two of the donkeys were focused on eating from a haystack. One, smaller in size, had brown fur, while the other was white and grey. They didn't respond to our presence. After a thorough examination, I was glad to notice that their physical features weren't so inconsistent with the images on Piko's slates.

'Can I stroke them?' I asked.

Thatem nodded.

As I stroked the warm forehead of the brown donkey, the feeling of life pulsing under my hand returned, even more intensely. It felt as though the donkey's existence was flowing into mine, and mine into hers. 'She has already bonded with you,' Thatem observed, amused, when the donkey performed a gentle nuzzling of her head against me. 'I worked hard at the workshop for three hundred days to get her. Nothing is more valuable than a donkey, Boz. Around here, they murder to steal a donkey. We need to be careful.'

Thatem helped me to hop on the precious donkey before mounting his own, and we set off towards the marketplace. It felt different now that, instead of leaving the house just for a short walk to the well, we were heading someplace far. As I was rocked by my donkey's wobbly pace on the uneven ground, I glanced back at the house at least twice to seal it in my memory, in case we never came back. When I saw Daffodil there, by the door, waving at me with a hint of concern in her eyes, I felt an urge to rush back to the safety and protection of the house walls; but I resisted, and tried to look as calm as I could under Thatem's attentive sideways glances.

We passed over the hill with the four mulgas, beyond which the land rapidly grew less barren, and there appeared wide swathes of yellowed grass, shrubs, herbs, and even a large colony of ants, at the sight of which Thatem allowed me to dismount to take a closer look. Hundreds of reaper ants meandered frenetically among a sparse patch of wheatgrass, going in all directions but with a clear mission: bringing wheatgrass seeds to their nest. The childish, joyous dance of the ants, revelling in their life under Sun, and apparently fearless, comforted me. Each of them, on their own, was vulnerable and defenceless – it seemed – but the colony as a whole looked dynamic and determined. After Thatem declined my suggestion to bring three ants with us for further study, we resumed trotting along until the might of Sun, now high above the horizon, had become unbearable. Thatem took a canvas out of his knapsack to put up the yurt under a solitary acacia tree, right beside a tall rock, where we found partial shelter against the growing light. He took a rusted bottle from his saddle bag and shared the tumbleweed soup with me. Not daring to leave the donkeys out, they stood with us inside.

'We must wait for Sun to fall,' Thatem said. 'Then we can walk again, until the dark arrives, and then stop again. We can stay outside the yurt only when Sun is between an altitude of five degrees below the horizon and twenty-five degrees above it, and again once it's nineteen degrees above the horizion until it descends back to five degrees below. The night is too dark and cold to travel.'

The yurt felt safer, like being within walls where everything was in my control, and I could find a hiding place, when needed. The outside offered plenty of marvels but could also be disorientating, and didn't always afford protection.

'Doesn't the plain ever scare you, a bit?' I asked Thatem.

'Your heart is pounding, right? … a knot in your throat … all that … right?'

'Right.'

'It goes away, in time,' he said, savouring his role of reassurer. 'And you get so used to the dust, the scents, the heat and the cold, that you would never go back to the corridors.'

After a pause, he added: 'I would never go back to the corridors.'

We waited for twilight to arrive. To pass the time, and distract us from the stifling heat, Thatem, resting his head on the folded knapsack, sang hymns of his own creation. One went like this:

Why should I live on dust, flies, and weed,
When they banquet on beans, cardoons, and mead?
I hide from burning Sun the most part of the day,
But around the palace grows the most abundant ley.
Draught after draught, our men wither of thirst and hunger,
Yet up there they somehow look heartier and plumper.
But a new friend has come from within the walls,
And he will ensure that a fair retribution befalls.

My imaginative friend would be a great fit in Cardenio's troupe, I noted – not least to make them laugh when needed, and to help escape the bailiffs after the first act.

Then, in a rare moment of silence under our yurt, Thatem asked: 'So, young man … what'll you do once you've ended your mission?'

I told him of my resolution to go back and bring Flox to the Land of … Earth.

'What … ?' Thatem's eyes clouded for an instant, before recovering their boisterousness. 'I left those damned walls for a woman … and you want to go back for one?' He was enraged. 'Are you mad, Boz … for heaven's sake!'

'*Heaven?*' I asked.

'Haven't you read the Bible?' he asked, his tone now subdued. 'No, of course, I traded it at the marketplace some-time ago. Shame on me! But I really needed those clay tiles for our house. Well, it's an amazing book. And the sequel, *La Divina Commedia*, is no less great. The author, a bloke called Homer, was a true genius …'

Thatem was a very knowledgeable man, I could tell. He had to know more about the intriguing palace sat atop the mountain. 'I can tell you what Bela told me,' he said, when I broached the subject. 'For some mysterious reason, it's never too hot there, and rain never forgets to fall, so that its denizens enjoy the most delicious food, swim in the cleanest water, and ride marvellous horses at their whim. They are attended by a multitude of servants, and spend their days singing, playing, having fun in a wonderful garden animated by so many amazing animals. That's a real *heaven*!'

'Have you ever been inside?'

'No, absolutely not,' he replied, snapping his tongue. 'Nobody who is fortunate enough to enter the palace would ever return here.'

'Then how do you know all this?'

'I'm only telling you what I heard from Bela. My guess is that some people sneaked into the palace, then got caught and were kicked out. But trust me: Bela always knows what he's talking about. Perhaps he's been there himself.'

We had brought two tomes to trade at the marketplace. 'These are more valuable than the donkeys,' he claimed. But the good thing about tomes, he added, was that, unlike the donkeys, you could trade one of your own for a new one, saving yourself some effort at the workshop. One tome told the story of a man gifted with the unique power of entering the minds of lunatics to root out madness. The other tome was an illustrated catalogue with more than one thousand herbal remedies.

'I didn't sleep for two full nights while deciding which books to give away ...' he confided.

'Why the catalogue of herbal remedies? It's very useful.' I frowned. 'It's wonderful. And it could save our lives.'

'We need new tunics. And I've learned all the remedies by heart, anyway.'

The temptation to challenge his memory was irresistible. I opened the book to a random page and read: '*Angelica.*'

'I believe it goes like this,' he answered. '*Angelica roots should be dried rapidly and placed in air-tight receptacles. The dried root is greyish brown and much wrinkled externally, whitish and spongy within and breaks with a starchy fracture, exhibiting shining, resinous spots. The odour is strong and fragrant, and the taste at first sweetish, afterwards warm, aromatic, bitterish and somewhat musky. Boil down gently for three hours a handful of Angelica root in a quart of water; then strain it off and add liquid Narbonne honey or best virgin honey sufficient to make it into a balsam or syrup, and take two tablespoonsful every night and morning, as well as several times in the day.* Unfortunately, I was never able to get hold of any honey. They undoubtedly have honey at the palace, though. But Angelica works even without honey, I heard.'

'What is the remedy for?' I asked.

'Climacteric.'

'What?'

'In time, Boz.'

I didn't get any rest my first night outside. The surrounding dark gave rise to disturbing thoughts about what I should do once I completed the mysterious mission given to me. Where I came from, the future wasn't a matter for consideration. You consumed your existence idling in the corridors, paired with a woman chosen by your genitors, until either the Juice ended or the bailiffs killed you. You made no choices. In fact, I had learned about the very concept of *future* only in Thatem's books; but its meaning was becoming clearer only now that I associated it with the need to find a direction. I was so afraid of having to make choices that I resolved to make one: after getting Flox out, we would build a hut, not far from Thatem's house. Or, perhaps, if life there was really so marvellous, we could live at the palace. As long as Flox was with me, everything would be fine.

'Why did your father choose me?' I asked Thatem.

'I think he likes rebels.'

He might be right, I thought. I had first met Mozart during one of my forbidden wanderings in the dark. No doubt, he had approved – if only because Piko would have disapproved. My two preceptors: so different from each other, they seemed to agree on one thing only – the absurdity of religion.

It was early morning when, after three days and nights of intermittent travel, we reached the top of a hill, from which we could survey our destination. Situated on a wide plain, the marketplace consisted of around thirty coloured yurts placed in a circle, connected by long lines of people who, like ants filing in and out of a crack, toured round the tents.

People, finally.

We put up our yellow yurt in the space left between two others. We hadn't even finished laying our merchandise on the floor when the first visitor entered. Thatem must have known the man already, because his dull greeting denoted a sheer lack of interest. After a lengthy browsing through the tools – which, I could see, annoyed Thatem even more – our unwanted visitor finally spotted something of interest.

'Mmh …' he muttered, picking up an item for closer examination. 'A magnifying glass!' he then commented in delight.

'Yes,' Thatem confirmed, glancing at the entrance in the hope that other, better traders would come in.

The dealer, holding the magnifying glass in his hand, looked at me.

'You've a new assistant, Thatem?' he asked.

Thatem nodded.

'I congratulate you, then … your trades must be going very well. I'm happy for you.' The dealer smiled. Then, after a slight pause, he said triumphantly, 'Listen to me carefully: I'll offer you for this magnifying glass … listen well … no fewer than … twelve large bags of exceptional tumbleweed!'

Thatem almost snatched the magnifying glass from the man's hand and placed it back on the floor. The dealer left the yurt, though not before having raised his offer to fifteen large bags of exceptional tumbleweed.

An entirely different visit took place shortly after. When the second trader walked into the tent, Thatem stepped forward to hug him. 'Welcome back to my tent!' he even said. The visitor eyed the merchandise, then pointed rather quickly at an old long metal tool that Thatem had recently painted in white at our workshop.

'What is it?' he asked.

'A faucet,' Thatem replied. 'It makes water run in houses.'

Despite an attempt to conceal his interest, the man's darting look betrayed it all. He wanted the item. After shaking Thatem's hand with a cordial smile – however – he left the yurt without making any offer. I was disappointed, while Thatem seemed completely indifferent to the man's behaviour. Perhaps he already knew the man would return.

'I can give you five steps of cloth for the faucet,' he indeed proposed on his return, not much later.

Thatem shook his head. 'No fewer than seven steps.'

The other nodded without hesitation, and went back to his purple yurt to fetch the agreed lengths of cloth.

'Now … he only needs the water.' Thatem winked at me.

With so many hagglers coming in droves from the other yurts, in no time the trading grew hectic and noisy. While Thatem was engaged in bartering, I helped him by keeping an eye out for the many thieves that, he insisted, hid among the crowd. In a safe corner we placed all the valuable goods received in exchange for our stock: cloth, oil for lamps, unguents, pans, two hoes, and one sheep's eyeball for Bela.

In the late morning, everybody went back to their yurts to let the heat abate. Thatem had just lain down for some rest when two men entered. He turned with a start. Tense, though not hostile, glances were exchanged inside the yurt. The two visitors might well be father and son, with the latter having lived roughly my same length of life.

The older man looked at me, then asked: 'Is this him?'

Thatem nodded.

'He isn't much more than a child,' the other said, sceptically, mimicking a baby's cradling.

'But he's clever, and very skilled with the azbuki,' Thatem replied with a very rare compliment, which made me shiver inside.

'The twins at the palace will soon be four thousand days old,' the man said. 'Their preceptor must already be on his journey to the palace. His name is Ghiorghio.'

Thatem nodded again, and this was all that was said before they left. As if I shouldn't have overheard his conversation, Thatem didn't look in my direction for the entire afternoon. Only when Sun had reached about six degrees above the horizon, by which time we had concluded our bartering, he addressed me: 'I've a surprise for you, Boz. Follow me.'

We walked to an orange yurt on the far side of the marketplace. Right in front of the entrance, Thatem blew through his folded hands to make a suffocated, warning sound that, he would later tell me, was the imitation of an elf owl's hoot.

Inside the yurt, a woman was in the process of loading up her donkey. She turned and smiled at Thatem, who reciprocated. It was strange: other than to deploy his peerless sarcasm, Thatem rarely smiled.

'I'd like to show my young friend Boz the valuable present I gave you sometime ago,' he said. 'Do you still have it with you, Lamezia?'

'Of course,' she answered, still smiling. 'It's always with me … it reminds me of you.'

If not for the hair concealing his whole face, I would've said that Thatem had reddened.

I was about to leave the two of them alone in the yurt, but the unexpected sight of a telescope being carefully extracted from one sack stopped me. Lamezia gave it to Thatem, who examined the tubular instrument like a passionate mother would inspect her newborn.

'I built it …' Thatem said. 'It took me twenty-two days of travel to get the finest lens from the greatest glassmaker.'

'And I'm grateful to you, Thatem, because your gift has bestowed on me so many enchanting journeys through the starred sky …'

'Shall we try it now? Sun has set, and the sky is clear,' Thatem suggested in my direction.

He didn't need to wait for my answer.

'But it's better if we watch the stars after breaking bread together, Boz,' proposed Lamezia, who seemed to me a very welcoming and amiable lady. Although there was no bread available, dividing the meal with Thatem and her took me back to the merry gatherings with Bebro and his troupe. Lamezia had laid a wide cloth on the ground, under the all-embracing night sky, and while Thatem switched on the portable oil lamp, she placed a large vessel with tumbleweed

soup and a generous bowl of dates on the cloth. It was understood that I was her guest, and that I should just eat the
meal and enjoy the stars, for which purpose she gave me the
telescope.

I handled it with hesitation, fearing that, if its body slipped
through my excited hands, the lens might break.

'Aim at the sky, Boz, not at the ground. It's not a magnifying glass: that has gone to the brown tent already. And you've
to look into it, remember,' Thatem said.

So, I brought the narrow end to my eye, and simply
looked up.

Now that the stars were bigger, they seemed even more
real, almost as if I could reach out and touch their surfaces.
I can say that only in that moment did I perhaps grasp in
full the extent of my journey: for most of my life, I had seen
only flaked walls around me; and here I was, examining with
a telescope an immense expanse of dotted lights that didn't
even belong to Earth. I felt a sense of regret for my inability
to touch them with my bare hands, but then I stopped myself,
reminded of how greedy I was, and thought of what Piko had
said about our ancestors shamefully failing to appreciate that
Earth was enough for them. Perhaps it was the boundless space
above and around me, or my first trip far from the house, but
it was then that I first realised how much I wanted to see other
lands. It was too late to share my intention with Thatem, who,
judging from the sounds coming from behind, was rather
more invested in Lamezia.

When Thatem and I woke up the next morning, ours was
the last remaining yurt on the plain. Everyone had gone. We,
too, left on the donkeys and went back to our solitary house.

XIV

MISSION

Two-hundred days had. passed since the marketplace when, one morning, three loud thumps on the door startled us. It wasn't windy, our donkeys were safely sheltered inside the shack, and the earth hadn't trembled: it could only be a visitor.

The first since my arrival at the house.

'Him?' Thatem asked Bela, who stood up and went to the hall, leaving his steaming tumbleweed soup on the table. The others remained still. We heard the sound of the door opening, and whispers from outside. Daffodil and I exchanged a look of alarm; the fear that the bailiffs might take us back to the corridors had never left us. Thatem, instead, looked nervously excited, as if he had long waited for this visit. We heard movements inside the house, and footsteps drawing nearer, then Bela reappeared in the kitchen. Next to him stood a man in a white tunic, though yellowed by the dust, evidently tired by his journey. I guessed the man's length of life to fall somewhere between Thatem's and my own.

'I beg for your hospitality,' the visitor said in a feeble voice, slowly laying his bulging rucksack on the floor. 'My donkey fell ill. I've been walking for five nights, and my water bottle is almost empty. I'm heading to the palace. My name is Ghiorghio.'

I stared at him intently, though he failed to notice. Thatem gave me a chastising glance to silently remind me that I shouldn't even consider remembering his conversation at the marketplace.

'Join us,' Thatem invited Ghiorghio, who bowed his head in gratitude, while Bela placed a fifth bowl on the table. Our guest had just taken a seat when, noticing Daffodil next to me, he tensed up. But his hunger overtook everything, even his surprise at seeing a Congoid at the table, and he lowered his eyes towards the bowl. We all resumed our meal.

'What's taking you to the palace?' Thatem enquired after five spoons of tumbleweed soup.

'The twins of the Ealdorman will soon be four thousand days old. I've been entrusted with the responsibility of initiating them in the azbuki.'

Thatem gave him an impressed look – albeit a contrived one.

'I come from the Schola of …' our visitor continued. 'I was chosen from among two hundred and eleven preceptors for this delicate duty. The Ealdorman is eager for his offspring to acquire the highest understanding of the azbuki.'

Thatem recomposed his fascinated expression.

'Have you ever met the Ealdorman?'

'No. It will be a true honour for me. I've never been to the palace.'

In the ensuing silence, I could hear the sound of our spoons against the bowls. To celebrate this rare visit, Bela served an exceptional second round of soup.

'I'll have to borrow a donkey from your shack,' Ghiorghio added, less meekly now that he had revealed his forthcoming role at the palace. 'I'm already late. They are expecting me.'

'Sure,' replied Thatem, no doubt aching at the prospect of letting a donkey go.

'And may I make use of your latrine?' Ghiorghio added.

'I'll show you the way.' Thatem stood up, and Ghiorghio followed.

Nobody spoke in their absence – and I was still trying to make sense of what the man at the marketplace had told Thatem – when I was unexpectedly called from the latrine.

'Boz, come here!'

His rugged forehead uncommonly dotted with sweaty beads, Bela gave me a nervous nod so as to confirm that I should go.

The door of the latrine was wide open. Ghiorghio lay on the floor, his tunic soaked in blood, his eyes open but unmoving. Thatem, standing calmly alongside the still body, was passing his knife through a strop.

I *don't deprive men of their existence, unless for a greater cause,* I remembered Bebro saying, and a donkey didn't seem to me a good enough reason for a murder.

'Why?' I asked Thatem. 'Why the killing?'

But the bloodshed had nothing to do with a donkey.

'You'll take Ghiorghio's place, and go to the palace to teach the Ealdorman's twins the azbuki,' Thatem said, while rummaging in Ghiorghio's tunic, from which he removed a thin folder that he then placed inside a pocket of his own robe. 'That's why you're here.'

Bela and Daffodil reached us. 'We must bury him,' Thatem instructed. 'Then you and Bela will leave for the palace. I will take Daffodil to join the village of the Congoids.'

He handled Bela a wad of white cloth taken from a closet, and told him to prepare a new garment identical to Ghiorghio's tunic. We buried the corpse not far away from the shack, using two hoes received at the marketplace for the magnifying glass. The soil proved very hard to dig, and it took quite a while to complete the work. As we finally dispatched Ghiorghio into the ground, I concluded that Thatem had acquired both the hoes and the white cloth in anticipation of what would later happen at the house.

'How did you know that the preceptor would come here?' I asked.

'He had to,' Thatem replied, while looking at his blood-ied hands impassively, before cleaning them with a dirty cloth. 'Only our house stands in the path between the Schola of … and the palace. We built it here on purpose. And it has been twenty generations, or so, that whenever a child of the Ealdorman reaches four thousand days of life, the Schola of … sends a preceptor to the palace. We received some visits from errants in the past, but when I heard knocking, I knew it was him.'

When we got back inside, my new tunic was ready: it fitted my body to perfection, and was exactly the same as Ghiorghio's. Bela was also a gifted tailor, I realised, trembling with excited fear at the prospect that I would soon impersonate a preceptor at the palace. My second performance after the interpretation of a bailiff to rescue Flox and the twenty-two stranded girls.

I missed Flox, and I missed Bebro, too, and now the diffi-cult moment of separating from Daffodil was also coming. We had gone through a lot together.

I felt her cheek trembling as she hugged me tight. Unusually for Daffodil, she was scared. I tried to console her by sharing what I believed would be a blissful future ahead of her: 'You'll be fine. And very soon Flox and I will come to visit you. Perhaps you'll have a child in your arms by then …'

'Life has been better since you left the cage – I'm sure – and it will be even better at the village,' Thatem said, trying himself to comfort Daffodil. 'And you're certainly in better shape than him,' he added, pointing at Ghiorghio's rucksack on the floor.

Not that my future seemed certain, but I was prepared to leave the secluded house, and admire the wonders of the palace's garden, even if they were only half as marvellous as Thatem recounted. The outside was no longer a novelty to me, and the awe that I had initially felt whenever stepping into the vast landscape had faded. Furthermore, I had come to realise that, no matter how much I satisfied my curiosity, it always led me into an unyielding search for the unknown. I was ready for my mission.

Thatem rummaged in Ghiorghio's rucksack, which, despite its small dimensions, contained apparently limitless items: a foldable tent, one miswak, an adze, two hornbooks, a copper flask with the engraving of a griffin, a compass, one bedroll, a comb, three loincloths, a board of senet (making me happy), one water bottle, and a flask of cactus oil (a strong aphrodisiac, Thatem said).

I busied myself on my last day at the house studying the hornbooks, which included useful notes on the Schola's doctrines and, no less essential, a code of rules to follow at the palace. I also played senet with Daffodil, and observed, not without pleasure, that she still didn't take losses very well. When Sun was eventually in decline, Bela and I left the house on the donkeys. I took Ghiorghio's rucksack, lightened of the cactus oil and the copper flask (which Thatem kept for himself), but containing the clepsammia, a tool that could still be useful to measure time.

Bela was predictably less conversational than Thatem. We had travelled for one day before he spoke to me. 'We'll have to make a diversion,' he warned. 'It'll take a bit longer to reach the palace. But we must first meet someone.'

Gravelled flatlands were our unchanging landscape, traversed by swathes of parched grass that, from a distance, seemed to be tinged dark green, only to reveal their undeniable brownness whenever we got closer. Despite the wide and boundless surroundings, at times the choking sense of loss that had taken hold of me during the passage through the dark tunnels with Daffodil resurfaced: once again, I was leaving everyone and everything behind, unaware of what lay ahead.

Sun was low when we reached a shallow pond, the first in our path, next to which was a sign of human presence – a hut made of weathered wood – that brought me some relief. As we drew closer, and the hut's decaying became even more evident, a woman calmly walked out, followed by a man three steps behind. They had seen us.

Bela got off his donkey, and both the woman and the man hugged him in silence.

'The kid's name is Boz,' Bela said, pointing at me while I dismounted. 'He comes from within the walls.'

I glanced around nervously before accepting that nobody could ever overhear us in such desolation. The woman released a thin, friendly smile, while I detected curiosity, or awe, or perhaps both, in the man's gaze. Though I knew Bela would never disclose my origins to someone he shouldn't, being stared at was a source of embarrassment.

'She's Yirah,' Piko told me. 'And her man's name is Kashmin.'

Yirah's smile widened, and she encouraged us to go into the house: 'You'll stay with us for the night?'

Bela nodded.

'Then we should break bread together.'

The hut consisted of a single room, though quite large, featuring a kitchen alcove at the left end, a table in the middle, and two aligned beds on the right. Kashmin invited us to sit, while Yirah moved towards the kitchen, whose shelves held far fewer utensils than ours; yet the sight of a flask and a cylinder on a stool next to the fireplace caught my attention.

'Yirah is the greatest chemist ever,' Bela said.

Yirah chuckled, feigning modesty, then commanded to the full room: 'You'll have to help me prepare the meal!'

Bela had never let me go near his kitchen utensils, so I relished the opportunity. Yirah took two small tubes from the pantry and motioned for us to follow her outside under a wooden overhang projecting from the rear of the hut. Beneath its far edge lay a pit oven, while another corner within the shaded area was piled high with stones. When Yirah began shifting the stones aside, Bela and I crouched to help her. A hidden clay bowl soon emerged. 'The pan, Kashmin,' Yirah said sharply, glancing sideways from her hunched position. 'I shouldn't even have to ask.'

When Kashmin had returned with the pan, Yirah opened the unearthed bowl, filled up to the brim with a dense, lumpy powder, and transferred the powder into the pan with a ladle. Then she added some water from the pond, mixing powder and water with her strong hands until it had grown into a ball of thick paste, which to my delight, I was asked to roll against the base of the bowl for a further smoothening.

In our kitchen, Bela lit the fire by striking a sharp piece of flint repeatedly against one slab of steel, but here Yira showed me her alternative method. She took a pinch of a dark powder from one of the tubes and piled it on a flat stone inside the ground oven. 'Potassium permanganate,' she whispered to me.

'Where did you get it from?' I whispered back.

'We are not short of deposits of pyrolusite here. I enjoy searching for minerals to use in my experiments – and there isn't much else for me to do in the area, anyway,' Yira answered, opening the second tube to get a fistful of some granulose powder. 'Sugar,' she informed me. 'I got it at the marketplace.'

Having mixed the two powders with care, she finally crushed the resulting solution with a pestle. 'What are you doing?' I asked, intrigued.

'You'll see,' she replied, delighted by my persistent curiosity. I didn't have to wait, because a tiny flame quickly rose from the stone. Kashmin hastened to drop a bunch of dried leaves over the flame to turn it into a proper fire, while Yira placed the flattened paste to bake on a steel pedestal over the burning oven, and not much later we found ourselves breaking actual bread inside the hut. Preceded by a fragrant scent that filled the room with promise, the warm bread brought me the most exquisite burst of flavour I had ever encountered. 'The enset has fermented for seven hundred days,' Yira told us. 'We keep it for very important occasions.'

'A man from within the walls is a very important occasion,' Kashmin commented.

Yira nodded.

I blushed.

'Where are you heading to?' she asked me, smiling at my flushed cheeks.

I remained silent.

'He's going to the palace,' Bela said, anticipating the impact of his revelation on our hosts. Caught off guard, they said nothing, merely exchanging glances. But Yira quickly dispelled the awkwardness in the room by announcing that she had something else in the kitchen for us to try.

'Agave juice. It's good. Drink!' she commanded, after pouring a clear liquid into four small cups, and downing hers in one swift motion. I was hesitant, but when Bela and Kashmin drank their juice, I followed. And, in no time, fire invaded my mouth and throat. Choking, I bent over, stomping and coughing uncontrollably.

Yira must have poisoned me with some chemical preparation – or so I thought. But her laughter was even louder than my coughs. 'Don't be afraid, Boz. It's normal ... the first time!'

My throat still ached, but after pacing the room for a while, I felt slightly better, and noticed Bela's flushed expression as, slouched in his seat, he smiled to himself. Kashmin, standing by the window, seemed likewise euphoric. It was then that, from her armchair, Yira asked me to tell them about my life in the corridors. She had known since her childhood, albeit vaguely, of the people living within the walls, but never had she encountered one of them.

So, I spoke of the unyielding cycle of artificial light and real darkness, the meaningless lives of idlers, our dependency on the Juice, my encounter with Mozart, the agony inside the shelter, my run with the thespians, and my final decision to leave the walls. I chose not to mention Flox, so that I wouldn't give away my plan to go back to the corridors to free her. No one in the room dared to interrupt, and even Bela, who must have heard similar stories from Thatem, listened attentively.

'Two guaranteed meals every day without doing a thing? Not bad. I can't even count how many days we have had without food here,' said Kashmin, stroking his belly with one hand.

'What?' Yira, who had watched me with commiserating eyes throughout the entire story, scolded him. 'A life without Sun? And your parents picking someone for you to love? I chose you – what a fool I was – but at least I made a choice! I like our lives here, as they are.'

Though not daring to overtly disagree with her, Kashmin didn't look convinced; but Bela intervened: 'I think Boz alone knows whether it's better there or here.'

His question would never have occurred to me. Despite the many thousands of days passed inside the corridors, in fact, the outer life had already affected me so deeply that I by now struggled to conceive of any other form of existence. Sun, the darkness of the night, the sand, the ants, even the tumbleweed had all become a part of me, and the scents, flavours and sensations discovered since my flight from the walls already seemed crucial to my survival.

Though I hadn't realised it when still inside, life in the corridors never really moved, or changed, and it was only after escaping through the manhole that I had begun to feel alive. At times, I even suspected that a hidden part of me had always known that a habitable outer world existed, and this was why Mozart had come to me. After experiencing the variety of the outside, I didn't believe my soul would ever fit back inside the corridors – whatever Thatem had meant by *soul*. I remember Thatem saying that, not long after his arrival in the Land of Without, he had started counting the days enjoyed outside, because it made his new life look even more real. I had taken to doing the same, and he was right.

'Kashmin: prepare the beds for Bela and Boz,' Yira, still absorbed in mulling over my troubled past in the corridors, ordered. 'They'll have to leave before Sun grows too high. The road to the palace is long.'

At dawn, while Kashmin, who had poured himself more than one glass of agave juice before the sleep, hugged me tightly ahead of my departure, across the room Yira, muttering something I couldn't quite make out, handed a small metal box to Bela.

'It's what you asked me for,' she whispered. 'Will you use it at the palace?'

Bela nodded, hiding the box in his tunic; and we left.

After two days of walking, during which the harshness of Sun had receded, and the surroundings had thus grown less barren, the donkeys brought us before a range of hills, over-looked from the rear by a mountain, whose flat peak was covered in thick green. The palace must be up there, I guessed. But to reach the mountain we first had to pass through a steep gorge. As we penetrated the narrow chasm between the hills, scarcely illuminated by the first light of dawn, Bela kept glancing around with a hint of apprehension. A little later, I noticed a sudden movement between two rocks on the slope to the right of our path, followed by another swift movement not far off, at roughly the same height.

'Did you see that?' asked Bela, without turning.

'Yes.'

'Bandits,' he whispered, just as I saw another two shadows scurrying on the opposite flank of the gorge. We couldn't possibly escape them, so the men – I counted eight of them – made a leisurely descent from both sides.

'They want the donkeys,' Bela mumbled when the pack of men had reached a distance of no more than thirty steps from us. With hindsight, we should have run away, leaving the donkeys there: perhaps the bandits would've left us alone. But we didn't. And, without his donkey, Bela would never have been able to reach the palace, or go back to the stone house, in any case.

The bandits surrounded us. 'We're heading to the palace ...' Bela started, but they didn't let him go any further: one man, wearing a surcoat over his torso, secured at the waist by a strip in which a curved knife was sheathed, rushed to drag Bela off the donkey, while the other three took turns kicking him on the ground, first in the stomach, then in the backbone. The rest of the bandits watched – one of them calmly taking Bela's donkey away from the assault.

I too watched, powerless, and got off my donkey in haste for fear that their rage might turn against me. To my relief, the men, already bored of attacking, left me alone, and headed back up one of the hills with our donkeys and the water from my rucksack.

I crouched beside Bela, who writhed on the ground.

He gave me his rough hand, and I clutched it tight.

'I will carry you to the palace, Bela.'

Bela shook his head, almost imperceptibly. It then took him quite some effort to find the strength to speak: 'It's too far to carry me up there ...'

He had resigned himself to the fact that the wounds, and the coming heat, would kill him.

'But you can make it, Boz,' he said with a renewed burst of energy. 'You're young and your will is strong.'

He asked me to search inside his tunic, where I found Yira's metal case.

'What is it?' I asked.

'In time, Boz.'

I carried him, already unconscious, to the shaded flank of the gorge. I couldn't help him anyway and, with no more water in my rucksack, my time was running out. After caressing his listless face, I began my ascent of the mountain under the strengthening sunlight, and never looked back.

XV

PARROTS

The white of the polished walls was so pure and gleaming that, as I walked along the corridor that divided the palace, I feared my very breath might soil it. Although the paint from the previous whitewash was still untarnished, the entire palace had been hastily repainted, ahead of the Ealdorman's forthcoming return, by no fewer than one hundred and eighty servants.

I stopped when about to walk into the twins' rooms, and inspected my tunic in search of imperfections. Although a fresh, pristine tunic, exuding a faint scent of daffodils, was laid beside my bed by a different servant every morning, I never once wanted to risk presenting myself to the twins in anything less than flawless attire. When, seven hundred and thirty-one days before, I had become their preceptor, the Maid of the Bedchamber had indeed warned me: 'The Ealdorman forgives no stain, hole, crumble or fold.'

I had never met the Ealdorman, who had left for a long journey the very day before my arrival, and still hadn't come back. But his return was now due, they had finally announced. I say *finally*, despite being very anxious back then at the idea of his scrutiny. The Ealdorman was a man of a very selective and strict disposition, I was told, though also fair and generous, albeit on his own terms.

I had been away for days – my only time outside the palace since arriving. When I stepped into the library, Lela stood up from the desk, bowed politely, and returned to sketching the parchment in front of her, already marked with several lines of *mislite*.

'Nice execution, Lela.'

'I am much obliged to you, Master Ghiorghio.'

'The *mislite* celebrates the supreme power of thinking,' I told her. 'Thoughts make you who you are. They're yours – just yours – and nobody, not even the mightiest man on Earth, will ever take them from you, not even if they put you inside a cage. Thinking can't leave you, regardless of your will: you cannot give it up! The neater and tidier your thoughts are, the wiser and more productive your actions will be. And my duty is indeed that of helping you learn to think about … thinking.'

'Even when the thoughts are … scary?' she asked, hesitantly. Lela had once confided in me how she feared that, despite the reassurances of the others, her father would never come back.

'Thoughts are like lions,' I said in a soft voice, mimicking feline paws with my hands. 'Invisible creatures among the tall grass of the prairie, silent, in an apparent doze. But, then, out of nowhere, they lift their heads up and let out the loudest roar, swat their paws on the ground, and run after you, headlong, prepared to attack. And there you are: prey, stilled by fear. But remember, your own thoughts can hamper you but never truly harm you. Why kill the hand that feeds them? You give birth to your thoughts, and even if you never really tame them, you'll survive them.'

Lela smiled and, despite the lingering silence, seemed convinced. Having passed so many days with the twins, I had learned to read their emotions, and perhaps they, too, knew how to interpret mine.

As had become all too common lately, her brother's desk, placed alongside Lela's, was vacant.

'Where is he?' I asked.

Lela looked over my shoulder towards the toy room. I frowned in amused frustration. Since the accident at the menagerie, Robbo had been passing most of his days alone there, barely speaking to anyone and, worse still, neglecting my assignments.

As I made my way to see him, I glanced at the fifteen shelves crammed with books that ran down all sides of the twins' library. While every night the servants carefully dusted the books with ostrich feathers, the children and I alone were permitted to browse through the precious pages. Once, climbing down the precarious ladder with a cumbersome Almagest in my grasp, I had even fortuitously sighted a copy of the Bible on the twelfth shelf to the right. I couldn't say whether it was Thatem's former possession that had found its way into the library – but, awkwardly enough, there was no mention of Homer on the jewelled cover or anywhere within the book's pages.

The shape of his back blurred by the intense light from the glass balcony door, Robbo sat cross-legged on the green carpet that covered most of the marble floor. In front of him a replica of the palace was taking shape, made of little wooden bricks lacquered in white, on which he had been working intensely for thirty-three days. The replica was based on a very detailed sketch of the palace he had made me draw on parchment as we strolled around the garden. A present for his father, Robbo was desperate to complete the model before the Ealdorman's return. The miniature meant so much to him that I didn't want to question the time he had taken away from the azbuki to build it; but, still, I could no longer bear the sight of a boy shutting himself away. I approached him from behind, knowing he had heard my steps.

'I'm back ...'

He didn't turn, or acknowledge my presence in any manner; he simply added two bricks to the replica, slowly building towards the ceiling. Early on, Robbo had encountered a problem with his work: the palace was circular in shape, but the tens of thousands of bricks crafted by the palace's carpenter had all been rectangular. Realising the gravity of his mistake, he had ordered the carpenter in a fit of rage to prepare a new supply of rounded bricks.

Robbo left the replica only to eat, and whenever he emptied the tall sack containing the bricks placed next to him, a servant would hasten to replenish it, so as to ensure that no time was wasted in completing the miniature. I knew how to persuade him to join me outside, though.

'The parrots have arrived ...'

Robbo sprang to his feet, and started off towards the balcony, which gave access to the ground floor via a short ladder. I followed him to the garden under the bluest of all skies, though a tiny breeze moved the air, a sign that heavy rain would join us that night. The temperature was always warm, and the scorching heat of the plain just a distant memory. A large group of servants were trimming the hedges, while others pulled carts ripe with groceries up the gravelled path to the kitchens. I liked watching the servants work, and observing the kind of unspecified harmony in their labour, though they weren't allowed to reciprocate the stare – not even a quick glance – and this felt somewhat unfair, both to them and to me.

On reaching the menagerie, I came up beside Robbo. He nodded at me, and after twenty steps in brooding silence, asked: 'Do you think my father will like the replica?'

'He certainly will do,' I said, but after ten more steps I added: 'He will be even more glad if you resume practising the azbuki.'

There was no reply.

To our immediate left was the lowest terrace of the garden, punctuated with admirable yet slightly boring precision by long stretches of palm trees. More diverse was the adjacent upper terrace, shared by holm oaks, olive trees, and chestnuts, sufficiently generous to leave room for an abundance of spleenworts, spikemosses, and other ferns, which would've fit wonderfully in my unit within the walls. But my preference was for the furthest terrace, where domineering conifers thrived in the cool air, creating perennial shade in which I occasionally hid, seated with my back against a pine trunk, musing on the troubles of my past or thinking about Mozart's story about that child who moved to the treetops to leave all human evilness behind him. But my time at the palace had been peaceful, and everyone treated me with no less than respect – including the prominent visitors who, unaware of the Ealdorman's absence, kept coming to the palace in the hope of seeing him. So, I wasn't tempted to make the woods my home, at least not yet.

Beside the menagerie flowed a stream – the one Thatem had told me about. It was narrower than in his description, but the water as pure, transparent and fresh as he had said. 'Shall we bathe?' Robbo had suggested during our first walk in the garden, shortly after my arrival. I had already noticed by then that he preferred sharing silent experiences with others rather than engaging in conversation.

Keen not to show any hesitation around water (the real Ghiorghio might well have been accustomed to streams), I had sat with Robbo on the torrent's bed. Him in his braies, me still in my tunic.

'Why aren't you taking it off, Master Ghiorghio?'

'The Schola doesn't allow us to remove our tunic in daytime, Robbo.'

He had nodded, persuaded only in part, but far from imagining that I never took off the tunic in front of others to prevent them seeing the long scar traversing my back, the one tangible legacy of my former life within the walls.

But, despite the layer of fabric, the motion of the water passing over my body, akin to a solidified cold wind trying to possess me, aroused a contradictory sensation of pleasure and fright, with the first naturally prevailing: born in water, we're drawn to water.

Robbo didn't enjoy the practice of the azbuki. Not because the azbuki wasn't to his liking – I still can't even conceive of such a possibility – but because of the pain he associated with it. Robbo had grown up playing in the garden with tens of children until, two days before my arrival, the Ealdorman had abruptly sent the other children away, lest his son be distracted from his journey into the azbuki. Thus one morning, without any warning, Robbo had found himself alone in an unusually empty and silent garden. And the following day his father, too, had left the palace. No doubt the azbuki signified loneliness to Robbo. But we shared the same passion for animals, and through such passion I had acquired his trust.

Until the incident.

Forty-four days earlier, a most prominent merchant and his escort had reached the palace to present the Ealdorman with gold, frankincense and myrrh procured from very far places. To compensate the merchant for his disappointment upon learning that the recipient of the gifts was away, we had shown him into the wonders of our menagerie – whose reputation had spread throughout the land and far beyond.

Walking through the opening wood, where a sizeable group of coatis followed us with skilful leaps between flimsy tree branches, we made our way to the four half-striped quaggas who, aligned perfectly, keenly grazed on star grass among the varied greens of their enclosure. Fifty steps later, the merchant stared in amazement at two black cranes parading before us, and was enraptured by Robbo's wide knowledge of such rare creatures. Throughout the entire visit, the merchant praised every new breathing marvel he could catch sight of, and more than once expressed his gratitude to the Ealdorman's son for the opportunity he was given to learn about the impressive occupants of the menagerie, also including ocelots, beavers, capuchin monkeys, white peacocks and myriad other creatures.

Elated by the intense flattery, Robbo was as voluble as I had ever seen him, and spared no detail in answering the many questions on how the various creatures fed, grew, reproduced, aged, and eventually died. But, just as Sun was preparing to set, an extemporary request from the merchant marred everything: 'I would be delighted to see the parrots ...'

There were no parrots at the menagerie. Parrots were rare, and difficult to locate. As if in search of support, Robbo looked blankly at me, but I couldn't do anything other than reciprocate his powerless glance. Stunned into silence, wounded by his failure to honour the merchant's wish, Robbo, to the surprise of everyone, ran away. His own seclusion inside the toy room began that day.

Finding parrots for the menagerie wouldn't be easy; but the merchant, moved to pity, tried to help, and recalled seeing two of them with turquoise feathers in the dining room of a lodge situated four mountains away from the palace. I had to go there, and bring the parrots to the palace, so that Robbo, and his soul, would return to us.

I gave Lela enough assignments for the azbuki to work on during my absence and left in the morning. After five days of travel on my donkey, and with my favourite leopard in tow to keep me company, I finally reached the lodge. I looked around the dining room, but no parrots were to be seen. It had been at least two thousand days since the merchant had last seen them there, he had warned me, so I wasn't surprised.

'Are you staying the night?' the innkeeper, seeing me at the door, enquired.

I nodded, taking a seat at one of the five empty tables.

There was absolutely no movement around.

'What do you want to eat?' he asked, curtly.

'What do you recommend?' I asked.

'We only have tumbleweed soup.'

'Can I have some tumbleweed soup?'

'Yes.'

He brought me the tumbleweed soup. I was hungry, and finished it immediately.

I waited for quite some time before he took the empty bowl away. That's when I asked him: 'Am I the only guest tonight?'

'You've been the only guest for forty-five days in a row,' he replied, and upon dropping the bowl somewhere in the kitchen, he asked from a distance: 'Where are you from?'

'The palace.'

'Ah!' he exclaimed, slowly pacing back to the dining room, while passing his hands over his worn apron. 'Sometime ago, a convoy with the Ealdorman stayed here for the night. They took all the rooms.'

It had to be when the Ealdorman had left the palace for his journey.

'Really? Have you met the Ealdorman in person?'

'No ... he slept inside a closed carriage. A huge carriage with four horses. I tried to sneak a look inside from here, but couldn't see a damned thing,' the innkeeper said, pointing to the nearby window and glancing at me, his eyes widened with an unexpected spark of excitement. 'The Ealdorman never came out, nor even approached the windows. His cook asked to use our kitchen, and brought in cereal grains, dried peas, beans and lentils to prepare a sumptuous meal for the Ealdorman. Under the condition that I wouldn't tell anyone, he even allowed me to try the dish, and trust me, I couldn't believe what I was tasting: damned good!'

It was getting late, and I thus moved on to the reason for my being there. 'I've met a merchant, who says you keep two parrots here. I don't see them, though.'

The innkeeper put his hands on his waist, shaking his head. 'I don't know what you're talking about.'

'Sure? He says they had turquoise feathers, and stood in a cage.'

The innkeeper rolled his eyes, and kept shaking his head, until his eyes suddenly sharpened. 'Ah! Yes,' he exclaimed, kind of amused. 'I even asked that Congoid if he wanted me to cook the birds, but he refused. Shame: it would've been quite a stew!'

'A Congoid?'

'Yes. From some village. He stayed here one night, then went away with the birds.'

'You wouldn't know where to find this Congoid?'

'No … I never move from here …'

At that moment, the door of the lodge opened, and the innkeeper, rather surprised, went away to check. After some whispering from the adjacent room, I heard him raise his voice: 'Two guests in one night! I can't believe it …'

The innkeeper came back with the second guest.

I had seen him somewhere before.

Yes: the tumbleweed dealer that Thatem had treated so dismissively at the marketplace. I tensed at the unlikely possibility that he might recognise me.

The tumbleweed dealer bowed, and I reciprocated, though looking away as quickly as felt polite. 'I will seat you together, if you don't mind,' said the innkeeper, without actually leaving much room for objections. 'It'll be easier for me.'

So, the tumbleweed dealer took a seat right in front of me.

He looked keen to talk. 'You must come from the palace,' he said, staring pointedly at my clothing. 'I come from the marketplace right behind the mountain,' he continued after my nodding. 'Quite a journey. I'm starving.'

'What do you want to eat?' the innkeeper asked, interrupting.

'What do you suggest?'

'We only have tumbleweed soup today.'

'Can I have some tumbleweed soup, then?'

'Yes.'

The soup arrived in no time. The dealer brought the bowl to his mouth, and as he drank the soup, glanced at me intermittently. 'Do we know each other, perhaps?'

'I don't think so,' I replied, looking up as little as possible. 'But I have three twin brothers.'

'What do they do?' he asked, trying to place where he had seen my face before.

'Everything.'

The dealer frowned at my answer, then looked around with an even dumber stare than at the marketplace.

'Are the donkey and the leopard outside yours?'

'Yes.'

'I have some tumbleweed for the donkey. It's not expensive.'

The innkeeper, who had not moved from his position by the other end of the poky room, interrupted: 'Are you trying to say that … you feed donkeys the same tumbleweed you give to me?'

The dealer winced, but found a way out: 'No, it's processed differently.'

After gazing at the dealer suspiciously, the innkeeper told me: 'He may well know where the Congoids live.'

'Do you?' I asked the dealer.

'Yes ... I've been doing some trade with them ...'

'Would you be able to tell me the direction, please?'

'Of course. I'm heading not too far away from the village. We can leave together early in the morning, and when it's time I'll tell you the shortest path to get there, right?'

I agreed, and the following dawn, after he had paid for his soup and stay with a bag of tumbleweed, the two of us left the lodge.

We descended the mountain – my feline following us at a distance, looking around for traces of springbok or impala.

'Does the leopard have a name?' the dealer, who rode a cart pulled by a donkey, asked.

'Onofria.'

After a quick ponder, he put forward an offer: 'Fifty bags full of tumbleweed for Onofria!'

'I don't wish to insult you ...' I said, after feigning giving serious thought to his proposal, 'but we eat much better at the palace ...'

The dealer laughed loud.

The vegetation was still thick around the stony descent that was rapidly bringing us to the expanse of sand and occasional shrubs of the plain, and I kept looking down in search of plants or grasses that were unavailable in the palace's garden. When I spotted, at roughly ten steps from us, a white shape barely visible among two large clusters of lemongrass, I got down to see, treading carefully on the green, mindful not to crush any hidden flower or harm any insect beneath. Hiding behind the lemongrass was a ghost orchid – meaning that, regardless of whether or not I would later find the parrots, my journey had already been fruitful. I took the small vase that was always in my rucksack (just in case I made some worthy discovery) and slowly transplanted the extremely rare flower into it. I was confident that, with proper care, the ghost orchid might survive in the palace's garden.

'Have you ever thought of diversifying your trade?' I asked the dealer, when back on my donkey, slightly annoyed by the fact that he had looked bored throughout my entire work with the ghost orchid.

'I'm good with tumbleweed,' he replied simply, before adding: 'Never leave an old road for a new one.'

I was really the wrong man to say this to.

'What are you looking for in the village?' he then asked, as we resumed our journey.

'Parrots. Apparently, they have two with turquoise feathers.'

'Oh! Parrots …' he commented with pensive enthusiasm. 'I may offer up to twenty tumbleweed bags for one of them!'

'I hope we don't have to start a bidding war,' I said.

The dealer laughed again.

We stood silent for some time, and with the only sound now being that of the trader's cartwheel rolling on the stones, my thoughts went to the Ealdorman, and to the fear that I might be missing his return to the palace. 'By any chance, have you come across the Ealdorman's convoy during your travels?' I asked.

The dealer shook his head.

'There!' he said right after, pointing towards a smaller road to our right. 'I'm headed straight, but that's the way to the village of the Congoids.'

And, so, after promising the dealer that I would persuade the palace to start buying from him the tumbleweed needed for our forty-two donkeys, I left the old road for a new one. Alone, once again.

The path had meanwhile levelled out, and the surroundings had grown parched, reminding me of the time I spent at Thatem's house. It was getting dark when I saw a wide group of tents on the flat horizon. The land was so lifeless there that I wondered where the villagers might find water, or something to feed themselves with, in that desert. I rode closer, and saw two young Congoids keeping watch right in front of the first tent. Onofria snarled. She had never seen men with dark skin.

'Let me deal with them,' I reassured her, and the snarling promptly subsided.

The suspicion had to be mutual, because the two guards, unnerved by Onofria's presence, raised their sticks to warn us. I stopped twenty steps from them. The dealer had recommended I should ask to speak directly with the village chief.

'I'm here to trade with your chief!' I shouted without preambles.

At hearing my voice, other villagers exited their tents.

'Is that creature dangerous?' one man asked, raising his voice, but not excessively, for he clearly didn't want to upset Onofria.

'Only when she's provoked,' I replied. 'Or if you're an impala in disguise.'

The man chuckled lightly, and gestured to the guards to let me in.

So, I walked into the village, under the attentive though not minacious eyes of ten Congoids. Onofria followed me closely, sniffing left and right at the tents as she passed.

The man who had let us come in was leading the way. We reached a much larger tent than the others in the middle of the village. Next to it was a narrow, circular enclosure made of stones, topped with a crossbar from which a bucket hung.

'Our chief lives here,' the man indicated, and he nodded when I asked his permission to walk inside.

The donkey remained outside, but I took Onofria inside with me.

Moderately lit by a lamp on the floor, the little interior of the tent would have perfectly suited Mozart. But, instead of him, at the centre of the tent was the burly chief of the Congoids, cross-legged on a circular carpet, wearing an azure kaftan and a short round cap in the same colour.

'So, you want to trade with me,' he said in a firm, heavy voice.

I spotted them almost immediately: the parrots, gently pecking each other inside a cage suspended behind the chief, and unaware of my aim to take them away.

The chief glanced at Onofria, yet remained unfazed, as if his role prohibited him from showing fear.

Thatem had explained to me, at the marketplace, that if you were interested in an item, you must nonetheless show indifference, so that the trader didn't know which item you were going for. But the problem was that nothing other than the parrots was visible in the tent.

'Yes, I'm interested in them,' I said, after taking a bow.

The chief shook his head.

'It's impossible, I am loath to say.'

'Why?' I asked.

'I am too fond of these parrots. And they complement my kaftan perfectly.'

There was another rule Thatem had shared with me: flatter the other trader.

'Indeed,' I remarked, giving another bow. 'The details of your clothing are exquisite. Where did you find such a master-piece of tailoring?'

'A dealer,' the chief answered. 'He used to source the finest kaftans for us. But now he only deals in tumbleweed. Easier to transport and no problems with the sizes, he says.'

'I think I know this particular dealer.'

Despite his apparently unbending opposition to parting ways with the parrots, the chief remained silent, looking at both of Onofria and me, as if he wished not to cease the conversation. I wanted to take advantage of his disposition.

'I come from the palace,' I said. 'We have four marvellous Cochins in our menagerie. Very fluffy, very cuddly. One of them has dark blue feathers that shift in colour throughout the day, changing with the light: this particular Cochin would pair very well with your elegant kaftan. A Cochin in exchange for your parrots?'

The chief shook his head again.

'Why not?'

'I wouldn't trade two animals for one. And if I were to take the Cochin, she would stay with me inside this tent, day and night; so her feathers wouldn't really have the opportunity to change colour.'

I couldn't argue with his logic.

I was thinking about which other creature I might offer for the parrots, but the chief was one step ahead of me.

'I may be interested in her, though,' he said, pointing at Onofria.

Robbo will kill me if I come back without Onofria, I thought. I had to divert the chief's attention from her.

'The leopard hasn't been well for quite some time. We may well have to take her down, once back at the palace – I regret to say.'

Onofria growled.

'She seems fine to me,' the chief commented.

'A sparrowhawk? She will glide marvellously among the tents of your village before landing softly in yours.'

The chief shook his head.

'A red-eared slider? She's not noisy, doesn't eat much, and you can play toss the turtle with the other villagers!'

The chief shook his head.

But, after a negotiation that lasted until Moon was already dominating the sky, we finally agreed that I would get the parrots in exchange for one Cochin, two sparrowhawks, and three red-eared sliders, plus my strict guarantee to visit him with Onofria, if she recovered well, at least every two hundred days.

The delivery terms were another issue. The chief insisted I should go to the palace with three of his men to retrieve the Cochin, the sparrowhawks, and the red-eared sliders, and only after that would they give me the parrots. But I couldn't imagine presenting myself at the palace with three Congoids: I didn't know how the guards would react (perhaps even worse than the idlers). It was too dangerous. I also struggled to find an explanation that didn't risk insulting the chief.

Had she not spoken in that exact moment, I may have failed to find a way out of that tricky situation.

'He's an honest man. I can vouch for him.'

I turned.

Daffodil.

She was wearing a gorgeous cobalt blue dress, and a likewise impressive basket hat embroidered with sophisticated golden squiggles. I didn't know when she had entered the tent, but I was elated to see her.

The chief was evidently surprised that Daffodil knew me, but without asking anything in that regard, he simply made the lightest of comments: 'If my chiefess tells me to trust you, then I will trust you.'

Daffodil reached us at the centre of the tent.

'You may bow and kiss her hand,' the chief ordered.

I did so, though it felt a bit awkward.

It is of great regret, but Daffodil and I couldn't properly speak when the three of us broke bread together to celebrate the agreed deal, and I've never seen her again. Nonetheless, I was relieved to see how content she appeared to be, and to my utmost pride, the chief even referred to her as … Daffodil.

A villager brought in food, but when he lifted the lid of the pan and Daffodil saw what was inside, she recoiled, saying: 'I don't think this dish will be suitable for our distinguished guest!'

The chief's eyes widened in affronted surprise. 'But stir-fried scarabs are a rare delicacy!'

I tensed up, and my horrified stare betrayed my shock.

'I believe that the rules of the Schola of … don't allow preceptors to partake of scarabs,' Daffodil intervened. 'Not even to watch others eating them. True, Master?'

I nodded, unable to speak for the protracted shock.

'But I've been waiting seven days for the scarabs,' the chief complained, before eventually giving in; and, to my relief, the stir-fried scarabs were soon replaced with a bowl of very tasty stink bugs. But when the villager offered me some water, I, remembering my initial misadventure with water at Thatem's house, braced myself. Accustomed for quite some time to the clear running water at the palace, I feared it might happen again. Daffodil came to the rescue once more: 'Our water is taken from the deep well that you saw next to this tent, and is very pure. You can drink it with no fear, Master.'

That night I indeed slept peacefully in the guest tent, and, at dawn I left with the parrots, who had spent their last night with the chief and chiefess.

I held the cage with my right hand while riding the donkey, and noticed that Onofria was eyeing up the parrots as if they were destined to be her next meal. Fortunately, Onofria's attention was soon diverted by some fresh marks to the right of our path. She sniffed them, looked over the edge of the road, and emitted a frustrated growl in admission of the fact that the creator of the marks was by now out of reach.

I thought about what awaited me at the palace. Robbo would be ecstatic about the parrots, and the renewed enthusiasm would make him work again on the azbuki, I hoped, thus soothing any sort of discontentment the Maid might have with the barter I had accepted – not exactly a fair one for the palace.

I estimated another six hundred days were needed before the level of the twins' azbuki reached mine (actually, five hundred for Lela, who was ahead of her brother); then, my mission should be deemed complete, and I could leave the palace to go back to Thatem at the house. He was the only one who could help me get back into the corridors to find Flox.

The journey back to the palace continued undisturbed until we reached the gorge where Bela had lost his life. Haunted by those dreadful moments, the steep edges of the road seemed even more intimidating to me than during the first journey, and my eyes darted nervously around for signs of the bandits. I didn't have to wait long before seeing four shapes coming down from the left flank, and four from the opposite side, no more than three hundred steps from us.

The bandits would never let me keep the parrots, I was sure, and would probably take my life, too. But I kept moving through the gorge. I think the bandits to our left – in line, one behind the other – had arrived at no more than one hundred steps from us when I resolved to deploy my only available weapon.

'Onofria, it's your turn,' I whispered.

Onofria began snarling.

The bandits stilled.

Then, she sprinted up the left flank of the gorge, reaching in no time the closest bandit and, before he could wield the curved knife in his hand, seized his right leg between her teeth. I have never forgotten the bandit's shrieks of pain as he fell to the ground. But Onofria, instead of biting again, just withdrew. The other bandits behind him were already on the run. And when I looked at the opposite flank of the gorge, not one man remained.

XVI

BURNING MIRRORS

In the preceding three hundred and twenty days of my stay at the palace, I had believed that, unlike in the corridors or on the plain, violence would never have a place there. But the act of retribution I witnessed that cloudless morning completely changed my perspective.

'Master Ghiorghio, could you join me?' the Maid of the Bedchamber asked with a mannered firmness.

I was in the middle of a lesson with the twins, and her interruption was so unexpected that, much like everyone who's acting in disguise and sees threats to his imposture lurking everywhere, I interpreted the Maid's call as a sign that she had found out. I left a quick assignment for the children, gave them one of those glances that suggested it might well be my last, and followed the Maid through the corridor, walking two paces behind her, as Ghiorghio's hornbooks prescribed.

'The twins mustn't see what's about to happen,' she said, without turning. 'It would upset them immensely.'

I didn't know what to make of her words, but they sounded rather ominous in my state of mind of that moment. We reached an open courtyard behind the palace. It was a large expanse of gravel, the only area around the palace devoid of vegetation or animals, and was normally left vacant. I had been there just once, not long after my arrival, for a full day of celebration of Sun: on that occasion, the entire palace had been feasting, chanting, playing, swimming in stone pools – exactly as Thatem had once described – and a joyful atmosphere, very much unlike the sobriety that normally imbued the palace, had taken hold of all the celebrants, me included.

It was different, this time. When the Maid and I walked out into the court, all the servants and the guards, lining the walls in multiple rows, were waiting for us in silence. At the centre of the courtyard was a cabin made of wood and coated with black tar, still fresh on the surface.

They all stared at us, and I naturally believed I had been summoned to be chastised for my betrayal in front of everyone. Then, the Maid, who had positioned herself at the front of one of the rows – and I beside her – spoke: 'Bring him forward.'

Three guards led a young man to the centre of the courtyard. He walked slowly, yet without offering any resistance. The crowd buzzed, but not at length. I recognised him, though only after taking a prolonged look: the younger of the two visitors to Thatem's yurt at the marketplace, whose father had teased me, saying that I didn't look much more than a child.

'Last night, this servant was caught trying to sneak out of the palace,' the Maid announced. 'The guards stopped him while he was climbing one of the walls with a rope.'

The crowd murmured, and I noticed expressions of disapproval on many faces, the servants included. 'He deserves a proper punishment,' the Maid continued, and the onlookers hummed in approval. The servant, whose arms were held tight behind his back by the guards, was now shaking and sweating, and staring at the Maid with hatred.

I was relieved that the gathering hadn't been called to behold my punishment; but still, I feared that if the servant knew about my mission, he might betray me to improve his own fate. But even if he had wanted to there was no time, because the guards bound his arms and locked him inside the black cabin, from where he began yelling something I couldn't quite make out.

'The mirrors!' the Maid, who had never raised her voice before in my presence, exclaimed.

From a nearby storeroom, one after the other, the guards pushed twelve circular mirrors into the courtyard, encased in wheeled copper surrounds. A fine expression of metalworking, the mirrors were positioned in a concave line before the black cabin. The people standing by the cabin moved away, placing themselves behind the mirrors.

I glanced at the Maid, who seemed indifferent to the screams of anguish and rage coming from the black cabin. I still didn't know what they would do to the servant, and the uncertainty over his punishment reminded me of those moments of vexation inside the shelter when the bailiffs had argued endlessly over Father's destiny.

From behind the Maid there appeared the shape of the palace's astronomer, walking hastily in our direction, carrying a large case in both hands whose weight caused him to stagger a bit. After apologising profusely to the Maid for his lateness, he opened the case to retrieve a sextant.

Crouching on the floor, the astronomer looked into the sextant's lens, apparently using the flat roof of a warehouse to one side of the courtyard as a reference point to measure the angle of sunlight. It was a cloudless late morning. Under the crowd's unyielding scrutiny, and beset by the incessant screams of the imprisoned servant, the astronomer, bobbing nervously, kept tweaking the direction of his sextant with trembling hands. He turned to the Maid four times, always shaking his head. Though she didn't speak, I could feel her impatience. When the astronomer finally nodded, the crowd sighed in anticipation. For her part, the Maid signalled the guards, and they began to adjust the angle of the twelve mirrors until the sun's rays hit the exact centre of each reflective surface.

Only moments passed before narrow threads of smoke were wafting over the black cabin, which was being seared by the sunlight that the mirrors were projecting on to its surface. I gazed at the scene with admiration, just like everyone else, until the smoke was abruptly replaced by small quivering flames, and my attention was thus switched to the ill-fated servant. I clearly remember the moment when he realised what was happening, and his shouting spiked in strength and frequency, swiftly turning into a continuous howl. I looked around at my fellow onlookers, and despite what the servant may have done, they appeared ill at ease in beholding the man's torture. Only the Maid showed no reaction, perhaps even enjoying the gruesome process.

Soon, the cabin was engulfed in steep flames, spreading a tangible heat throughout the entire courtyard, and the servant's screams subsided. I was still staring at the blaze, unable to take in the full gravity of the event, when the Maid gestured for me to follow her back into the palace.

We walked many steps in silence through the corridor. 'I don't understand,' she said with an air of detachment, glancing at the white ceiling as if to emphasise her lack of comprehension for the servants. 'Preferring the heat, drought and famine of the plain to the plentiful food, crystalline water and astonishing beauties of our palace ...'

'Does it happen often?'

'It happened just before your arrival. We caught one servant boring a hole in an outer wall. He, too, was punished the following day.' There was a brief pause before the Maid continued. 'Another servant tried to escape last night. But he avoided the guards, and is still inside the palace.'

She turned to me. 'You're often at the menagerie at night-time, they say. I wonder if you were there last night, and saw anything unusual, Master Ghiorghio?'

I didn't know whether her question had some other intention, but the night before I had been reading in the library, and retired to my room quite early, and this is what I told the Maid.

Clad, without exception, in a white gown and a white corset, the Maid spoke only if strictly required, and her tight smiles, even rarer than her voice, were directed at the twins alone. I had initially believed that the Maid's sole responsibility was to care for the children, but it soon came to my attention that she also oversaw the kitchen's activities, made decisions about the menagerie, dealt with traders, organised the celebrations of Sun, welcomed the most prominent guests, and, in essence, ran the palace while the Ealdorman was away.

She treated the servants with harshness, even those who didn't dare try to escape. I once saw her scolding a young girl, bringing a basket full of apples to the kitchen, simply because she had slowed her pace to contemplate a blooming magnolia tree; and I also witnessed her ousting an aged gardener from the palace for having simply picked an overripe strawberry for himself.

The Maid acted with a cold politeness towards me, and on those rare occasions where, perhaps letting my guard down too much, I tried to establish a conversation, she did not show the least intention of opening herself up. The circumstances of my arrival at the palace hadn't helped: she first saw me in dismal conditions – ragged, dirty, exhausted, hungered, thirsty – after a four-day solitary trek up the mountain. An occasion in which, despite the safe conduct taken from the real Ghiorghip's robe, I still don't understand how I succeeded in persuading the guards to let me in.

Lela, the twin daughter, likewise sensed the Maid's inaccessibility, and asked me those questions she didn't dare ask her. Lela's curiosity towards life, and her unconditional trust in my knowledge, made this sensitive girl all the more endearing to me.

'What is it like outside?' she once asked.

Lela had never left the palace, and it was unlikely she ever would. Aside from the Ealdorman, in fact, those born at the palace could not step beyond its gates. Hence, unless she became Ealdorwoman – an event that could only happen if her brother, the heir apparent, passed away before her without leaving any offspring – Lela would never see the outside.

I told her about the plain, where people could only tolerate the open air during very restricted parts of the day, and everybody endured tasteless food and toxic water. I also mentioned the bandits, and many other threats, some of which I invented, repeating over and over that her curiosity towards the outside made little or no sense, because she was definitely better off at the palace.

Much like those existing within the walls, Lela had been deprived of the power to choose where to live, although the former lived in what Thatem would call *hell*, while she was born in *heaven*, and the contrast was considerable. But regardless of how I tried to diminish the world outside the palace, she kept asking me about it, a bit like when I had pestered Piko with questions on scarabs. So, I decided that if her desire to see the plain didn't wane, I would consider taking her with me when I left the palace.

Only a handful of children lived at the palace, after the Ealdorman sent most of them away so as not to disturb the twins' learning of the azbuki. One was the carpenter's daughter, with whom Lela had bonded immensely, and so she often asked me to accompany her to the workshop to see her friend.

I had first met with the carpenter when, returning from a visit to the enclosure with the ostriches, I saw him replacing a group of planks in one of the barns along my path.

'Can I help you?' I asked.

He turned to me in surprise. 'I would never ask a Master to help me with such a humble job.'

'I'm offering my help. You have not asked for it.'

He smiled at my logic.

So, I helped him, holding the planks steady as he nailed them, and we immediately got along. I enjoyed that occasional work outside, as an alternative to my endless days in the library. For this reason, I was happy whenever I accompanied Lela to the workshop. The children played near the entrance, while I stayed inside, observing the carpenter at work and checking on them intermittently.

The carpenter seldom paused his work when I was there, but didn't seem displeased at my presence. He had numerous responsibilities around the palace – mending a fence whenever an animal went wild, fixing the windows shattered by the occasional rainstorm that hit the summit of the mountain, fixing a pipe when a faucet ran dry, and other tasks that reminded me of Father going back and forth around the perimeter as a keeper.

I had tried to talk with others at the palace – the gardener, the guard commander, the saucier, the head groom – but they had all quickly withdrawn from conversation. I wondered if they had decided they shouldn't talk to a Master on account of his higher station, or whether the palace discouraged them from engaging in unnecessary communication. The carpenter had reacted differently, though, showing a willingness to talk.

He hadn't been born there, and had first arrived at the palace around three thousand and six hundred days before, as part of a convoy of ten carriages accompanying the Malgrave of Draudes in his visit to the Ealdorman. The carpenter had dealt with maintaining the coaches, clearing any obstructed paths, gathering food for the convoy, and other tasks essential for the continuation of the Malgrave's journey.

The first night, while the Malgrave and his retinue were welcomed at the Ealdorman's table for a sumptuous meal, the carpenter and the other members of the convoy remained downstairs, inside the carriages positioned just past the main gate. Late in the night, though, when the carpenter was asleep, one of the Malgrave's attendants woke him up in haste.

'The Malgrave needs you upstairs,' the attendant said.

The befuddled carpenter put his clothes on, rushed up the stairs, and walked into the dining room, very intimidated by the attentive stare of the entire table and of the five servants encircling it. Not only was the carpenter unsure of what they might ask of him, but he had never been addressed directly by the Malgrave before. He didn't know the protocol and, when he drew too close to the table, the attendant gently tugged at his arm to halt him.

From the furthest part of the table, the Malgrave spoke: 'Are you the builder of our coaches?'

The carpenter nodded, confused.

'I've decided to present the venerable Ealdorman, who is hosting us so generously, with the greatest coach your skilled hands may ever craft,' the Malgrave continued. 'We've agreed that you will remain here at the palace as long as necessary to build a coach that will be unrivalled. It shall be endowed with unique elegance, and possess the solidity and strength to withstand thousands of journeys up the windy, steep road that leads to the palace.'

The carpenter kept nodding to the floor, mesmerised by the enormity of the unexpected task imposed upon him, and ran downstairs as soon as the Malgrave curtly dismissed him. He didn't get any sleep that night, he told me.

The day after, the Malgrave and his convoy left the palace – but, as instructed, the carpenter remained.

It took two hundred days of hard work and precision to produce a coach that, according to the carpenter's own account, surpassed in beauty and sturdiness any vehicle he had ever crafted. It was thirty steps long, and covered by a roof of embroidered fabric infused with gold thread, which the palace's tailor had prepared upon his instructions. To build the body and wheels, he had used the resistant yet light wood of the tallest balsa tree in the garden, which he himself had (regretfully) felled, cut and whittled, while the palace's chemist had helped him to compose a most resistant varnish to protect the coach from heat, wind and rain.

The Ealdorman met the delivery of the wonderful coach with such astonishment and enthusiasm that he never asked its maker to leave the palace; and, in light of the subsequent failure of the Malgrave to enquire about the carpenter, the palace regarded him as part of the gift to the Ealdorman.

In the same period, and with the essential help of one of the kitchen aides, the carpenter also produced a daughter. To his eternal dismay, however, the mother was taken away by the hard labour of the kitchen when the girl was still a toddler. So, he raised the daughter on his own, though she was always enveloped in the care and affection of the entire palace, and the girl was never deprived of anything.

When the Ealdorman banished most of the children from the palace, the carpenter pleaded with him to let the girl stay; or else he, too, would have to leave. His plea was accepted, and the palace retained the greatest carpenter in the land.

I asked him to tell me more about the Ealdorman, and the carpenter said that he used to stay in his apartments most of the time; yet whenever he took one of his walks in the garden, the Ealdorman never failed to walk into the workshop. He wouldn't speak, but instead just look at the carpenter handling his tools, exactly like I did – though not for the same generous length of time. For his journey, the Ealdorman had taken the coach made by the carpenter and, given the length of the trip, the latter anticipated it would require significant repairs upon its return.

I once asked him who the twins' mother was, but he couldn't say. And when I – perhaps too influenced by Bebro's boundless imagination – suggested that it might be the Maid who had given them life, the carpenter shut down, rather abruptly, what he deemed was an inappropriate conversation. After this unfortunate episode, he acted coldly towards me for many days, and I thus learned that from then onwards I should avoid expressing my curiosity in front of him.

He probably hadn't liked my insinuation because he, in the first place, wasn't entirely transparent about his past.

When I looked at him at the workshop, I indeed couldn't help but notice how he organised his work and handled the tools very much like Thatem. Like him, for instance, he hammered each nail thrice: the first tap barely hard enough to dent the surface of the wood, while the second and the third blows, coming quickly one after the other after a brief pause, drove the nails firmly into the plank. And, with regard to the tools he used, and how they were positioned on the shelves, his workshop seemed very much a replica of Thatem's.

Moreover, he didn't speak like anyone else at the palace, or on the plain, and his tone carried the subtle strain of someone who wants to hide an accent – something I recognised all too well, since I was doing the same. Moreover, whenever I tried to learn more about his past before his arrival at the palace, he dodged my questions – which in some way was good, because it meant he would never enquire about the Schola of …

And the faint pallor beneath his skin – which I occasionally thought I noticed, much as I saw in my own reflection – was yet another sign that the carpenter might not have come from a distant village as he claimed, but had perhaps made the same long journey through the tunnels as I had. In that case, another question surfaced: if my mission was to teach the twins the azbuki ... what was his?

Yet I held back, and never went anywhere close to making an insinuation about his past. I didn't want to lose the only person I talked to other than the twins. Thatem had once said that the people at the palace knew about the corridors, but it didn't seem so to me. I hadn't found any mention of where I came from inside Ghiorghio's hornbooks, or in the library, and no discourse or action from the Maid or anyone else at the palace had betrayed their knowledge about us.

In any case, after the carpenter had told me that the Ealdorman wore a huge white beard, I had grown mine. I wanted to be liked by the Ealdorman, so that he would allow me to remain at the palace even when my mission was completed, perhaps as a librarian, or even to teach the azbuki to Robbo's children. I would then take a leave and bring Flox to the palace to live with me.

I still thought of Flox often, but whereas I had dreamed of her nearly every night while on the plain, her presence in my dreams had become less frequent as I spent more time at the palace – for the emotions and delights stirred by the marvels of the menagerie and the life in the garden had partially crowded her out. And, though no single detail of my past within the walls had been forgotten, my memory tended not to linger too much on a place that I ultimately associated with the killings of Father and Mother, Piko's rejection of me, the bailiffs' cruelties, and the brutality of the Crier. I had risked death to escape the corridors, and I wouldn't allow my thoughts to take me back there.

XVII

COJO

When I entered the great hall for the last meal of the day, an unexpected visitor was sitting opposite my chair. It wasn't rare for guests to break bread with us, but this time, unusually, the Maid hadn't informed me. I bowed to our guest – as Ghiorghio's hornbooks instructed should be done with anyone I met, apart from the servants. The man, dressed exactly like me, stood up, returned the gesture, and assumed his position once again.

From her seat, the Maid announced: 'We are honoured to share our repast with Master Cojo from the Schola of …'

I almost flinched – yet succeeded in holding it back. With his long face, crooked nose, and sparse hair on his shiny temple, Cojo stared at me. The inner part of my lips trembled, and so did my legs beneath the table.

'Our fellow scholar Master Zoro speaks so highly of you, Master Ghiorghio,' he said solemnly. 'I'm so honoured to make your acquaintance. Finally! In my three hundred and twenty days at the Schola, I heard so many praises sung about you.'

I sighed with relief; at least he had never met the real me.

'I hope your journey was safe, Master Cojo,' I responded cheerily.

'Yes, Master Ghiorghio.'

'Glad to hear it,' I commented, with no change in my expression. 'Regretfully, the journey that brought me here seven hundred and thirty-one days ago wasn't a peaceful one: the bandits attacked me at the base of the mountain, and stole my donkey.'

'My donkey is resting safe in the stable,' Cojo said reassuringly.

Without speaking, the Maid lightly gestured to a servant that he should bring the meal in, and he hastened towards the kitchen.

'Before joining our Schola, I belonged to the Schola of ...' Cojo informed us.

'Both are prominent Scholas, Master Cojo,' the Maid gushed.

'Very true, Maid.' Master Cojo smiled, bowing his head slightly in acceptance of the compliment. 'Though, as you may already be aware, since time immemorial the two Scholas have been engaged in an intense rivalry, combating each other on countless doctrinal matters, and still refuse to acknowledge the other's authority. So, it wasn't easy for me, coming from the Schola of ... to gain acceptance with the Masters of the Schola of ... , despite my show of unconditional loyalty to them since my inception.'

'When did the conflict between the Scholas begin?' the Maid enquired.

'Aah ... the strife goes a long way back ... to their notable founders ... who disagreed first and foremost on the meaning of the *pokoy* ...'

'The founders of the Schola of ... believed the *pokoy* to signify calmness of the human soul, and the inescapable yearning of every man to achieve his own gratification, even at the cost of deceiving others. The founders of our Schola, instead, traced the *pokoy* back to a vision of perennial harmony between creatures, where everyone is aware of the others, and coexistence without prevarication is possible.'

The Master paused, then added: 'Two unreconcilable interpretations, I must admit. And this was only the first of many items of contention between the Scholas. The friction, as I said, remains to this day.'

Noticing my unusual silence, the Maid addressed me: 'What is your perspective on this delicate matter, Master Ghiorgio?'

My previous reading of Ghiorghio's hornbook proved quite opportune, and I put my memory to work by repeating his notes: 'The *pokoy* can only be understood as evidence of a shared intent among all living beings to honour Earth,' I remarked. 'This is the very reason Sun forgave humanity, despite our wrongdoings, and spared us from inevitable ruin. Viewing the *pokoy* as merely tied to individual sensations would be overly reductive.'

Despite Cojo's convinced nods of approval, I felt it wise not to let this dangerous conversation linger, and I moved on to praise the produce of the palace's garden, and told Cojo how the flavours he was about to try would never be forgotten.

Robbo avoided gazing in our direction, and I inferred from the light restlessness of his body that he feared Cojo might be there to take my place. I wondered that myself: and, had that been true, I would certainly have been torn between sadness at leaving the twins, to whom I had become very attached, and joy at the prospect of returning to Flox.

'What brings you here, Master Cojo?' I asked.

'I'm heading to the marketplace,' he answered, pointing with his finger towards the valley just beyond the mountain. 'The Schola has dispatched me to procure ink, scrolls and acetone for the copying of important manuscripts. While on my journey to the marketplace, I deemed it appropriate to pay my respects to the Ealdorman. But, just before you arrived, the Maid informed me – much to my regret, as you can imagine – that the Ealdorman is currently away. Though he is expected to return soon; and we all hope that will be the case.'

And I hope you'll leave even sooner, I thought to myself.

Meanwhile, one servant, avoiding our gazes in accordance with the palace's rules, brought in a crock of pottage.

'You must be starving, Master Cojo,' observed the Maid, as he slobbered like a mongrel over his bowl before the servant had even filled it.

The warm pottage was sublime. Slowly moving the first mouthful around my palate, I easily identified cabbage, carrots, onions, peas, beans, artichoke and leeks within the jumble of bold flavours. Despite having been at the palace for a while, I was still amazed by the variety of food the garden could produce, and the ability of the kitchen to blend it into extraordinarily fragrant dishes. No soil existed where I came from, and out on the plain, even where it did exist, the ground failed to produce much more than dust; at the palace, however, the garden's munificent earth was a continuous source of bright colours, enchanting smells and satisfying tastes.

'You were right, Master Ghiorghio. I've been travelling most of my life, and visited many palaces, but rarely have I tried such an exquisite dish,' Cojo said approvingly. 'I'm sure I will miss these excellent flavours the very moment I leave for the marketplace.'

'You shouldn't go to the marketplace, Master Cojo. The palace has everything you need,' the Maid hastened to propose. 'Our servants will bring the supplies of ink, scrolls and acetone to the Schola. Please accept our offer. The Schola has done so much for us in the past. You don't need to go to the marketplace, nor tire your donkey with an unnecessary burden.'

It was an uncommon display of sympathy from the Maid, who was typically reserved and diffident, and Cojo expressed profuse gratitude in accepting her unsparing offer. Lela, too, appeared to welcome Cojo's presence, and was openly captivated by his manner of speech – all of which stirred up a touch of rivalry in me.

'Do you ever feel lonely on your long journeys?' Lela asked Cojo.

Robbo cast a stern glance towards his sister. He had seen in the question a nod to their father's long absence, and the ensuing melancholy it had caused within them, and clearly was not pleased that his sister was bringing all this up with a stranger.

His chin covered with pottage, Cojo looked at the Maid, as if to seek her approval, then answered: 'I can feel lonely at times, Lela, but the missions the Schola assigns me prevail over my sentiments ...we have to sacrifice ourselves for the higher good ... what's a little loneliness against the duty to work together?'

'Master Cojo must be very tired,' the Maid interrupted. 'We should let him retire to his room.'

Lela lowered her eyes.

I, however, was content to part ways with him.

But Cojo – his eyes assuming a humble softness – intervened: 'Actually, Maid ... I've heard such fabulous stories about the palace's menagerie, and the living wonders it contains, that you would have all my gratitude if I could visit it before Sun sets. Tomorrow I shall leave at dawn.'

'I would have been truly delighted to come with you, Master Cojo, but my duty is now to ensure that the twins are settled for the night. Especially Robbo – he has a habit of sneaking out of bed to go to the toy room,' she said, before glancing at me. 'Master Ghiorghio, would you be so kind as to accompany Master Cojo to the menagerie?'

'I would be honoured, Maid.'

Sun was in decline, and barely anyone was outside. Striding with me through the darkening garden, Cojo wanted to learn more about the palace, but I kept my answers to the bare minimum. I felt troubled, and knew my tension would not leave me until he left the palace.

We swiftly reached the enclosure that hosted the ostriches. Three sat in a group near the far side of the wooden fence, while a fourth ostrich was striding around, twisting her neck, pecking the grass, showing all the suppleness of her stout body.

'The irony of it: of all birds, the largest cannot fly,' Cojo said with a dismissive laugh, his arms resting on the high wooden fence. Now that he was alone with me, he had abandoned the contrivance shown with the Maid and the twins.

'But they can run faster than horses,' I observed, unwilling to accept any demeaning of these admirable creatures. 'That one there, with the black feathers and the dark red beak, once flew over the fence. It took ten days for the servants to catch her, and she gave them quite some kicks. We had to raise the fence.'

Cojo chuckled.

I chuckled, too, but nervously, impatient to see him gone.

We stood there in silence, observing the behaviour of the ostriches, then he spoke. 'Some time ago I visited a marketplace far away, in the middle of the plain. I went through the crowded yurts, but couldn't find what I had been tasked to procure for the Schola: gold, frankincense and myrrh. When I reached the last yurt, and was surveying the merchandise laid out on the ground, I saw an item that shouldn't have been there.'

The dark ostrich headed closer to our side of the enclosure, and stretched her neck out towards us, seemingly interested in what he was saying. 'A copper flask with a griffin,' Cojo continued, still with his back to me. 'I knew that copper flask very well, and all the scratches time and travels had left upon it. That flask belonged to my friend Ghiorghio.'

I stiffened, and quickly looked around to see if someone might have overheard him; but there was nobody about.

'Ghiorghio would never have given away his copper flask, not even under the greatest of threats. I saw him crying once, when he couldn't find it at the Schola,' Cojo continued in a firmer tone, still without turning to me. 'So, I bought the flask, and many other useless items merely to please the trader, before asking him where the flask came from. He said he had acquired it from a man living alone in the middle of the plain, and even gave me very precise directions to find the man.'

Cojo was getting too close to the truth. I clutched the clepsammia in my right pocket, where it had remained since saving my life in the tunnels.

'I travelled as fast as I could to the house on the plain, where I feared Ghiorghio might have been taken,' he said, his eyes still on the ostriches, 'but I found it abandoned, empty, as if nobody had ever been there. So, despite a great sense of foreboding, I came here to see if Ghiorghio had made it to the palace. But I found you in his place …'

I stepped forward, and struck the back of his head twice with the clepsammia.

Cojo briefly clung to the fence, then fell down.

I wanted to hit him again, as Thatem would've done, but I chose to stop, as Bebro would've advised. I was panting, no longer able to discern what I should do for the best.

'I'll take care of him,' a firm voice behind me said.

I turned, and ten feet away was the man Thatem had spoken with at the marketplace, and whose son I had seen being sacrificed with the mirrors.

He wore the clothing of a servant.

Together, we dragged Cojo, still unconscious, to an empty barn roughly one hundred steps away, where we locked him in, our movements calmly observed by the unconcerned ostriches.

'You'll be long gone by the time they discover him,' the man said. 'Had he found out about you?'

'Yes.'

'How?'

'Thatem traded Ghiorghio's copper flask at the marketplace.'

'How foolish …'

I nodded. Reassured by the man's presence, my thoughts were starting to flow again, and with them my awareness of the problems ahead. Thatem was no longer at the house, apparently. I was sure he was fine, but where was he? I needed him to show me the way back to find Flox, I told the man.

'I know the way,' he revealed.

'Really? Will you lead me there?'

'Yes, but first we must find a way to get me out of the palace …'

I pointed at the barn, and winked. He didn't grasp my plan immediately, but then widened his eyes, almost smiling. 'You're as clever as Thatem said; perhaps even more so.'

After agreeing we would meet in that place at dawn, he went inside the barn, but as I was walking away, he came back outside.

'Boz: do you still have the tiny steel box Bela gave you?'

'Yes.'

'Bring it tomorrow.' And he went back into the barn.

The palace was still. I climbed the stairs to my room in solitude. I lay on my canopy bed and, the moment I touched the linen, my hands were instantly reminded how they would never again rest within such a silky embrace. Once outside the palace, I likewise would no longer partake of the garden's generous produce, nor immerse myself in the smells, hues and sounds of the wondrous creatures of the menagerie. No longer would my curiosity be fed by the books of the library, nor would my senses appreciate the copious water springing out of my washroom's faucet. The pleasures of the palace had dulled me, I knew: my body had forgotten what thirst or hunger was and, while on no single occasion had Sun produced anything less than agreeable warmth in the garden, finding food on the plain would become a daily chore again; and the scorching heat of Sun was bound to curtail the time I could enjoy outside.

My fingertips met the surface of the clepsammia: slightly cracked, yet still intact. Had the glass broken against Cojo's head, I would have never forgiven myself for the destruction of the only tool that might help bring Flox outside.

I tried to persuade myself that I should remain at the palace until my mission of building the twins was complete – because, unlike Piko, I didn't want to leave anything incomplete. But I was too aware that, by remaining there, it would only be a matter of time before the Schola found out about my deception and condemned me to the burning mirrors under Lela and Robbo's betrayed eyes. If I disappeared at dawn, however, leaving some message of excuse, nobody would ever know, and the twins would never question my teachings.

Then, the door creaked, and for a moment I believed I had been caught. Before I could make out what was happening in the room, however, her scent reached me. She walked through the dark toward the bed, and after raising one side of the linen, glided in. 'The Ealdorman is near. It'll be the first and last night for us,' the Maid whispered, bewildering me: I had never thought she might like my flesh. Instinctively, I pressed the lips against her neck, realising that, despite my past conviction that we were indifferent to each other, the Maid's unexpected availability had stirred a sudden craving for her. I slowly removed her nightgown. My growing desire relieved any anxiety over my imminent flight from the palace, allowing me to appreciate those moments of pleasure in undisturbed fullness.

When, some time later, the Maid quietly stood up, and the creak of the door confirmed she had gone back to her room, I felt relieved there would be no embarrassed glances between us that day. And it suited my plan, as she would assume I had left the palace because of what we had done together.

While preparing my rucksack, I decided to see the twins one last time. The first servants were walking through the corridors, so I hastened to reach Lela's room. Looking at her in bed, I tried to imagine the pure emotions flowing behind the occasional twitch of her closed eyes. Lela was an innocent soul, unable to conceive malice, and I would miss her curiosity and enthusiasm. I looked for Robbo, too, but he wasn't in his bed. I found him where I was sure he would be – the toy room – but I hid behind the door, observing him working on the palace's miniature. Even though I really wanted to tell him I was going on a mission and couldn't possibly stay there, so that he would perhaps forgive me, I wisely thought better of it.

I walked to the menagerie, where the servant was waiting in Cojo's clothes, next to the donkey. The guards wouldn't question two preceptors leaving the gates of the palace on their donkeys.

'I need to get one for me,' I told him.

He shook his head. 'You don't need a donkey,' he said.

'What?'

'You aren't coming with me today.'

'What?' I said with irritation.

'You first need to complete your mission,' he warned. 'Have you brought the silver box?

I nodded, despite not grasping where our conversation was heading.

'Open it.'

The little box contained three phials.

'Don't touch them with your bare hands,' he warned, a hint of apprehension in his eyes. 'It's poison,' the servant revealed.

I stretched out the arm holding the box, instinctively, so as to distance myself from the poison.

'The Ealdorman. You must give it to him,' the servant instructed. 'This is your mission, the reason why you're here.'

'So ... why ... are there three phials?' I asked.

'You must take the twins' lives, too.'

At that very moment, when it hit me that I wasn't at the palace to teach Lela and Robbo the azbuki, but to kill them, I plunged into despair, and failed to find the strength to utter anything more than: 'Why the twins ... ?'

He looked at me sternly, as though he didn't appreciate my questioning of his clear instructions. 'For twenty generations, one after the other, the Ealdormen have held our people in captivity. We're too scared of the Tenets to find the courage to break free, and are kept in check with the damned trick of the Juice. But Mozart uncovered the enormous lie we live in, and he's fighting it with all his strength. His son Thatem, and me, like you, fled the walls to pursue the same mission.'

'But why the children?' I repeated.

'The dynasty must end!' He raised his voice – at the risk of being overheard. 'Only then will we be able to free our people. I've sacrificed the blood of my blood for our mission, and won't allow you to ruin it. Before your first meal with the Ealdorman, you must dissolve the pills in the water that he and the children will drink. The poison will overtake them, slowly, in their sleep. You'll then leave the palace, and join me at Thatem's house on the plain. From there, I'll take you back to the walls to find your woman. And we'll free our people.'

He took a bulging cloth from his pocket and handed it to me. I unfolded it – a curved knife. What he told me then was even more appalling: 'I need the head of the Ealdorman.'

XVIII

DOPPELLEBEN

I vomited four or five times, alone in my washroom, memories of gaiety and laughter with the twins only reinforcing my pain at the prospect of harming them. I remembered Robbo smugly trying to climb a sycamore in front of us, just to get stuck on the lowermost branch, nearly in tears as he called out for help. And when, during the celebration of Sun, Lela and the carpenter's daughter had sung a hilarious chant with the palace's jester, upon hearing which, even the Maid had been forced to show the trace of a smile. Or the image of Lela suppressing laughs when, during a class, Robbo had confused the ᛪ with the ᛃ – because, even though no matter even indirectly connected to the azbuki should be taken light-heartedly, her reaction had certainly been amusing.

I owed so much to the palace. Nowhere had I felt so respected as in this calm and harmonious place that had allowed me to grow undisturbed into manhood. The library fed my knowledge, and the garden my senses, while the menagerie had finally brought to life the once immovable content of Piko's flint slates. And now, to my disbelief, I was being asked to murder a man I didn't even know, along with his two children, so dear to me; and to put the palace's very existence under threat for apparently no good reason.

I wanted to believe the servant had lied, and that it was only his son's unbearably painful death that had led him to such an insane resolution. But the phials of poison seemed to prove otherwise: Bela – and likely Thatem as well – had known from the start that my true mission wasn't to teach the twins the azbuki. As a strict condition for my escape from the corridors, however, I had promised Mozart I would never question the content of the mission, whatever it might be. And I wanted to free Flox, together with as many idlers as I could, from their truncated lives within the walls. When viewing my situation from this latter perspective, I was no longer sure whether the duty of establishing what should be done or not fell to me. Perhaps I should just accept the instructions received.

A scream came from the garden: 'The Ealdorman!'

My heart pounded even harder. I left the washroom, and peered out of my window. The guard who had shouted was running in crazed circles around the lawn, while dozens of people surged towards the palace gate, where a crowd had already formed. My room wasn't the best position from which to observe, but I could make out in the far distance the bright purple of the Ealdorman's coach inching through the excited crowd. The oblong vehicle had to stop several times, obstructed by the people's excited swaying, before coming to a halt next to the main fountain.

I didn't want to raise suspicion by being the only one not celebrating the Ealdorman's return, so I quickly moved downstairs, the sounds from the garden faintly echoing within the empty palace. When I reached the dining room, I stopped, and took a few hesitant steps beyond its threshold. Nobody was there, and the large table that had hosted Master Cojo's final dinner just the evening before still had to be prepared for the Ealdorman's first meal upon his return – the one where I should kill him. I gently grasped the box with the phials inside my pocket, though I was unsure whether I would really use them.

I wanted to see the Ealdorman's face before he was able to see mine, so that I would feel better prepared when the man I was meant to murder first looked into my eyes. Would I be able to hide my tension and sense of guilt, or would the Ealdorman see right through me, like Piko or Mozart had always done?

But when, not without difficulty, I reached the stationary coach, the Ealdorman had already retired to his rooms. My disappointment at being late soon faded as I studied the astonishing craftmanship of my friend, the carpenter: the long journey had in no way tarnished the coach, whose still-polished surface was adorned with floral motifs so intricate and precisely detailed that one might question whether such masterful carving and chiselling really came from a human hand. No less impressively, the fine golden decorations around the roof had survived the harsh sunlight of the plain, while the wooden spoked wheels, a delicate masterpiece of proportion and grace in form, had proved sufficiently sturdy to survive the uneven slope that ascended to the palace, and the rocky paths encircling the mountain.

The crowd around the coach had already thinned out when I heard the usually taciturn saucier confer with the smith: 'He's still magnificent. And hasn't aged a bit since his departure.'

The smith, nodding to confirm, replied in an ecstatic tone: 'He almost smiled at me. Almost!'

'I believe he will address us all tomorrow,' the saucier added. 'He did so after his last journey.'

The smith, about to respond, was interrupted.

'Shouldn't you be in the kitchen to make your contribution towards a most sumptuous meal?' The voice firmly addressed the saucier.

'Yes, Maid.' The saucier lowered his head, and headed towards the kitchen.

She was behind me, but I hesitated to turn around.

'And you, Master Ghiorghio ... you'll be late to your class ...'

I glanced at her, and she gazed in my direction but failed on purpose to meet my eyes. I went back inside and climbed the stairs to the library, wondering whether I would run into the Ealdorman – and how I might react if I did. Throughout my entire stay at the palace, my frequent thoughts about my future encounter with the Ealdorman had always been filled with curiosity, and with the hope that he would take a liking to me. Now, however, knowing what my mission was, I felt threatened by his arrival.

For once, I was glad that Robbo was in the toy room, and not in the library. But Lela sat at her desk, anticipating reuniting with her father for the last meal of the day, and smiled in a manner I had seldom seen before, her hands fidgeting with excitement, her joyful frame of mind only strengthening my guilt.

I had prepared a class on the Ⴀ, the *tverdo*, a mark that, among many interpretations, signified the importance of placing trust in others. I, the one who was about to breach Lela's trust with a murderous act against her family – or, if I decided to spare their lives, the one who would renege on my agreement with Mozart – was in any case destined to commit a betrayal. I, who had foolishly entertained the dream of living a blissful existence with Flox at the palace, might instead end up devoting my entire life to Mozart's rebellion, hiding or fighting somewhere on the plain, for the guards would surely pursue me. I couldn't see any light in my future.

I spoke to Lela without any genuine thought or spontaneity, all the while obsessing over whether Mozart truly believed in the azbuki, or had merely used it to plant me inside the palace. Lela felt my absence of mind, my failure to be entirely present, but apparently misinterpreted the cause of my restlessness: 'Master Ghiorghio: you, too, are so excited about my father's return – yes?'

I dragged myself to the end of the class, and, no longer trusting my own clarity of mind, retreated to my room to rest. As soon as my head touched the cloth bag atop the bed, I resolved that no one would die that evening. One or two days wouldn't make any difference. The decision calmed me, and I fell into a deep sleep.

In the dream that ensued, which I still remember in every detail – for it was my last as a free man – I was seated with Thatem in his kitchen. Just the two of us. Thatem was whistling one of his soothing melodies when the hall door opened with its familiar creak. He didn't seem to care, and kept on whistling, but I, worried, left the kitchen to investigate.

Lela and Robbo were standing in the hall. Their clothing was torn and soiled – a sight I would never have witnessed at the palace, where the servants gave them new clothes upon the appearance of the tiniest stain. In the back of my mind I knew that Thatem's house was not a place they could possibly be, especially Lela, who wasn't allowed to leave the palace.

I was about to ask why they were there when a second door in the hall – which I didn't remember ever existing – opened.

And through it stepped Bruttho and Flox. It was like being on a Bebro stage, especially given that Flox was masquerading as the boy in *Dead of Night, Life of Men*. Bruttho was wearing his usual worn robe, upon which, however, lay Mozart's necklace with the three scarabs pointing towards Sun.

Once inside, Flox pulled from her pocket the curved knife that had once belonged to her father and, with a glare in her eyes that was so unlike any remaining image I had of her, took a few menacing steps towards Lela. 'You have everything. I have nothing,' Flox said, almost pinning her against the wall. 'I've lost my father. You'll soon meet yours again. I had to give my body and soul away to survive, while you're still a spoilt child playing silly games …'

Lela looked at her, frightened but also slightly bewildered, for she had no comprehension of what Flox was referring to. No one could possibly imagine, in fact, what occurred within the walls, unless they had seen it first-hand – least of all a girl who had never set foot outside of the palace. Flox appeared to disagree with that line in the Bible according to which children should never be put to death because of their fathers: 'It's your father who keeps us imprisoned!' she yelled, drawing even closer and pointing the knife at Lela's throat.

Seeing his sister in peril, Robbo rushed to the adjoining workshop, whose door had been left ajar, and came back in a matter of seconds holding an adze. Positioning himself between the two, and waving the adze in the air, he succeeded in making Flox retreat. But when Bruttho finally intervened, Robbo was no match for the much bigger kid bred in the corridors of Breathitt, and Bruttho easily snatched the adze from him, throwing it on the floor. Disarmed, Robbo was left unconscious by Bruttho's punches in no time.

I wished Daffodil was there. She would easily have ejected them from the house without anyone getting hurt. I, on the other hand, stood still, because, despite my will to protect the twins, I couldn't bring myself to attack Flox, even though she only vaguely reminded me of the quiet, pensive girl whose misfortune had once moved me to sympathy – and soon after, to love. I couldn't tell whether her transformation was due to the presence of Bruttho, who was casting conspiring, possessive glances at her, or it was just the dream that was making her behave differently.

Thatem's whistling had grown closer, and when I turned, he was standing at the kitchen threshold, casually leaning against the doorframe. He looked entertained, and not the least concerned, by the ongoing fight in the hall. He then gave me a mischievous glance, and whispered flippantly: 'Your past is killing your present, Boz. And be warned: a man without past or present has no future ...'

Back then I couldn't grasp what Thatem meant, and even now, after all the time I have invested in pondering over his warning, its true sense still eludes me. In the end, Flox didn't commit Lela's murder; and not due to any action taken by someone in the room, but because of Sun's intervention.

Flox was again drawing close to Lela, the knife still in her grip, when the outer light that illuminated the hall suddenly intensified. There was no distinct sound or vibration, and the temperature didn't change, as I recall, but the soft brightness in the room rapidly became an ever-increasing glow. I remember a puzzled Bruttho turning towards the doors to see what was going on, and Lela glancing at me, scared, but very soon the white light around us became so blinding that we all screamed.

Then I was out of the dream, lying on my back with my eyes shut, still lingering in the dream's after-image, when a slight restriction in the movement of my body prompted my eyes to open.

The Crier!

There was no mistake, this time. It was him, towering over my bed with his giant physique and piercing eyes, though his beard was now white, and not purple. There was likewise no trace of purple in his green embroidered kaftan, and he clutched a long iron rod in his right hand.

'I'm known as the Ealdorman, here,' he said.

Such was my astonishment in seeing the Crier at the palace that I began to question whether my dream had truly ended, and even now, after thousands of days, I still wonder which events fall within the boundaries of my dream and which do not.

The Maid of the Bedchamber stood behind him, gazing at me impassively.

'These were meant for us?!' The Crier held up the three phials in one hand.

They had found out; denying would have been useless. I lay silent.

'You're the son of that thief, right?'

Though fear and impotence weighed on me, his renewed insult of Father ignited the last spark of anger I had left in me: 'If you had given Mother enough calciferol, Father wouldn't have broken the Tenets!'

Very few found the courage to speak to the Crier, and even fewer in that manner. Staring at me with his sharp eyes, he hurled the box with the phials to the floor. 'The Tenets must be followed, not resisted!' he yelled, getting closer, but when he lifted the iron rod to hit me, the Maid intervened, placing her hand on his shoulder to halt yet another act of brutality from him.

As soon as the threat of violence had receded, she addressed me: 'You don't understand. Life in the inside can continue only if you all behave the same, and no one tries to take more than the others. Because the greed of those who crave more, like your father, imperils the delicate harmony of the inside.'

She paused and, in contrast with the silence of the room, I heard the sound of the carts moving on the gravelled paths of the garden, ahead of the celebration for the Ealdorman's long-awaited return to the palace.

'And if we hadn't punished your genitors as they deserved for stealing the nutrients,' she continued, 'others would have followed the same path. Even without sunlight, bad habits take root very easily in the inside.'

Trying to persuade them of Father and Mother's innocence was pointless, I realised, but still I believed the punishment inflicted had been brutal and excessive beyond belief, and to prove it, I recited the Tenet used by one of the bailiffs inside the shelter: 'If the right hand has stolen, cut it off and throw it away.'

'Lax sanctions will never discipline the inside,' the Maid responded, dismissively. 'And your actions, Ghiorghio – or whatever your name is – prove it: despite your genitors being condemned to death, you still chose to leave and sought to kill my brother and his children. You haven't learnt from their mistakes.'

'I never meant to harm you or the twins!' I shouted, turning my gaze to the Crier. 'I gave all of myself to guide them through the azbuki, and to help build their souls, and if you put them to the test, their abilities will shine, especially

Lela's. And, yes, I left the corridors, responding to my desire to see the joys of nature – once a gift to all humankind, but now denied to most. This is the reason why, every time I savour the produce of your garden or stand in awe before the creatures of the menagerie, I wonder why only a few men can enjoy what Sun still bestows upon Earth with such generosity.'

I was deliberately provoking them, aware that my journey was nearing an end, and thus no longer fearing their reaction – not even the Crier's brutality.

'You don't understand,' the Maid answered with disappointment. 'Unless restricted, humans are fated to destroy Earth.'

'What do you mean?'

'Unlike all other creatures, men aren't satisfied with the existence gifted to them by Sun. It's in their ravenous nature to devour more than Earth can give, occupy all space, procreate with no restraint, and finally bring the other beings to pain and extinction …'

'Men are like rats, just bigger and stronger,' the Crier interjected, speaking as though he weren't one himself.

The Maid walked over to the window and gazed outside, closing her eyes in contemplation: 'Earth was on the verge of collapsing, and most humans had already been lost to the relentless scourges and cataclysms of many centuries, when the first Ealdorman, our forefather, persuaded the few survivors to find refuge in the inside. He requested a gesture of trust, though: in return for protection, shelter, light, food, and everything necessary for survival, they would have to give up wandering around Earth, plundering the land, creating machines to serve their laziness, reproducing themselves more than they could sustain, and they would renounce all their other vices …'

'Enough! He doesn't deserve to know more!' the Crier shouted, raising the rod to his sister, who, for the first time since I had known her, blinked with fear before withdrawing into silence.

They both left the room without saying anything more.

Strapped to the bed, I wondered what my fate would be. Perhaps dying of thirst and starvation? But, in the full day that I remained confined there, a servant came twice to feed me. Alone, barely able to move, wondering what might become of me, the long wait in bed ate away at me. When the night arrived, I hoped Mozart would appear, and take me with him somewhere else.

At first, I couldn't figure out how I had been exposed, but in time I've become fairly sure it was the long scar on my back that betrayed me – that night with the Maid. Or perhaps the clepsammia. I will never know.

The following morning, four guards pulled me from my bed, and I was escorted down to the main corridor. We passed by the library, and I wondered if Lela was waiting for me at her desk, or had been warned that she would never see me again. As I walked with the guards, the servants in the corridor now felt entitled to quietly stare at me, and the sudden loss of respect pained me; but not for long, because I soon understood where I was being taken.

Everyone was waiting. The courtyard looked even more crowded than for the execution of the young servant. I couldn't see the Ealdorman, but the Maid stood in her usual spot, and the astronomer wasn't late this time. The procedure was unchanged: he made his nervous measurements and, when the sunlight was at the right angle, nodded. But, unlike the servant, I didn't shout when they locked me inside the cabin; it was useless and, even if I had tried, pure terror was blocking my throat, and no sound could have escaped from there. The dingy cabin was already searing under the intense sunlight when I heard the mirrors being wheeled through the courtyard and, sweat-soaked, I began to shiver uncontrollably in anticipation of what was to come. Moments later, the crowd fell into a sudden, unnatural silence. Then, the Ealdorman's mighty voice resonated in the air: 'Halt! This man is destined for another punishment.'

XIX

WITHIN

'The spectacle! The spectacle has arrived! Boz is with you!' I yell whenever I enter a new corridor. I've never learnt to do music with the cans, but still, as I pass by, the idlers come rushing out of their units to see what I'm up to. They say I am a great thespian, perhaps the greatest thespian the inside has ever seen, but I believe they would think differently had they met Bebro.

When the Crier sent me back, it wasn't in perimeter ᴜᴜꞋ⊖ᴏ. I had been relocated. The idlers I asked didn't even know about my old perimeter. I felt lost and miserable, and wandered without a purpose through the corridors for quite a while, even contemplating ending my life. But I willed myself to resist, because Flox might still need help, and I wanted to be there for her.

I visited the local Master of the Known, and asked for permission to browse through his slates, so that at least the azbuki would busy my mind and lift my spirits. He possessed no slates, though, and never had, because – he boasted – his powerful mind allowed him to do without them. But his powerful mind was also a defective one. When we talked about flower chafers, for instance, I noticed he couldn't name a single tribe. Or, upon switching our conversation to mammals, it was clear he couldn't tell a genet from a ringtail. When I thought it correct to apprise him of the patchiness of his knowledge, he turtled up, and commented drily that we should no longer talk to each other, for I wasn't his peer.

With such an abundance of unoccupied time, and my knowledge proving apparently useless, I regularly went through what the Maid had said about the origin of the perimeters. I did so for the most part to understand the later developments, of which she hadn't spoken.

Based on her account, the first Ealdorman offered people a refuge within the walls to escape a collapsing world. In return for survival, however, the fleeing men relinquished their freedom to move and enjoy what Earth still offered – the bounties of the land, the vastness of the seas, the smell of the seasons, the company of other creatures, and innumerable other blessings. But I suppose what these men could not have foreseen was that they would also forfeit something equally precious: the vast knowledge humanity had amassed through millions of days of effort, trial and sacrifice. Generation after generation, in fact, the people within, oppressed by ever-stricter rules and precluded from cultivating their own minds and souls, eventually forgot about their true past, and how to pursue a future.

In my period outside, I didn't see any of the machines accused by Mozart of ruining Earth. No remains of a factory, skyscraper, airplane, or those small engines described so thoroughly in Thatem's books came to my sight, not even in the faint shape of some ruin or wreckage. Yet I can't possibly know how wide the portion of land I saw was in comparison to the whole Earth, and it was quite possible the signs of human voracity lay elsewhere.

There was no zoo in my new perimeter, just the museum with the image of a clouded sky, and I had outgrown the stone ball. Still, I needed a solution to satisfy my starved curiosity, unless I wanted to wither inside like all those damned idlers. I also needed a way to locate Flox. And it was precisely for these reasons that I became a thespian: I can travel through the perimeters, entertain myself and the idlers, and meanwhile search for Flox.

I have no troupe. It's just me. I sing Thatem's songs, or the hilarious chants I heard from the palace's jester, or perform soliloquies created upon my return. I always survey the crowd in the hope of seeing Flox, perhaps disguised. I've gone through hundreds of perimeters, and staged just as many spectacles, but Flox hasn't shown up yet. I'm not giving up, in any case. I want to reunite with her, and leave the walls again.

I miss the artichokes, the strolls under warm sunlight, and bathing in the stream, or the slowly awakening in the twilight. Once, dragged from my sleep by the harsh illumination, I burst into tears and hit my head against the wall many times to quell my despair.

I wished I had never been outside. A man without nature is an incomplete man, I can say. The corridors looked so wide and long when I was a kid. But now, after the outside, they don't seem much more than burrows. Thatem says that men in the Land of Without used to lock those who misbehaved inside a place called *jail*, so that they would only harm each other. I think I live in similar circumstances, even though I certainly never behaved badly.

So, the first Ealdorman offered people a refuge within the walls to escape a collapsing world. But he and his kin remain outside, nestled in the beauty of the palace, indulging in life's pleasures to the fullest, and they surely don't subject themselves to the same sacrifices and restrictions of those inside the walls. Why shouldn't some of the people from the corridors be allowed to live in the sunlight? There's plenty of space outside – and enough tumbleweed – for many more to live there.

Nobody in these new perimeters knows about the Crier. When I make mention of him, and describe his frightening appearance in accurate detail (though I leave out his cruelty, as idlers can be quite impressionable), no one seems to have ever seen him, or even heard his name. So, I wonder where the relocation has really brought me, and how far I am from my old perimeter, and even whether it still exists. Perhaps I'm in a place from which ᏌᏌᏊᏫ cannot be reached, and I will never meet Flox again.

Admittedly, I don't possess Bebro's never-ending well of creativity, and as such, there are moments when I find myself less than fully inspired on stage. On one occasion, for instance, after performing two hilarious chants, I ran out of ideas for the spectacle. But, despite my blank staring at the crowd and their puzzled reaction, the silence didn't last too long. I redeemed my temporary lack of inventiveness by remembering aloud one moment I had enjoyed in the Land of Without.

'I was advancing barefoot, each step plunging among the fine, caressing blades of a tall grass, when the single cloud staining the blue sky decided to let out a drizzle of rain over me,' I told the sparse gathering of idlers, not quite sure myself where the story was going. 'I enjoyed the attention the cloud was giving me, and the tickling of the water on my skin was far from unpleasant, but, when the drizzle quickly turned into a pour, I resolved to find shelter under a solitary oak tree. My tunic was already soaked, and, with nobody around in that part of the garden, I took it off. My body instantly sensed the freshness of the air, and I immediately felt stronger and happier, though the sudden scraping of the oak's rough bark against my back caused me to wince (but my inner smile didn't wane). I stood there, my eyes closed yet not asleep, cherishing the earthy smell of the rain, at ease in being by myself for some time, though starting to shiver a bit. Suddenly, something hit me on the head, and landed on my right leg. An acorn. I looked upwards: from a branch, a motionless chipmunk was eyeing me with interest. I threw the acorn up towards the branch, and the chipmunk rushed away. It was getting darker, and so I put my tunic back on, leaving the tree.'

In the silence that followed, the idlers stared at me, stupefied. They had never heard anyone speak speaking that way. The idlers knew what a cloud was because of the museum, and trees were mentioned in the hymns, but they had never listened to a description of Without before the apocalypse. One man asked me which animal the *inner smile* was, and I explained that it's not an animal, but simply feeling so satisfied by your own state of mind that hardly anyone or anything can disturb it. I'm not sure he understood what I meant, but he nodded. Other questions followed. It had never happened before. Later, the idlers left the spectacle in a quiet hum, and I spotted more than one smile in the crowd, but I didn't know for sure whether they had liked it. None of them could really imagine that I had been to the Land of Without, and seen all that nature before me.

I repeated my story at the next spectacle, this time with no improvisation, and at the following spectacle, again, and the ten after that. The reaction of the crowds, which had meanwhile grown a lot in size, never changed. In every perimeter, they stared at me, almost ecstatic, and asked questions afterwards. I didn't attach much importance to what was happening until that one spectacle where I left the story out. At the end, one upset idler asked why I hadn't spoken about the chipmunk and the acorn. The crowd insisted I tell it. I didn't even know why I still remembered that story, which would have sounded quite ordinary to those outside, but it clearly meant a lot to the idlers. In hindsight, I should have known why: my story was bringing Earth into the corridors.

Time went on, and I no longer dared to omit recounting the chipmunk on the oak tree story; though, apparently, it wasn't enough, and the idlers began asking if I had more stories like that. After an initial reluctance, quite unjustified I must say, I granted their wish, and developed other stories, in part based on my experience, in part fruit of my imagination.

One of these tales, for which I took some inspiration from a recurring dream, goes like this: 'I'm heading through a pass between two mountains, at the edge of a large forest, when I hear a young voice calling me from deeper within. He knows me by my name, but I can't place him, and I can't say whether he's calling for help or just wants company. I move forward towards the voice, and forty steps later I find a wide gap to the right of the pass. It appears to be the entrance to a cave, spacious enough for me to wriggle in. The voice keeps calling from the cave, its tone unwavering – as though he's certain I'll come to him, and sees no need for urgency or alarm. I take a torch from my toolbox, and make my way through the cave. I'm not afraid; I've lost the fear of the dark long ago. The voice is getting closer, but I can feel that he is not moving, so it must be me who's drawing nearer. And, indeed, I finally reach him. He lies curled on the ground, tucked into the corner of a vast clearing. I stand still, but he catches sight of me almost immediately. As soon as my eyes get used to the darkness, I notice that one of his legs is chained to a wall. "Boz, finally ..." he says. Being chained, he can't harm me, I think, and so I get a couple of steps closer, where I can now see his face better, and realise that ... he's identical to me! I jump, but, unlike me, he shows no surprise at our uncanny resemblance. I even touch my face to make sure I'm not in two places at once. I ask him what he's doing there. He seems amused by my question: "I'm chained, don't you see?" I answer that I can see it, but who has done it? He seems even more amused. "Who chained you?" I ask again, and his answer astounds me: "You did it. You chained me, Boz. Don't you remember?" I'm overwhelmed. I don't recall ever doing anything so evil, and why would I have harmed him? But he seems sure; and he holds the answer: "You did it because you wanted everything for you, Boz: the sunlight, the food, the animals, and all the rest. You don't want to share anything ... you're greedy ..." What he says hurts me ... I can't stand his accusation ... so I take a hammer out of my toolbox, and strike the chain right next to the ring around his ankle with all my force. He yells in pain a couple of times, but the chain breaks. I want to free him from the cave ... even though he can barely stand up ... he must have been chained for long ... so I give him my hand, and he grabs it, smiling, with no trace of resentment in him. Together, we slowly walk out of the cave ... towards the free life he deserves.'

I have told this tale just once. The many idlers around me listened attentively, yet with unusual silence, and no questions came afterwards. They just left, and I remained alone in the widening, where an unwonted sense of emptiness made its way through me. I took my things, and moved to another perimeter, in a corner of which I unfolded my sack right before the lights went out. I was particularly tired, and overslept.

When I woke up in the artificial light, a bailiff was standing next to me. I hadn't seen one in a long time, and the sight instantly reminded me of the sorrowful time in the shelter. The bailiff informed me that I would no longer be permitted to hold my spectacles. I had violated the Tenets, he argued drily, with no animosity. He also informed me that I shouldn't step outside my perimeter. No more wandering, in light or darkness. When, alarmed, I asked what had happened, he offered no explanation, and only said that he would always remain by my side to prevent further breaches of the Tenets. And, indeed, wherever I go in the perimeter, the bailiff follows me. I can't get rid of him. He listens in on my dull conversations with the other idlers in the corridor, though without ever commenting on then, and just leaves me alone when the dark arrives (he sleeps in the unit next to mine).

I think it's now more than a hundred days since the bailiff first appeared. What is most exasperating is that he never speaks, but just stares at me blankly. If he spoke, he might at least be some kind of company. Despite the silence and his apparent lack of emotion, I can still feel the bailiff's ruthlessness. So I avoid doing anything that could appear even as a remote violation of the Tenets, because I don't want to be struck by his club or, worse still, end up in a dungeon. And when I speak to the idlers in the corridors, I no longer make comments or ask questions that might stir their curiosity – I keep everything to myself. I must have become very tedious, a far cry from the entertainer who once excited throngs of idlers with his stories of the Land of Without.

So, with no prior warning or sign, I suddenly lost the spectacles, and the freedom to search for Flox through the perimeters. I quickly plunged into a thick boredom that felt like an inescapable trap – and, unable to express my creativity, became alien to all forms of enthusiasm. The agreeable memories of the outside, initially a refuge where my mind could find some solace, grew into an obsessive getaway from a reality devoid of curiosity, pleasure, or joys of any sort. My existence had shrunk to nothing, and I no longer saw a purpose to bring me forward. I even resumed thinking about terminating my own life.

But I'm glad I haven't, because last night – yes, I still count time – a jangly voice spoke in my dark unit.

'The Juice may nourish you, Boz …'

'The Juice may nourish you, Mozart …' I reciprocated.

ABOUT THE AUTHOR

Alan Rhode is a former journalist, lawyer and digital entrepreneur from Italy, now living in the UK. Born in Genoa, a chilled-out town on the north-west coast of Italy, Alan spent many years in the more hectic Milan before moving to London, where he wrote his first novel, *The Eagle and the Cockerel* (2023), a geopolitical thriller that has stirred the curiosity of the public and media alike, establishing Alan as an exciting new voice in British literature.

His second book, *Within* (2025), is a post-apocalyptic thriller that delves profoundly into the often-conflicting relationship between man and nature, portraying a world where humans are secluded inside a maze of viewless corridors, longing for a no-longer existing natural world.